Scharlette Doesn't Matter and Goes Time Travelling

SAM BOWRING

For Amy

Everything is gonna be all kay.

1. Lucky Guess, Book

Scharlette was almost permanently annoyed, pretty much because her parents were morons.

After she was born, her mother and father had spent a long time arguing over what to call her. Her father wanted Scarlet but her mother preferred Charlotte. In the end they had compromised by welding the two names together into something that no one really knew how to pronounce.

It was annoying.

It was annoying when she had to introduce herself, annoying to spell it out for people, and super annoying wearing it on a name tag all day at work. She was sick of hearing 'that's an unusual name', and having to tell the same stupid story about her parents being indecisive idiots who would rather destroy their first born daughter for life than go with something nice and simple like 'Sarah'.

At least her sister Jenelope had understood.

She tried to put it all out of her mind. Beyond misted shower doors her dull existence awaited, the opposite of any life she had ever imagined for herself. She scrubbed absently at a love heart on her shoulder with a banner through it that read 'Jam' – testimony to the danger of breaking up with someone called James in a tattoo parlour. As soon as she left the safety of the steam it would be time to put on a grey uniform, eat a bland breakfast, and race to catch an overstuffed train. Bleak as the endless cycle was, today it was tinged with a sadness that made it even harder – for today was the day Jenelope had died, ten years ago.

There was no one to talk to about it. Her ever-and-increasingly-useless parents switched off whenever she tried to bring it up, suppressing their emotions and probably turning them into gallstones. She wasn't remotely close enough to any of her work colleagues to broach the subject. They might think to themselves, 'Scharlette seems a little more morose than usual today', if they could even pronounce her name correctly in their heads, but that would be that. Her few real friends had been supportive in the past, but she couldn't harp on about it to them forever. What would she even say? 'Jenelope's still dead and I'm still sad'? In which case, what could they say back? 'We're still sorry'?

She looked at her hand and clicked her fingers, the sound reverberating off the shower walls. It was a little trick she had devised to help her get through something she wasn't looking forward to. She would click once, and then, after whatever it was had come and gone – in this case, the whole damn day – she would look at her hand and click again, and it would seem like no time had passed at all. It reminded her that whatever lay on the horizon would soon be behind her, and was the closest thing she could get to time travel. She did not use the power lightly – dull as her life was, she did not wish it away – but today was an exception.

There was a knock at the door.

'Dammit,' said Scharlette, scrambling out of the shower. She was expecting the parcel delivery of a remote control helicopter, which she thought might be fun to fly off the balcony of her apartment. Maybe it could even deliver a note across the street to the muscular fellow who lived in the block opposite, mostly with his shirt off? Or, when she decided not to do that because it would be way too desperate and creepy, she could wait for a car with a 'Baby On Board' sign to drive past below, and crash the helicopter through the driver-side window.

She hastily wrapped a towel around her as she ran dripping to the door. A glimpse through the peephole showed nothing outside but beige corridor. Wondering if she had heard a knock on a neighbour's door, which happened sometimes while living in such close confines, she opened hers and looked out. There *was* a package on the ground, wrapped with brown paper and string. Why hadn't the delivery guy waited for her to sign?

She dumped the parcel on the dining table and set about getting dressed, her shirt patchily wet where she hadn't bothered to dry herself properly. Her uniform was a bit tighter than was comfortable, as had been the case for several weeks, but she tried to ignore the fact she was putting on weight. She'd gone to the gym once or twice earlier in the year, but had found it ate up too much time between finishing work and bottles of cheap wine on the couch. Maybe she should force herself back there. Where was her membership card again?

She prepared for her cereal regime. Since Scharlette thought of cereal as a joyless fuel that took ages to chew properly, her habit was to shovel in a huge mouthful and then attend to other chores while she masticated. Some chores were timed to one or two mouthfuls, like wiping down the kitchen bench, or brushing her boring brown hair. Others, like ironing a pair of pants, were more like a three mouthful chore. This morning, however, opening the package was going to be allocated 'all mouthfuls', because she wanted to read the helicopter instructions.

As she set about undoing the string, she noticed the package did not have a regular postal sticker. In fact – she frowned as she turned it over – there was no name or address written anywhere. Scharlette supposed that, given she worked as a security guard at the airport, she should be naturally wary of mysterious unmarked packages. She also knew, however, that she was so bored and in need of distraction that she was going to open this one anyway. She began to suspect it might be from the short bald guy (Clive?) who lived down the hall and made awkward small talk whenever he saw her.

'Hey,' he had said to her recently, as she'd stepped into the elevator beside him, 'did you know that if a female ferret goes into heat, and she can't find a mate, she dies?'

'I did not know that,' said Scharlette, in a flat tone of voice that implied she didn't want to, either.

'Yeah. Imagine if it was the same with people. If only! Ha ha.'

Sharlette had stared at him until the nervous little smile had dropped from his face and he had edged away.

As she tore the parcel open, she wondered if there was a dead ferret inside with a pink bow on its head to signify it was female. Instead, it was a book. Was this disappointing or not? Perhaps she had been secretly hoping for something weird. Or at least the remote control helicopter, after all.

The book was bound in brown leather and the cover was completely blank. She flipped open to the first page and discovered a handwritten message.

To Scharlette Day
Let's do it all again sometime.
Love,
Theodorus

Sharlette frowned. She didn't know anyone called Theodorus. In fact, she *certainly* didn't know anyone called Theodorus. It wasn't the kind of name she'd forget, being unusual and silly like her own.

She took a second spoonful of cereal and turned the page.

It was welcome to have a momentary distraction.
Something to amuse, perhaps, or even intrigue.

But perhaps neither of those things were really necessary. Perhaps finally, deep down, she had begun to realise it was time to let go.

The rays of sunlight through the glass seemed cold, somehow. Was it them, or what they showed up? White benches and tabletops, white walls and carpet, shelves somewhat bare for all the time she had lived there, a few scant motes floating about minding their own business. The apartment was clean, certainly, but the stark light made it feel barren, almost unlived in.

Scharlette grunted and stared through the glass doors that opened onto her balcony. The words resonated with her – the winter light entering her place carried no warmth. She noticed that her washing was still out on the clothesline, which she had forgotten to bring in the night before. Shirts and underwear hung motionless, probably frosty by now. The thought of sliding on a pair of icy knickers made her shiver involuntarily, then chuckle at her own reaction. She decided she couldn't be bothered dealing with the clothes right now, because she didn't want to eat that much cereal.

The demands of a burgeoning day began to present themselves in her thoughts. Too much delay and she'd be late for the bus. Late for the bus and she'd be late for the train. She resented these prosaic worries stealing focus from the deeper sorrow in her heart, but what point was there in dwelling on it? She needed to step back into the flow of things, even if life moved like a polluted river, snagging her with branches caught in sluggish currents and dragging her reluctantly onwards.

Scharlette chewed slowly and stared off into the distance. She was surprised by the vague threat of a tear pricking the back of her eye. *Silly girl. You're like someone who hears song lyrics after a breakup and thinks they're all about you.*

'Although I *am* going to be late for the bus if I don't hurry up,' she muttered, glancing at her phone. 'Thanks for reminding me.'

She took the final spoonful of cereal and stood, her eyes sliding over one last sentence.

She finished her cereal and put the bowl in the sink before heading off to work.

Scharlette stared at the words. Then she shook her head.

'Lucky guess, book,' she said, and dumped her bowl in the kitchen sink.

2. Wormholes at the Airport

'If you'll just remove your watch, sir, and check whether you have any metal in your pockets – any coins, jewellery, things of that nature – then we'll try this again.'

The businessman was already rummaging through his suit, evidently irked about being put through any of this. *Can't you see I'm not a terrorist?* his body language seemed to say. *I'm wearing a tie for Chrissakes.*

He dumped the contents of his pockets in a plastic tray on the conveyor belt next to his carry-on luggage.

'Step through the detector again please, sir.'

The man walked through the metal detector and it beeped loudly.

'All right, sir – you may proceed.'

'Scarlet!'

'Hmm?'

Scharlette glanced at her co-worker Barry, who was working the scanner. Like most people, he had stopped trying to get her name exactly right moments after meeting her.

'The alarm went off,' he said, crossly. 'As in, metal was detected.'

'Oh!' Scharlette blinked. She had been running on automatic while her mind wandered elsewhere. She turned to the businessman. 'Sorry, sir, it must be something else.

Are you wearing a belt?'

The businessman scowled and fumbled for his belt. *You think a terrorist could afford a nice leather belt like this?*

'Actually,' said Scharlette, and then stopped. 'Terrorists usually belong to very well funded organisations,' was what she had been *going* to say, before realising she was about to rebuke the guy for thoughts she had attributed to him in her own imagination.

'Yes?' The businessman paused mid-fumble.

'Er, continue,' she said.

'Actually, continue?' the businessman said derisively. He held his belt out as if it were a dead snake.

Scharlette glanced at Barry, who treated her to a brief shake of his head. She hoped he wouldn't tell their supervisor about her screw-up. Letting someone waltz through the metal detector after metal had been detected was high on the list of things not to do when working the metal detector. She suspected Barry wasn't just going to drop it.

Sure enough, once the irate businessman was finally through the checkpoint, Barry raised his eyebrows to a ludicrous height.

'What was that about?'

'Just a mistake, Barry. You know, like everyone makes, from time to time.'

'Quite a big mistake though. I should probably ... well ...'

'What, report me to Alan? Fine. Maybe he'll also be interested in how regularly you frequent the storage closet with what's-her-name during your lunch breaks.'

Barry turned red. 'Just promise me it won't happen again.'

Scharlette didn't care much for his officious tone, but she also didn't like herself for weaponising secret staff relations. God knew she didn't begrudge anyone for doing whatever they had to in order to get through the day, even if they were a ruddy-faced arsehole like Barry.

'Sure, Barry,' she said. 'Let's get this next lot through.'

She tried to stay focused on the queue of waiting travellers. She was never far outside her own head on Jenelope's deathversary, however.

It's just a date, she told herself. *Dates are just abstract measurements created by humanity to try and make sense of the endless march of time. It's probably not even really ten years since she died. There have been at least a couple of leap years since, so her real death was yesterday or tomorrow or something. Plus, the last thing I need on top of everything else is to lose this boring job I hate.*

She forced herself to continue on with method and formula. She asked the standard questions, confiscated scissors and aerosol cans, waved people through the gate and generally ensured that no insane bombers were trying to board any short domestic flights out of Sydney with grenades in their carry-on. Maybe she would have felt more job satisfaction if she found one every ten bags or so, instead of never.

'Hi there.'

The handsome traveller smiling at her made her forget her troubles for a moment. He was dressed in tight black fatigues which looked vaguely like a military uniform, but carried no badges or insignia. His short brown hair was neatly cropped, his face very pleasant, his boyish grin wide and toothy, his blue eyes sparkling and present.

'I'm Tomothy,' he said, and she felt a little flutter.

Plenty of handsome men went through the gates, of course. Sometimes she checked out their butts as they passed, but asking them to take off their belts was as intim-ate as it got. They did not normally introduce themselves.

The man peered at her ID badge. 'Very nice to meet you, S-charlette.'

Scharlette had never heard her name pronounced correctly by a stranger before. Not even she was always able to manage it. She experienced a moment of profound amazement.

'Is everything all kay?' asked the man.

'Ah ...' She could not, in that moment, think of any way to adequately explain her surprise to him. Also, had he just said 'all kay'? She must have misheard him over the airport bustle, or maybe because of his strange accent she couldn't quite place? It had a sort of understated clarity to it, like every word was spoken precisely as it should be, without idiosyncrasy.

And what about his name?

'Did you say that your name is ... Tomothy?'

'I did.'

Scharlette wondered if she had finally met someone else with the same problem.

'Are your parents mentally deficient also?'

'Sorry?'

'Er ...' Awkwardness made her revert to formula. 'And are you travelling with any carry-on today, sir?'

'No thanks.' He answered as if Scharlette had offered him something. 'So, how does this work?' He was inspecting the detector. 'Sort of a funny old thingjiggy, isn't it?'

'Um ...'

If anyone was flip or humorous about anything at all while going through the checkpoint, it was Scharlette's task to inform them that all jokes would be taken seriously, so they had better watch it. Tomothy hadn't really made a joke however, he just seemed inexplicably amused. What was the protocol for that? She supposed she could tell him to be careful what he said, but she didn't want to seem uncool. She decided to simply plough ahead.

'Do you have any sharp objects on your person, sir? Anything metallic or dangerous?'

Tomothy seemed to consider this.

'Please put anything like that in the tray provided,' said Scharlette, pushing a white plastic tray towards him.

Tomothy put in some coins and, as he did, his sleeve rolled back to reveal a metal band around his wrist dotted with tiny flashing lights. Probably some new mobile phone or fitness thing?

'I'm afraid that will have to go in too, sir.'

Tomothy touched the device and frowned. 'Are you sure?'

'Yes, sir.'

'Is there not some other way?'

Barry, who had been watching this whole exchange with mounting suspicion, cleared his throat. 'I'm afraid not, sir. All phones and accessories must be scanned.'

'But couldn't you scan this perfectly harmless diddle-dabbit while it remains attached to me? It's very hard to remove, you see.'

'Either you take it off,' said Barry, 'or you don't go through the checkpoint. Sir.'

'Oh.' Tomothy seemed slightly worried. 'Well, all kay then. I mean, I don't want to miss my plane, which I definitely intend to get on, so ...'

He closed his eyes, seemed to concentrate for a moment, and the wrist thing clicked open.

'That didn't seem too hard,' said Scharlette.

'Hmm? Oh, that's not what I meant.' Tomothy deposited the wristband in the tray. 'Can we be pretty high speed about this, please?' He glanced at his device again fretfully. 'I really shouldn't ...'

The device began to beep.

'Why is it making that noise, sir?' asked Barry, his hand going to his walkie talkie. Tomothy had probably earned himself a round a questioning before he got on any flight.

'That's a good question,' said Tomothy. 'I've never heard it outside of training, but I believe it's the sound of a universal recall. But why would ... ooooh, crumbs.'

Scharlette followed his gaze and her eyes grew wide. A few metres away, a pulsating purple wormhole was opening in the air. She had watched the odd series of Star Trek, so she had the right word for it – but what she did not have, what she *did not have*, was an explanation for why she was seeing one appear right there, in real life, at her place of work.

'Snipers!' shouted Tomothy, and dived to the floor.

A glowing green laser bolt shot out of the wormhole, narrowly missed him, and blew up Barry's scanner.

'Everyone take cover!' shouted Tomothy, as he rolled to his feet. Several more wormholes opened, shooting more laser bolts at him as he ducked and weaved through the rapidly panicking crowd. Somebody's luggage exploded, and a cloud of burning underwear filled the air. Guards ran this way and that drawing their guns, but nobody knew what was happening or how to respond.

Tomothy raced through the airport doors to the street outside.

'There!' shouted Scharlette, pointing after him, but amidst the shouting and sizzling and shooting, no one paid her any attention.

There was nothing for it but to follow him herself. She moved warily past a sputtering wormhole, but no more laser bolts shot out of it. In fact it seemed to be losing stability, its edges rapidly fizzling and shrinking. A moment later it collapsed to a dot and disappeared entirely.

Scharlette burst through the doors into the short term pickup/drop off zone. There people huddled in fear amidst several more shrinking wormholes, while smoke oozed from burn marks on the pavement and several waiting taxis.

There was no sign of Tomothy.

'Crumbs indeed,' said Scharlette.

3. Violated Brain Molecules

Scharlette arrived back at the gate to find Barry being helped to his feet by what's-her-name, a pretty young info desk clerk called Kelly. The soot in his eyebrows made his glower seem somewhat comical.

'Thanks for making sure I wasn't badly injured before running off,' he said.

'Oh!' said Scharlette. 'Sorry about that. I was chasing ...'

'What on earth was that?' said Kelly. 'I've never seen anything like it. It was like something out of a fantasy movie.'

A sci fi, you mean, you little idiot, thought Scharlette.

Everywhere people scurried about, airport guards were trying to work out what the hell, melted technology sparked and crackled, and police were beginning to arrive on the scene. It did not look like anyone had been seriously hurt.

'Are you seriously hurt?' Kelly asked Barry. 'We should have someone take a look at you.'

'Mmf,' said Barry, casting a final glare at Scharlette as he allowed himself to be led away.

'Attention all passengers,' came an announcement through the PA. 'Please remain calm. All flights are delayed until further notice. We are just trying to ... well, to figure out … er, please stand by for further information.'

Scharlette took a closer look at the exploded scanner. From the appearance of its mangled interior, no person would have survived a hit from a laser bolt. The conveyor belt was warped and heat damaged, and plastic trays were scattered over the floor. Inside one of them, Tomothy's wrist device twinkled away without a care in the world.

Scharlette bent to pick it up. It was a segmented chrome band with two interlocking parts, and a small screen which flashed the word 'disengaged'. It didn't seem to have a speaker or keypad, so maybe it wasn't a phone after all? She turned it this way and that, but no new angle revealed its function.

Maybe some kind of diving watch?

She thought about trying it on, even though she knew airport security guards probably shouldn't voluntarily attach unknown technology to themselves.

But it probably is just some kind of fancy diving watch or something, right? So what's the harm?

Impulsively, she snapped the device around her wrist. Immediately the segments drew closer and tightened. She gave a yelp of surprise and tried to take it off, but the thing was firmly affixed – not painfully, but definitely.

'Well,' said Scharlette, 'that was a pretty dumb thing to do.'

PRIMING, the little screen flashed happily.

What do you mean, priming? Is priming a bomb word?

A soft blue light began to shine from inside the band.

Oh shit, it is a bomb. I need to get away from everyone. Or maybe I can cut my hand off. Did we confiscate any machetes this morning?

Before Scharlette could have any more panic-fuelled thoughts, the light pulsed so brightly that it seemed to shine through her skin – and then there was nothing 'seemed' about it, for she could actually *see* the arteries and bones inside her own translucent flesh.

It was enough to give her pause.

ANALYSING TEMPORAL IDENTITY, the screen informed her.

'What?'

BRAIN MOLECULES UNVIOLATED.

'Well, that's good, I suppose.'

VIOLATING BRAIN MOLECULES NOW.

'*What*? Wait!'

Frantically Scharlette searched for a way to get the wristband off, but no clasp nor button revealed itself. She thought about calling for help, but how would she explain her predicament to anyone before this thing did whatever it was going to do?

The light blinked off and her skin returned to its natural opacity. The message on the screen changed again.

ALL KAY, it said.

Scharlette stared at the screen. 'All kay? So did you violate my brain molecules or not?'

'Charlotte?'

She turned to find her supervisor, Alan, bearing down

on her, flanked by two police officers.

'This is where the first one hit,' he told the cops, gesturing at the murdered scanner. 'Charlotte, these officers want to speak with you.'

'No problem,' said Scharlette, struggling to adopt a casual tone as she hurriedly smoothed her sleeve down over the brain-violating deep sea wrist watch.

Police made Scharlette nervous, which was strange, given they were on the same side. Perhaps it was a feeling left over from her largely unsupervised youth, during which her hippy-ish parents had been so caught up with their own progressive ideals that they had pretty much let her and her sister roam free.

'We don't believe in mollycoddling our children,' they had proudly told their friends over glasses of wine while passing around joints. 'They have to learn about life for themselves, you know? Make their own mistakes.'

As a result, Scharlette and Jenelope had made plenty of mistakes. They had run with a pretty ragtag crew, broken into abandoned buildings to get drunk, smoked weed stolen from their parent's stash, vandalised the odd bus stop, gone to bush raves and warehouse parties, frequently skipped school, and had the occasional run in with the authorities. In retrospect, a bit of mollycoddling would not have gone astray. Once she had realised it was the only truly rebellious thing to do, Scharlette had thoroughly cleaned up her act. Ever eager to emulate her older sister,

Jenelope had done the same. Together, they had moved on from petty acts of civil disobedience to more scholarly pursuits. Scharlette had, much to her teachers' surprise, done extremely well in her final year of school, and had absolutely resented her parents' assertion that their hands-off attitude was finally paying dividends.

'What about the device your partner mentioned?' the guy cop asked. 'The one this ... Tomothy ... was wearing?'

'Um,' Scharlette said, as her wrist itched traitorously, 'I think it was just a fancy watch of some kind. Probably one with GPS or stealth detection or something.'

'Stealth detection?' said the girl cop. 'What makes you say that?'

'Oh, nothing. Just that it was ... you know, technological. I, er ... it probably wasn't stealth detection, because I don't even really know what that is. I was just using it as an example. Of this watch looking technological.'

The cops glanced at each other.

'Are you sure you weren't hit in the temple by a tiny piece of debris?' asked Guy Cop. 'That happened to a buddy of mine once, and nobody realised until hours later when he attacked a pool pony with a speargun.'

Scharlette shook her head.

'And you're sure he said his name was Tomothy?' said Girl Cop.

'Yes.'

'Not Timothy? Or just Tom?'

'I'm sure he *said* that's what his name was.'

Girl Cop stared at her closely. 'There's no history of mental illness in your family, is there?'

'Look what my parents named me,' said Scharlette, tapping her ID.

Girl Cop frowned. 'Maybe we should have a medic check you out,' she said, putting a hand on Scharlette's shoulder. 'Just to be safe.'

Scharlette noticed Alan returning, this time with a swarthy fellow in the same black fatigues as Tomothy had been wearing. Alan pointed her out to the guy, who nodded, then cocked his head as if listening to something only he could hear. A moment later he spun on his heel and walked away, leaving Alan looking somewhat put out.

'Come on,' said Girl Cop. 'Let's get that bump on your head looked at.'

Scharlette didn't have a bump on her head, but she let herself be helped up anyway.

'... very strange,' she overheard a woman say to her husband as they passed by. 'One of those glowing bullets was coming right at me, but then it just disappeared. Or fizzled out. Or something.'

'I'm sure it just looked like it was coming at you, dear,' said the man.

'I'm telling you, one moment it was heading towards me, the next it was gone. It was like it hit an invisible barrier.'

'Yes, dear,' said the man, patting her hand. 'Well, at least one thing's for certain ...'

They passed out of earshot, and Scharlette was annoyed she didn't get to find out the one thing about this day that was certain.

Scharlette sat on the train home, trying to resist pawing at the still-firmly-attached device. She had kept it hidden the whole day, barely daring to look at it herself, yet now her hand kept disappearing up her sleeve to poke and prod at it. She wondered if she would be able to smash it off with a hammer.

'And then it will explode and kill me.'

She realised she had spoken out loud. She tried not to look at the people sitting to either side of her, who would no doubt affect some reason to move away very shortly. She also wasn't helping her image as a Normal Sane Person by constantly scratching at her wrist as if there were insects burrowed under her skin. Sure enough, the businessman to her right suddenly thought it was time to go and stand by the doors, even though the next stop was a good few minutes away. She scowled at him for being so transparently fainthearted, then caught herself and smoothed her features, trying to relax.

It was impossible. Almost as impossible as it had been trying to maintain any semblance of normality at work. Nobody had any explanation for what had happened, and with no indication of an ongoing threat, the pressing concerns of the airport had soon begun to take precedence again. Staff had reorganised queues of passengers, baggage carousels had whirred into motion, and planes had returned to the skies. Distressed people had told news crews about glowing holes that spat green bullets, which would have sounded pretty wacko if there hadn't been so many corroborating witnesses. Someone had asked about security tapes, and Scharlette had experienced a fearful moment as she imagined footage that clearly showed her removing evidence from the scene of a crime. It had been a great relief that, when she had finally been allowed to go to lunch and kind of resume a regular day, she heard a rumour in the cafeteria that all the eyes-in-the-sky had been wiped. She had leant back in her chair and taken a deep breath, staring up at a digital clock on the wall that read 2:45.

As she sat on the train thinking about that moment, another clock superimposed itself on the memory. This one was round and analogue, and had hung on the wall of Alan's office. She remembered looking at it and wondering how much longer Agent Hudd was going to keep questioning her. The time on the clock had been 2:45.

She shut her eyes, confused – how could she have seen two different clocks in two different places at exactly the same time? Unless they had been running entirely out of sync?

Agent Hudd?

'What the fuck?' she whispered, her hand going to her forehead, as if to hold her sanity in. She had a second, and distinctly different, memory of the afternoon, which somehow occupied exactly the same period of time. It was as if it had been waiting, buried – but now that she had somehow uncovered it, it was as clear and real as any other memory, *except that it had never happened*. And in this second memory, she had never made it to the cafeteria for lunch.

The old lady to her left got up and moved off, clutching her handbag in fear.

4. Agent Hudd

Scharlette tried to keep it together as she thought through her alternative memory of the afternoon, mentally reliving each moment in hope she could work out what the bejesus was going on:

As Girl Cop and Guy Cop were finishing up with her, Alan arrived with the same black-fatigue-wearing-swarthy-stranger who she also remembered not being interested in her at all.

'Scharlette,' said Alan, 'this man wants to speak to you.'

The man had flawlessly smooth olive skin, an impeccably neat beard, long black hair and startling jet black eyes. He looked very serious, as well as a bit like someone in a rock band.

'Agent Robin Hudd,' he said, flashing a badge which she didn't get a good look at. 'I'm told you observed the incident first hand. Can we talk somewhere private?'

He spoke with the same unpretentiously exact accent as Tomothy had.

Alan had eagerly offered up his office, and that was where they had gone.

'Please,' said Hudd, gesturing at the seat behind Alan's desk.

Scharlette felt a little uncomfortable in her supervisor's

chair, not least because of Alan's propensity to sweat. She also could not help staring at Hudd's eyes, which really were totally black – not just the pupils, but his whole eye.

'It's a genetic disorder,' said Hudd.

'Oh. It's very ... striking.'

'Thank you,' said Hudd, sitting down opposite. 'So, I'm told you spoke to Agent Dartle?'

'Who?'

'Agent Tomothy Dartle?'

'Ah. Yes. He didn't mention his surname. So, he's really called Tomothy?'

'Yes.'

'That's an unusual name.'

'Is it?'

'You don't think so?'

'Maybe where you come from,' Hudd said absently, which struck Scharlette as odd. She came from *here*.

'What did he say to you?'

'Nothing much. He was just another passenger going through the gate. He said something about it seeming funny.'

'Funny?'

'Yes. The metal detector. Not funny ha-ha, more funny-weird. That was my impression, anyway.'

'He's probably not familiar with this style of airport.'

Scharlette had been through a few different airports in her time. Not as many as she had once planned to, but still, a few. She tried to think of one that didn't have the exact same security checkpoints as all the others, and couldn't.

'You confiscated a device from him?'

'Not confiscated,' said Scharlette. 'He had to remove it so he could go through the detector. That is the style of airport we run.'

Her pointed tone seemed to wash over Hudd, who simply stared at her with his void-like eyes.

Must be some kind of try-hard coloured contacts, she told herself.

'Sorry, what ... department ... are you from, Agent Hudd?'

'And he didn't have anyone else with him?'

'Not that I saw.'

'He was travelling alone.'

It seemed more a statement than a reiteration of the question, so Scharlette remained silent.

'After the sniping started, you pursued him, correct?'

Scharlette frowned. Hudd was the only person besides Tomothy to refer to the incident as 'sniping'. She found herself growing irked about the lack of information coming her way, and decided to employ Hudd's own tactics against him.

'So what were those purple things, anyway?' she said, leaning back in Alan's chair. 'They looked like wormholes.'

Hudd remained impassive. 'Wormholes don't just open up in airports.'

'No? Then what did I see? What did everyone see?'

'I'm as uncertain as you.'

'Oh? Yet you're wearing the same uniform as Agent Dartle, so I kinda really don't believe you.'

'Let's just say I'm here on a highly classified government assignment, and it would be best for all concerned if you'd answer my questions as truthfully as you can.'

Scharlette thought about the device attached to her wrist. Did Hudd know it was there? Had he seen footage of her picking it up and putting it on, and was now making her sweat?

'Have you checked the security cameras?' she asked, trying to sound casual.

'They were turned off prior to the attack,' said Hudd darkly.

'What? By who?'

'Standard practice. Contains the ripples. Diminishes plimits. One moment.' Hudd closed his eyes and pinched the bridge of his nose. 'Hudd here. Where's the information I requested?' A pause – she couldn't hear any reply. It seemed, in fact, like he was talking to no one. 'That's not good enough, sir,' he continued. 'Anyway, I don't understand. The attack was a failure. Why not edit it entirely, if only for breaching non-interference policy?'

Scharlette glanced at the clock on the wall, wondering how long she would be subjected to this strange man. She was hungry – it was already 2:45 and she hadn't had any lunch.

'Sigh,' said Hudd. 'Well, all kay then. For the records I

don't think this is wise.'

He lowered his hand and gave Scharlette an exasperated look, as if she somehow understood what he was dealing with.

'Did you just roll your eyes?' said Scharlette. 'It's hard to tell, because of ... you know ... the blackness.'

'I did,' said Hudd. 'It's infuriating. As if this whole operation isn't complex enough.'

'I still have no idea what you're talking about.'

'They don't want to edit the failed attack on Agent Dartle because it caused some unexpectedly favourable ripples,' said Hudd.

'Well, that clears everything up.'

Hudd gave her a wry smile. 'Look, Ms Day, just two more questions and then you can go. I promise none of this will matter after you answer.'

'That doesn't sound ominous at all.'

'Did you see where Agent Dartle went after he fled? A general direction? Did he get in a taxi? Anything?'

'He was gone by the time I arrived in the drop off zone.'

'Unsurprising. All kay, did you see what happened to his PPC?'

'His what?'

'The device he took off.'

'Oh. Um, no, I don't think so.'

Was she insanely stupid for lying, she wondered? Maybe this man could tell her what the wrist thing did, or help her get it off? Then again, what if she got in some kind of trouble for tampering with evidence? She *really* couldn't afford to get fired right now, not with her mortgage continuously clocking up interest. Also, Hudd had irritated her by saying mysterious things instead of answering any of her questions, and she didn't trust him at all.

'Think carefully, Ms Day. It's very important.'

'Maybe it's in the rubble? Of the scanner that got blown up?'

'I already searched.'

'Maybe Tomothy took it with him?'

It seemed as if the ... PPC? ... grew heavier and more obvious by the moment, bulging on Scharlette's wrist as if trying to declare its presence to the world. She could simply pull back her sleeve and show it to him. Maybe she could make a deal – the truth in exchange for not being dobbed in to Alan?

'You didn't actually see him pick it up again, though?' said Hudd.

'Everything happened so fast. I mean, there were wormholes opening in the air and lasers zapping all over the place. Sorry, not wormholes.' She fixed him with an acerbic eye. 'I mean the pulsating purple openings to another dimension that definitely weren't wormholes of any kind.'

As Hudd searched her face, Scharlette hoped her annoyance was enough to mask her guilt, and the sweat that was beginning to prickle her brow. She almost wiped it away with her PPC-laden hand, but managed to catch herself in time.

'What a clusterfarm,' said Hudd, then raised his own sleeved wrist to his mouth.

'What are you doing?' she asked.

'Sending a message to myself not to bother with this conversation.'

'That seems rude.'

'Never mind, you won't remember.' He cleared his throat and spoke into his wrist. 'No useful intelligence gained from Scharlette Day.'

After that, nothing.

On the train, Scharlette frowned, searching her recollection.

What do you mean, nothing?

She had no memory of talking any further with Hudd, or standing up from Alan's chair, or leaving his office, or heading back to work, or anything. It was as if the memory simply ended.

In her 'real' memory of the day, she could recall having lunch, leaving the cafeteria, asking after Barry (half-heartedly, only because she knew it was probably right to affect some concern for his wellbeing), finding out he had been sent home to recover, and then going about her afternoon pretty much as usual. She had finished her shift, headed home, and now here she was, sitting on the train – but in the *other* memory, nothing.

'What's happening to me?' she said, but there was no one left sitting beside her to freak out.

5. The Personal Phase Compiler

Scharlette made it through her front door and wondered what she was supposed to do next. Her instinct was to confide in someone, but who? Her parents habitually dodged her calls on Jenelope's deathversary. What about her friends Gus and Nell, a debauched couple she knew from her university days? Or Ultra-Gay Steve, thus named because he was the grouchiest, least camp gay man anyone had ever met. If she told any of them the whole story, they'd probably think she had lost her mind. Maybe she could start with the wormholes – at least they had been on the news – and then see how believed she would be from there?

Or maybe she should try to smash the PPC off? The device was her best guess for where the strange memory-that-had-never-happened had come from. It had claimed, after all, to have violated her brain molecules. Perhaps the false memories were all in her head, so to speak?

I don't have a hammer, she thought. *I know that, because the last time I needed one, I didn't have one then either.*

Maybe a wine bottle would work?

Better not risk breaking a full one.

With that thought, she opened a bottle of cheap sauv blanc and took a big swig.

Scharlette wasn't the nerdiest nerd on the planet, but she had a passing interest in Dr Who, and didn't mind big budget space flicks. As a result, she had learned a few things from the sci fi genre – for example, if a strange device is connected to your brain somehow, it's probably a bad idea to brutally bash it off.

'I'm still going to drink all of this wine,' she informed the world.

Her eyes fell on the book which still lay open on the dining table. It had been an odd gift in the first place, but what with the accumulation of odd she had experienced since its arrival, it somehow now seemed even odder.

She took another gulp and went over to look at it.

> *She finished her cereal and put the bowl in the sink before heading off to work.*
>
> *Later that evening, as she stood in her apartment tempering her shock with booze – the events of the day were proving a lot to digest – Scharlette was*

Scharlette closed the book so quickly that the whoosh of air up into her face added to her list of surprises.

It's a coincidence, she told herself. *There are heaps of girls named Scharlette, right? That's why I've always hated the name – because it's so common. Remember last week, when we all met up at the Scharlette Club, the super exclusive place you can only get into with a valid photo ID proving that your name is Scharlette?*

Slowly, Scharlette opened the book again.

Later that evening, as she stood in her apartment tempering her shock with booze – the events of the day were proving a lot to digest – Scharlette was so surprised to see her own name in print that she snapped the book shut right there and then.

'Okay,' said Scharlette, rubbing her brow. 'Okay.'

However, being a brave and curious sort, she slowly opened the book again. Unfortunately, she did not have a chance to read much further, for a knock at the door made her snap it shut once more.

Scharlette frowned at the words. Brave and curious? She would never describe herself using such words – not in recent years anyway. She felt a moment of relief at this hard proof that the book couldn't possibly be about her. Then a knock at the door caused her to snap it shut again.

It was Agent Tomothy Dartle.

'Hello,' he said, smiling handsomely.

'Oh, thank God,' said Scharlette, waving him in. 'I think.'

Tomothy strolled into her apartment and glanced around. 'God is a strange concept,' he said. 'I'm surprised He endured for as long as He did. Are you a what-do-you-call-em? A religiousist?'

'What?'

'Do you believe in this God fellow for true?'

'It's just an expression.'

'Ah, good,' said Tomothy, picking up the wine bottle and sniffing it. 'Not one of the mad ones, then.'

'I don't know about that!' Scharlette half-shouted, making him start. She snatched the bottle back, then used it to point at him. 'All right,' she said. 'Talk.'

'Well, we outlawed religion. Seemed a rather destructive habit. Anyone caught practising it gets sent straight to Hell.'

'No, I mean ...'

'Ah.' Tomothy sat down on the couch. 'This is nice. Been on my feet all century. You know, I feel fortunate that yours was the only security checkpoint available within the plimits.'

'Look, what the fuck is going on?'

Tomothy stared her straight in the eye and said, very seriously, 'It's often hard to say.'

'What were those wormholes? What was with the laser bolts? What's this thing?'

She pulled up her sleeve to reveal the PPC.

His eyes widened. 'You, er ... you put it on?'

'Yes, and now I can't get it off! And why do I remember an interview with another one of *you*,' she jabbed the bottle at him, 'except that I remember it both happening and not happening?'

'Another one of me?' Tomothy was very interested. 'What, like, actually me?'

'No, of course not. I mean someone dressed like you.'

'Oh, another agent. Was it Hudd?'

'You mean he's real? That's a bloody relief.'

'Let me ask you this,' said Tomothy. 'Did the interview really happen but you also remember it not happening, or did it not really happen and yet you remember it happening anyway?'

'Um ... the second one, I think.'

'Ah. So he decided to edit it.'

'Why am I still answering your questions? It's about time you people answered some of mine!'

'I'm afraid I've already been far too flapmouthed. I usually remember not to be when dealing with past civilisations and alien cultures, but there's something about this place that seems so homely and quaint. It's put me off my guard.'

'Alien cultures?'

'I really should stop dropping clues so wildly. Although, I suppose it doesn't matter much, since ...' He eyed her inquisitively, then seemed to drop whatever he had been going to say. 'At any rate, I very much need my PPC back. I'll just have to disengage it from your brain molecules first.'

'What? No, no way. No one's tinkering with my brain molecules again until I find out what is happening here.'

'Sigh,' said Tomothy. 'I'm real-like sorry about this, but I'm going to have to insist.' He reached into his fatigues and drew out a ray gun. It was small, mauve and sleek, but it was unmistakeably – again Scharlette's passing know-ledge of sci fi proved useful – a ray gun. Its firing end was pointy and had little ray gun rings around it.

'You can't take that on the plane with you,' she said, staring at it.

Tomothy grimaced. 'My apologies for resorting to such vulgar tactics, but I must have my PPC. It could contain information of vital importance to the future of all humanity, not to mention, you know, the universe.' He waved the gun around to generally indicate the universe.

Scharlette had taken a self-defence course in Border Force College, although she had never actually faced a gun in the field. Still, either through instincts imbued in training, her growing frustration, or the wine, the moment the gun wasn't pointed at her, she lurched forward and planted a knee on Tomothy's outstretched arm, driving it down into the couch.

'Argh,' he said, his hand flying open.

She grabbed the gun and bounced backwards, pointing it at him.

'Ha,' she said, and took another swig of wine.

'Deft,' he said begrudgingly, rubbing his arm. 'Serves me right, I suppose. That said, I don't expect you've ever fired a Zappity 123 before.'

Scharlette considered the ray gun. 'Mmm,' she said. 'No. But maybe I'll just press buttons randomly while it's pointed at you until I figure it out.' She made a move as if to start doing just that.

'No, please!' Tomothy flung up his hands. 'You're right, it's not very hard. Even a child could do it.'

'Well, let's try this again. Who are you?'

'Agent Tomothy Dartle.'

'I don't just mean your name. *Elaborate*. And remember, I have a gun this time.'

'It's just that I really shouldn't tell you anything.'

'And I shouldn't know what melted scanner smells like.'

'I could get into a lot of trouble.'

'Guns,' she said, 'are not usually needed to make people do what they are perfectly willing to do in the first place.'

He stared at the weapon hovering before his nose. 'But you don't know what you're asking.'

'I ... don't ... care.'

'All kay, all kay. I guess I can always edit you later.'

'Excuse me?'

'Send a message back in time to myself to make sure none of this ever happens.' Tomothy lowered his hands into his lap. 'I'm a time agent, you see.'

Scharlette scoffed. 'Of course you are.'

'I am! I come from the very distant future.'

'How distant?'

'The number of years is so stupendously great, it would hurt your mind to think of.'

'What, but you can handle it?'

'No, no – it hurts my mind to think of, also. There are symbols involved.'

'Okay.' Scharlette almost used the gun to rub her temple, but realised what she was doing and stopped. She felt a touch of hysteria creeping over her – it was not as though the day's events did anything to *disprove* what Tomothy was claiming.

'All right,' she said. 'Let's play a little game called "I'll pretend to believe you for now". So, if you are indeed a *time agent*, what are you doing here?'

'A hugely important thing happens today.' He frowned. 'It doesn't seem super critical at the time, but it's very super critical to the future, it turns out.'

Scharlette gave the gun a little wave of 'pray, continue'.

'I had to stop Hudd killing someone,' said Tomothy. 'Which I did, I think. And capture Hudd too, if possible, although that's kind of a secondary objective. That's why I was at the airport. Hudd might have tried to get on the plane that Common Ancestor 6702ahjx445 was booked to board.'

'Who?'

'A guy who a lot of people in the future are descended from. If Hudd had killed him, my government would have ceased to exist, and probably a lot of other folk too.'

'Oh dear,' said Scharlette. She could always, she told herself, stop playing this game whenever she liked and call the police. 'So what were those wormholes with lasers shooting out of them?'

'Lorentzian snipers,' said Tomothy. 'They are what they sound like.'

'Humour me.'

'Agents who open up wormholes across time to shoot at targets in the past. But only my government has access to such tech. That's why it's so confusing.'

He stood up, and she kept the gun trained on him, but he wasn't paying it any attention. He wandered over to the balcony doors and looked out onto the street.

'What's confusing?' she demanded.

'Well, that they would try to execute me when I was only carrying out their orders. And why do it in a well documented and populated location? Must have been a fixed point drone piping through vision to the Meanwhile, I guess. Maybe there's a double agent in their midst, or else some mistake has been made along the line, or it's something to do with that universal recall ...' He spun around, '... or the answer lies in my PPC. Please, you have to let me have it back.'

'Why? What is it?'

'A Personal Phase Compiler. If you're wearing one when the timeline changes, you remember your alternative history.'

'When the timeline changes?'

'Yeah. There's only one timeline – that's the really zicky thing to get your head around.'

'Is it?'

'Especially if you're in the past before you were born, and you do something that affects your own personal history in the future.'

'Bah, I hate this time travel crap. It's always full of plot holes.'

A strange look stole over Tomothy's face. 'How do you know about plot holes?' His eyes glittered. 'Have you ever seen one?'

'What? No. Stop changing the subject. What does this,' she held up the PPC before his eyes and tapped it with the gun, 'do?'

'I told you already. It preserves memories from previous versions of the timeline. It can also send causality free messages through the 16th dimension. Look, say that you ... what's a good example? Trying to remember my Universe City days here. All kay, say you and I are walking down the street wearing our PPCS, and you've chosen to wear a rather fetching red hat. Then, when we pass the Robot Dog shop, you catch a reflection of yourself in the window, and decide that the red hat, while nice, is a bit over the top for this particular occasion. So you use your PPC to send a message back in time to when you're making hat-based decisions, and advise yourself that a blue hat would be much more appropriate. Your past self therefore puts on a blue hat, erasing the timeline in which you're wearing a red hat, and replacing it with a new blue hat reality. In this new timeline, once you and I get to the Robot Dog shop, we'll both remember – thanks to our PPCs hitting the same point in their internal chronology as when the old timeline ended – our alternative history, in which you looked a bit over-dressed in your bright red hat.

We have a laugh about your fashion faux pas and move on. Understand?'

'Kinda.'

'That is the most anyone can hope for.'

'But then ... hang on,' said Scharlette. 'If I was wearing the blue hat, I would no longer have a reason to send that message to myself about wearing it instead of the red hat.'

'Ha ha,' said Tomothy. 'That's the beauty of 16th dimensional tech. Causality free, right? Once a message passes through the 16th dimension, it will always arrive at the same chronological point to which it was sent, regardless of changes to the timeline that stop it needing to be sent in the first place.'

Scharlette frowned, but decided to let this little mind-bender pass for now. After all, this was all just nonsense spurted out by a madman, right?

'So,' she said, 'my interview with Hudd – it never really happened?'

'First it happened and then it didn't. The moment he sent an edit telling himself not to bother talking to you, he changed the timeline – ending the old one at the point he sent the message, rewriting the new one from the point the message arrived. If you hadn't been wearing my PPC in both timelines at the same chronological point as when the old timeline ended, you never would have remembered anything about Hudd.'

'But I didn't remember right away. I was on the train home when the memory ... popped up.'

'Memories are sneaky,' said Tomothy. 'Especially if you aren't trained to check for new ones on a regular basis. They kind of steal in and wait around to be had. You know what it's like – all of a sudden something pops into your head which you haven't thought of in years. Or something reminds you of something else. Or you have to deliberately cast your mind back to search a memory out. Memories don't always just muscle forwards and announce themselves.'

Scharlette sat down at the table. 'This is ridiculous.'

'Please,' said Tomothy, 'I need my PPC back. If the timeline changes again, I need to know how.'

There was a knock at the door.

'Agent Dartle,' came a voice. 'It's Agent Hudd. I'm here to give myself up.'

6. As Scharlette Lay Dying

Tomothy went very still.

'That's him?' said Scharlette. It was strange recognising a voice she had technically never heard before.

Tomothy nodded. 'Agent Robin Hudd. Displaying quite atypical behaviour.'

'Why, who is he?'

'The worst kind of time agent – a rogue. He would never willingly give himself up, not when the most lenient punishment he can hope for is being banished to Hell.' Tomothy held out a hand. 'Can I please have my gun back? I promise not to point it at you again.'

'How can I trust you?'

'I don't know about how, but *why* is so we don't get badly killed.'

Hudd knocked again. 'I can hear you in there, you know.'

'Good for you!' shouted Tomothy.

'I want you to take me back to Panoptica,' said Hudd. 'You can cuff me if you like, or I'll cuff myself. Look through the-little-hole-in-the-door-you-can-peep-through and watch me throw my weapon away.'

'Just one weapon? You don't have enough to make a pile?'

'I could blow the door to skerricks, Tom, but I'd prefer

you to accept my surrender peacefully.'

'All kay,' said Tomothy, 'say that I believe you. Why would you give yourself up?'

'Can we speak inside? There's a weird bald guy wandering around out here, he just told me something disturbing about ferrets in the elevator. Also, I think the plimits are closing in. I really don't want to get shredded.'

'Talk!' said Tomothy.

Hudd gave an audible sigh. 'I've failed my mission. You successfully protected 6702. I'd flee if I could, but the shield codes will have been changed by now. Basically, I know when I'm beaten.'

'What's he talking about?' whispered Scharlette.

'Our government,' said Tomothy, 'has all of Earth protected in a timeshield. It's impossible to get through without clearance.'

'So why not accept his surrender?'

'Because only someone within the government could have gotten him through the shield in the first place. Something's going on, and I'm not sure what. This could certainly,' he stared at the door, 'be some kind of trap. Listen, how about I make you a deal? If you give me my gun, and help me get away, I'll show you inside of a time travelling spaceship.'

'What?'

'Wouldn't you like to see inside a time travelling spaceship, Scharlette Day?'

Scharlette thought about her boring life for about one

second. The fact that she was half drunk and fairly certain she'd gone insane helped her adopt a rather cavalier attitude.

'Okay,' she said, and handed Tomothy the gun.

'Ha ha!' he said, turning it around on her immediately. 'You trusting fool!'

'Are you frickin' kidding me?'

He grinned at her outraged expression, and tucked the gun into his belt.

'Yep. Now come on, let's go!'

Tomothy led Scharlette out onto the balcony.

'We don't have long. Hudd will blow that door to fresh bananas once he realises he can't hear us inside any more.'

He twisted a dial on his ray gun and took aim at the balcony rail.

'What are you doing?' said Scharlette.

A thin red laser beam issued from the gun, which Tomothy used to cut the rail until it fell away and smashed through a car windscreen on the street below.

'Do you trust me?' said Tomothy.

'Of course not! Not even remotely. Are you crazy?'

'Jump into my arms.'

'What?'

'Jump into my arms!' said Tomothy, as he manoeuvred to try and sweep Scharlette off her feet. She was about to clock him in the face when there was a massive explosion in the apartment behind them. The interior door blew off its hinges, windows shattered outwards, and debris hurtled past them. An object thumped against Scharlette's shoulder and went spiralling down into the street. Dimly, she registered it as her new book. She staggered towards Tomothy, who scooped her up into his arms and stepped off the balcony. Scharlette screamed and clutched at him in panic.

'Quite a grip on you there,' he grunted. 'But please, relax. I have you.'

As they floated slowly towards the ground, Tomothy looked down and gave her a friendly smile.

'Standard issue time agent togs,' he said, 'complete with anti-grav stitching. Death by plummeting is so antiquated, don't you think?'

Scharlette was a bit self-conscious at being cradled like some fifty-kilo slip of a girl, instead of the overstuffed teddy bear she felt like. She wondered how she had the presence (or absence) of mind to worry about such a thing, but there was something undeniably nice about staring up into the face of a handsome man who was flying through the air, even if he was beginning to sweat from the effort of carrying her.

They set down in the street with barely a bump, and he lowered her to her feet. Vaguely, she wondered how she was going to explain what had happened to her apartment to the people from strata.

Then she noticed the book open on the pavement in front of her.

Stunned to find herself not splattered to bits, it was lucky that Scharlette retained the presence of mind to retrieve the strange book that continued to freak her out so consistently.

'No time to farm about,' said Tomothy. 'Hudd is still after us.'

'Wait!' she said. Not quite sure why, she picked up the book.

A moment later they were running down the street as lights flicked on in the buildings around them. It seemed as if the large explosion had somehow attracted some attention!

'Why are you escaping?' Hudd shouted from the balcony. 'Stop and accept my surrender! Accept my surrender or I'll shoot!'

Laser bolts went sizzling past.

'This way,' said Tomothy, steering Scharlette down an alley. 'Try to stay out of his line of sight.'

'Okay,' puffed Scharlette, as her gym membership flashed before her eyes.

The alley was long and straight without any side streets. There weren't even doorways or handy recesses to duck into. It seemed like line of sight was going to be difficult to avoid. Sure enough, when they were about halfway down the alley, 'Tom!' came Hudd's voice from behind. 'Don't make me fire a warning across your bow.'

'Why not?' Tomothy called over his shoulder.

'Because I'm a terrible shot.'

A red bolt sizzled overhead and pinged off a rusted pipe, exploding it to hot metal ash. Scharlette yelped as she ducked beneath the falling embers, frantically brushing a few from her hair. Ahead the alley opened onto a main road, but Hudd's pounding feet were closing the gap. She felt the heat of another bolt as it passed between her and Tomothy.

'Crumbs,' said Tomothy.

'I was aiming for your legs,' called Hudd.

'You missed!'

'Exactly! Imagine what would happen if I didn't aim for them!'

Ahead on the left was an illegally parked car.

'We should,' wheezed Scharlette, her vision starting to swim, 'get behind that'.

'And then what?' said Tomothy.

'I dunno, genius, maybe return fire? Otherwise why did I even give your gun back?'

'I was hoping it wouldn't come to that,' said Tomothy.

He reached the car first and darted behind it. Scharlette made to follow, but a laser bolt hit the small of her back, lifting her up and sending her flying with surprising velocity. The pavement flashed along below, then suddenly rushed up toward her. She hit the ground at speed and tumbled, snapping and splintering, until she came to rest in a battered pile.

As Scharlette lay dying, Tomothy began to shout.

'Time out! Time out!'

Was his voice angry, or just very, very firm? It was hard to tell, face down on the cold stone.

'Time out, Agent Hudd! Time out.'

Crisp echoes emanated from footsteps around her, like sonar pulses in the void. Voices were dim, somehow nearby yet very far away at the same time.

'... going to do? Look, it's *us* picking apples from the low branches here. We shouldn't involve her ...'

Her vision faded in and out. Under her cheek, bitumen shone blackly in the soft glow of street lamps. A warm liquid pooled between her fingertips. Beside her, the book lay open, its pages flapping in the breeze.

'... non-interference policy, anyway. *They* aren't even adhering to it. And you and I – well!'

'I know, we've both been terrible at adherence. Which includes, by the way, you grabbing this poor girl from her home and dragging her along with you.'

'For the love of Science, I didn't *grab* her. She's much too stubborn for that.'

There was pain too, and becoming aware of it made it intensify. It was everywhere, a miasma of burning and brokenness meshed together in horrible union. She retreated into herself, the remainder of her life force a flickering spark in the night. Soon, she knew, it would be snuffed out completely.

'... discuss each other's missions. You're hardly going to

answer my questions, like why I'm being sniped, and how you got the shield code in the first place. The fact is, an innocent is hurt, and there are *some* rules you didn't abandon when you went rogue.'

The snatches of pavement grew briefer. The voices grew softer. Unconsciousness seeped in like a dark tide.

'I mean,' said Hudd, holding his ray gun at a jaunty angle, 'what's to stop me from just, you know ...' He waved the gun at Tomothy, not quite enough to put him in its sights, but near enough to get the idea.

'Well, Robin,' said Tomothy, shrugging casually in a way which accentuated the fact that he also held a gun, 'as you said yourself, you're a terrible shot.'

Hudd scowled. 'It's true. Something to do with being blind, I suspect.'

'Could be, could be. Maybe your implants are badly calibrated.'

'At least I'm pretty good on the timeship guns.'

'Indeed,' agreed Tomothy. 'You are quite bang-wow on the timeship guns. I hope never to get into a timeship battle with *you*. But when it comes to the regular, hold-in-your-hand-type itty bitty ray guns,' he spun his Zappity around his finger and caught it aimed directly at Hudd's head, 'I wouldn't trust you to knock a flimswaggle off a zhog's back if it was standing right in front of you.'

Hudd grimaced and holstered his weapon.

'All kay, then,' said Tomothy, doing the same with his

own. 'Now we can have a civilised conversation.'

'I want you to know,' said Hudd, 'that I do land the odd shot.'

'I guess that's what makes it odd.'

'Also, I've checked the Server logs while we've been standing here.'

'Oh?'

'I wondered how we're both able to interact with her so comprehensively. Why she doesn't seem to be protected by plimits at all.'

'And?'

'She's got no ripples. And she's infertile.'

'Poor Scharlette. It's all a bit medieval round here, isn't it?'

'Tell me this isn't just because you think she's cute, Tom? That you don't think you've found a way around the whole "whatever you do, don't sleep with anybody from the past" loop-churning clusterfarm? Not to mention, hard and fast departmental rule.'

On the ground before them, Scharlette choked up blood and her eyes fluttered.

'You're hardly in a position to lecture me about departmental rules,' said Tomothy. 'Besides, whatever my reason, I know you're still going to save her. It's in your nature, so I don't have to convince you of anything, really.'

There came the sound of sirens approaching.

'Sigh,' said Hudd. 'All kay, I won't take that last shot. We'll resume after you get behind the car. But Tomothy ...'

'Yes?'

'Let's not do this all night?'

'Couldn't agree more. Hopefully, I'll have gotten away by now.'

Scharlette groaned.

'Hurry up,' said Tomothy. 'You're prolonging her pain.'

'Strange of you to care. She's not going to remember it.'

Tomothy looked like he was going to say something, then thought better of it.

Police cars screeched into the alley from both directions.

'I imagine the local authorities are on high alert all over the city,' said Tomothy, 'after this afternoon's strange shehooliganics at the airport.'

Police jumped out of cars brandishing weapons and shouting at them to put up their hands.

'Send the edit, Robin,' said Tomothy.

Hudd raised his PPC to his mouth.

'Don't shoot,' he said, and the timeline ended.

7. Non-Interference Policy

Hudd raised his gun and regretfully took aim at Tomothy's back.

Don't shoot, came his own voice in his head.

He paused uncertainly. He didn't usually doubt edits he sent himself from the future, but he wondered about this one. Regardless, the missive achieved its desired effect simply by distracting him, giving Tomothy and Scharlette time to duck behind the car. Whatever his reasons were for screwing up the shot, he would remember them soon enough.

He moved forward cautiously, hugging the alley wall. Tomothy could pop up at any moment, and unlike Hudd he was an excellent shot. Hudd dialled up the strength of his Zappity until it could explode the car to apples and oranges.

'Agent Dartle,' he called. 'You know that vehicle won't protect you. Best you come out and accept my surrender. Or I'll accept yours. I suppose it doesn't really matter at this point.' He inched a little closer. 'Tomothy? I'd rather not blow you both up. And we should also try to avoid gaining any more attention.'

No answer.

It wasn't like Tomothy to stay silent. Whatever else you could say about the man, he was chatty.

The sound of approaching sirens reached Hudd's ears.

'We're out of time, Tom,' he said, and darted around the car.

A metal grill in the pavement had been dragged back to reveal a dark hole into the city's squalid intestines.

'How wonderfully old fashioned,' said Hudd. 'If a little clichéd.'

He eyed off the hole and wondered if he was about to get his uniform dirty.

Don't bother, came another edit. *They get away.*

'Farm it,' said Hudd.

Scharlette stepped over the thin stream of garbage-strewn water that ran down the middle of the tunnel. What was she doing here? In fact, *what the hell* was she doing here, walking around the city's drainage system at a time when normally she was curled up watching Netflix? Still, beyond the disbelief and continuous suspicion of herself-going-mad, a part of her grew increasingly excited about what was happening. It sure beat watching TV until it was time to go to sleep with no one.

'So why,' she said, 'doesn't Hudd simply go back in time and head us off at the pass?'

'Yuck.' Tomothy winced as he stepped on something spongy. 'What do you mean?'

'You know, go to his timeship, go back in time, then come at us from the other end of the alley before we escape down here into the sewer.'

'Well, maybe he will do that,' said Tomothy, 'but he hasn't done it *yet*.'

'But even if he hasn't done it *yet*,' said Scharlette, 'we would still remember it *now* if he does eventually do it, right? Because, you know, it already would have happened to us in the past.'

'Nope, because it hasn't happened to us in the past *yet*.'

'You're being quite impenetrable.'

'Listen, don't worry about it. Time agents are extremely cautious about physically visiting our own personal pasts. When you help your own past self, you instantly change your own personal history, and therefore run the risk of changing your present *while you are living in it*. And if for some reason you don't shred against a plimit before you even come within sight of your past self, you could drive yourself timewarped or make your head explode.'

'Really? But then what's to stop him from going back even further then when we enter the alley, so he never sees his past self, and descending down into this sewer ahead of us, and waiting for us around this corner?'

Scharlette sprang around the corner, scaring herself even though no one was there.

'You show an impressive head for this stuff,' said Tomothy, 'but the answer goes towards what I was saying about him not beating us back in time *yet*. If we make it to my timeship before he gets to his, we could always oversee our own escape and ensure he does not interfere. But we can only do that if we get away, and if we do get away, we don't need to go back in time to make sure we get away, because we already did, right?'

'I think knowing you is going to be annoying.'

'It's much easier and safer to make edits via PPC. Much less chance of running into plimits.'

'What are these plimits you keep going on about?'

'Oh, look, here's a way out.'

An iron ladder led up to a circle of grated light above. Tomothy climbed its rusted rungs, pushed aside the grill, peered around, then clambered out. Scharlette tucked the book into her belt and followed. As she emerged from the gutter, she saw bitumen gleaming with reflected street lights. It reminded her of something.

'Scharlette? Scharlette, are you all kay?'

Tomothy, she was dimly aware, was helping her out of the hole. Had she almost slipped? She sat down heavily on the curb.

'You started shaking,' he said. 'You very nearly fell. What's wrong?'

It was strange to remember. An impossible impact, harder than a human body could withstand. The crunch of her own bones upon landing, the world spinning. The pain, which had lasted for longer than was merciful.

'I got shot,' she said.

'You look all kay to me.'

'No, I mean, I remember getting shot. On a ... different timeline?'

'Oh dear,' said Tomothy.

'Do you remember it too?'

'No,' he said softly. 'You're the only one of us wearing my PPC, remember?'

'I think I died.'

'Happens to the best of us. Come on, we better keep moving.'

She shrugged him off. Her heady enthusiasm of mere moments before had completely evaporated.

'Hudd shot me by mistake,' she said slowly, trying to piece it together, 'and you talked him into undoing it.'

'Well, that was nice of me, right?'

'I now know what it's like to have a burning hole in my back.'

'Look, I'm not sure what you remember, but it never really happened. Not here. Not in some parallel universe. Not in another dimension. Never, ever, and nowhere. The timeline has changed. The only place it happened is in your mind.'

'Wonderful.'

'Please, let's keep on. I wasn't joking when I said I'd like to make it to my timeship before Hudd gets to his.'

Scharlette allowed herself to be helped to her feet, but she was giddy, dazed, and could not help but relive the memory over and over. She began to recall snatches of Tomothy and Hudd's conversation, spoken over her while she faded away.

'Hey,' she said, 'what did you mean about non-interference policy?'

'Pardon?'

'You two talked a bit while I lay bleeding out.'

'Ah. Well, it is very rare for an agent to visit Earth prior to the invention of time travel. It's too risky, even with plimits in place.'

'What are ...'

Tomothy waved her question away. 'That's a whole other conversation. Just know that *paradox limits* prevent impossible loops from forming. I could not do anything right now, for example, that would stop time travel from being invented, and thus prevent myself from being here in the first place. It's one of the laws of the universe – actions cannot prevent themselves. For example, there's a historical film we watch in time agent training, which I think was released around this period – Terminator?'

'Yeah, that's been out for a while.'

'We study it as an example of something that could never happen. It's totally batso – sending your father back in time to get your mother pregnant with yourself? Who ever thought that made any kind of plausible sense?'

'It's just a movie,' said Scharlette, a bit defensively, though she didn't quite know why.

'It's ridiculex. Anyway, if you want to know about non-interference policy, it's just what it sounds like. Even within the plimits, it's possible to make changes that affect things in the future. Like I could step on an ant, and suddenly most of my friends will never be born. The change may not be enough to prevent me from being here to step on said ant, but I'll be a whole lot lonelier "after" I do it. Plus, thanks to my PPC, I'll start remembering all these people I love who never even existed. And while I might have different friends in the newly created timeline, maybe even better than my old friends, it's still a bad deal for the ones who get wiped out of existence. Thus, as a general rule, agents try to minimise all impacts of being in the past as much as possible – but, you know, it's *hard* to track a rogue agent across town without stepping on a few ants.'

'Tracking? That's hardly what you're doing. You keep running away from him! He couldn't have made it easier to find him if he tried. Actually, he *did* try.'

'He has me at a big disadvantage.'

'How so?'

'I'm not wearing,' said Tomothy meaningfully, 'my PPC.'

Scharlette might have paid more attention to the pointed look he gave her, had she not just remembered another snatch of never-had conversation.

'Hey! I'm infertile?!'

Tomothy's eyes softened immediately. 'How did that come up?'

'Hudd said something about a Server log.'

'Ah. He must have looked you up. The Server contains a big map of everyone's lives, which charts the ripples of influence individuals send into the future.'

'He also said I don't have any ripples.'

'Hmm. I guess that explains why it's so easy for me to

interact with you. You never have any children, you never do anything in particular with your life, and therefore you never have any impact upon anything.' Tomothy smiled widely. 'You don't matter at all!'

'Why are you smiling?' said Scharlette. 'That's the most horrible thing I've ever been told.'

'What?' Tomothy seemed genuinely confused.

'What do you mean, "what"?' snapped Scharlette. 'I find out I can never have children and that I don't even matter – and you think I'm going to like it?'

'Why not?' said Tomothy. 'There's no pressure on you to live up to any expectation. You're totally free to do whatever you like. Isn't that great?'

Scharlette opened her mouth, but couldn't quite think of what to say.

8. To the Timeship!

They headed across a quiet road into a stretch of parkland.

'I mean, I don't think I even want children,' Scharlette muttered. 'It would be nice to have the choice, though. Even if I did want them, it kind of requires another person to, you know, get it all happening.' She had another sudden remembrance. 'Hey, you also said you thought I was cute.'

'Did I? That certainly sounds like me.'

'Oh, wait – no, Hudd accused you of it. It's all a bit foggy, what with the agonising dying I was doing at the time.'

Tomothy chuckled. 'Well, I do think you're cute. Everyone in the future is so farming polished, whereas look at you – you're all overweight and messed up.' He grinned. 'It's refreshing.'

Scharlette gave him a hard stare. 'You really know how to make a girl feel special.'

'Thanks,' said Tomothy, failing absolutely to pick up on her tone. Scharlette wondered if they even had sarcasm in the future.

'Ah,' said Tomothy, 'here's a place that'll work.'

They arrived in a shadowed area of the park, surrounded by trees and free of lamps, with nobody else nearby.

'There's nothing here,' said Scharlette.

'Give me a minute, she's flying around up there some-where. I just have to ...' His gaze became distant. After a moment, he said, 'If you're wondering what I'm doing, I'm simply accessing the ship's security and navigation systems via my head computer.'

'I see,' said Scharlette. Perhaps if she just said 'I see' to everything, it would eventually become true.

'She's coming down,' said Tomothy.

Whooshing air hit them out of nowhere, rustling the grass and blasting Scharlette's hair, though she couldn't see anything.

'Is the ship cloaked or something?' she asked.

Tomothy gave her an odd look. 'Why would I put a cloak on a ship? To keep her warm?'

'It's just,' said Scharlette, 'that I can't see anything.'

'Oh. Well then, yes, the ship is invisibilised, if that's what you mean.'

The ground shook as something heavy set down, and the shape of four invisible landing pads flattened into the grass at equidistant points. The white glowing outline of a doorway appeared in the air.

'After you,' said Tomothy. He held a hand out through the doorway, and it disappeared as it crossed the threshold, making it look like he was cut off at the wrist. 'Don't worry, the ship is just maintaining maximum sneakiness. It's perfectly safe to step through.'

'I see,' said Scharlette. She took a deep breath, wondered if this was a good idea, and stepped through.

As if reality was nothing more than the thin sheen of a waterfall, she found herself standing in a luminescent blue chamber. Ahead of her was a sealed door, and from all around came a subtle thrum, as if she was – well – inside a spaceship.

A moment later Tomothy bumped into her from behind.

'Pardon,' he said. The external door slid closed behind him, in which a porthole window looked out onto the park. 'Well, what do you think? I bet you've never been in an airlock before.'

'I don't think so.'

'Not very exciting, is it? Come on!'

Tomothy strode towards the opposite door and it slid open. Scharlette glanced back through the porthole and was shocked to see the ground dropping away rapidly at a crazy angle some distance below. She had felt no lurch, no launch, no nothing.

'We ... we ...' She made after Tomothy, into a corridor lined by more doors, and lit blue by the walls themselves. 'We're ... flying?' She experienced a strange sense of vertigo as she imagined the ship perpendicular to the ground, even though everything seemed completely level.

'Indeed,' said Tomothy. 'You know the old saying – "leaving a massive spaceship invisibilised in a public park in the distant past is asking for trouble". Apologies for the lack of warning – I gave the take off instructions silently via my head computer. Even though you don't have one, by the way, you can still talk to the ship, and ask her to open doors and such – just use her name.'

'What's her name?

'Gordon.'

'Oh. But isn't that ...' Scharlette stopped herself from saying 'a boy's name?' Instead she said, 'I see. Um, hello, Gordon?'

A friendly feminine voice emanated from the air around her.

'The warmest of greetings to you, unidentified visitor.'

'Gordon,' said Tomothy, 'meet Scharlette. She can have clearance level, oh ... let's say W.'

'Clearance level W?' said Gordon. 'Are you sure?'

'Yes, Gordon.'

'Do levels of clearance coincide with letters of the alphabet?' asked Scharlette.

'They do.'

'So W is pretty low, right?'

'Indeed. We don't want you learning terrible secrets or accidentally sending us into the jaws of a Tyrannosaurus, now do we? W is all you need.'

For some reason, mention of a T-Rex filled Scharlette's heart with childish joy. It was such a classic where time travel was concerned that the thought of really seeing one almost made her laugh. It was a good thing, she decided, that she had only been assigned clearance level W, or she probably *would* have been tempted to fly straight to the Cretaceous. She pictured herself hiding behind the treeline of a prehistoric forest, looking out onto a field where a T-Rex stood bellowing at the sky, while the theme music from Jurassic Park played.

The good mood she had experienced down in the sewer began to return.

She realised Tomothy was smiling at her.

'Hey there,' she said. 'Can I help you?'

'I like how you just stood there for a moment giggling to yourself,' he said.

'Was I?' She grinned sheepishly. 'I haven't done that since ...' It took her a moment to remember the last time, which she could not believe, since it was something Jenelope had always teased her about. '... since my sister was alive?'

Tomothy's smiled faded. 'Oh. What happened?'

'She plugged in an old sandwich press and it exploded.'

'Ah. My condooblences.'

She quirked an eyebrow at him. 'You'll have to tell me about the etymology of that one sometime.' She glanced around. 'Well, this corridor is very interesting, but *I* want to see the view outside. Can you take me to the bridge, or whatever you call it?'

'The bridge?' said Tomothy. 'Why would there be a bridge on a timeship? There are no babbling brooks between here and the Piloting Area, I can assure you of that.'

'The Piloting Area!?' said Scharlette exasperatedly. 'Has anyone ever told you that everything in the future is named very literally?'

'Useful, isn't it?'

Tomothy led her up a stairwell – for some reason she found it strange that they still had stairs in the future – which emerged into a large hexagonal room with much more personality than the corridors below.

'This is Meals and Rec,' said Tomothy.

A jet black table in the centre showed evidence of a recent meal in the form of a dirty plate and cutlery; against the wall stood a lumpy, rubbery red couch, draped with a pair of hideously clashing orange pants; a bookcase contained books and discs and twinkling bright orbs on stands; a bizarre plant stood tall in some kind of computer-ised pot with a heartbeat monitor; something that might have been a bird in a birdcage chirped and chattered up near the ceiling; and generally lying about were a bunch of strange oddments from alien worlds the likes of which Scharlette had never seen.

'What is this?' she asked, picking up a thing that defied all logical description.

'Don't touch that!' said Tomothy, quickly taking it from her. A drawer popped seamlessly out of the wall, and he slipped the thing inside, never to be seen again.

Scharlette peered up at the talkative little creature fluttering about in its cage. Was it a bird? It *seemed* feath-ery. Well, it seemed to have *some* feathers poking out from between its scales.

'Gordon,' said Tomothy, standing by the dirty plate,

'why haven't you cleaned up? We have company.'

'For Science's sake, Tom,' said Gordon, 'don't you remember how annoyed you got the last time I recycled your plate before you were finished?'

'That's because I had half a rhinodon steak left! This is what, a couple daubs of mayo?'

'Well,' said Gordon, 'I wouldn't want to *presume* you didn't want them, just because they've been sitting there for days and would probably kill you if you ate them.'

'Come on, Scharlette,' said Tomothy, beckoning her to an upward sloping passage on the other side of the room. 'It's this way.'

After a short walk up a brief incline, they emerged into the Piloting Area – a dark chamber lit with flashing control panels and monitors, which faced a concave viewscreen that took up an entire wall. On screen was a rolling blue ocean lightly smattered by fairyfloss clouds, and a coastline that, after some inspection, Scharlette had to admit she had no idea what the hell country it was. Geography was not her strong suit.

'Have a seat,' said Tomothy, gesturing to a line of plush black swivel chairs standing before what she imagined must be called the Main Control Panel. She plonked down on one and found it very comfortable.

Tomothy took a seat beside her. 'Now please, put your hand in there.'

A small aperture ringed by blinking lights opened up in the panel before her. Scharlette peered at it suspiciously.

'So just stick my hand into this dark hole without any further explanation?' she said.

'It's a PPC reader. It will let me download any of my own memories that might be stored on the one you're wearing. Here, look.'

He opened a drawer and pulled out another PPC, which he snapped into place around his wrist. A second aperture whirred open in front of him and he placed his hand inside. There was a click, a buzz, and the circle of lights glowed more brightly.

'See? It's alllll all kay.'

Scharlette supposed there was not much reason to distrust Tomothy at this point. With a shrug, she put her hand into her own aperture. There was a click as something gripped the PPC in place, then a vibrating buzz, which kind of tingled – Scharlette was a bit surprised to discover this – in her anus.

'Eee,' she said.

'I know,' said Tomothy. 'Quite nice, right?'

In sync, the lights around the two apertures started turning from white to blue.

'Even though I wasn't wearing my PPC when the timeline changed,' said Tomothy, 'I may still be able to do a manual restore of my alternative memories from a previous point. That is, if the universal recall somehow left something behind. Which it probably didn't. Anyway, I'm also swapping the temporal identities of our two devices, so my new one will be my old one again, for all intents and purposes, and yours will be fresh.'

Scharlette didn't really hear him. She was too busy taking in the view of her *home planet* from the *timeship* she was *flying through space* in while she sat next to a *time agent from the future*. For a moment she was almost overwhelmed by italics. Was any of it even real? Tired as she might be – and she was tired, she realised – she was definitely not dreaming.

Her dreams were never this colourful.

As the last lights in the apertures turned blue, the buzzing subsided and her wrist was released. Tomothy leaned back in his chair and closed his eyes, which immediately began to twitch. Scharlette was curious about what he was doing, but decided it was better to leave him undisturbed.

She turned back to watch the Earth. After a while, its languid rotation made her eyelids grow heavy. On her chest, the book she had been clutching ever since it had exploded out of her apartment after her, began to rise and fall more slowly.

It had been a long day.

9. Tomothy Tries to Explain a Few Things

Scharlette awoke so wonderfully well rested that she was blissfully blank for a moment before she became entirely disoriented.

She sat up with a jolt.

She was in a nice big bed under clean blue sheets. The room around her was starkly futuristic. There was an empty built-in wardrobe with glass doors and keypad; a glass table by the side of the bed, upon which stood the book and a glass of water; a glass doorway through to what looked like an en suite; and a glass desk upon which sat a sleek and snazzy computer terminal. It was definitely not her stuffy bedroom with sheets left unwashed for slightly too long and empty water bottles all over the floor.

Her clothes were neatly folded at the foot of the bed. She blinked at them, coming to grips with the significance of their location. *They were not upon her body.* Or, in other words, *someone had undressed her.* She lifted the sheets and found that she was wearing amazingly soft pajamas that seemed to glide over her skin, the same blue colour as the sheets.

'What's with all the goddamn blue around here?' she muttered.

'Blue has a calming effect,' answered Gordon, making

her start.

'Jesus!'

'It is a peaceful colour and also, nice. I chose the shade myself. Are you feeling calm, Scharlette? If not I could make you some tea, or fill the room with anti-hysteria gas?'

'Er ... no, that won't be necessary, thanks,' said Scharlette. She rubbed her temples, hastily compiling information. She was in a spaceship, high above the Earth, speaking with an advanced AI from the future. Or perhaps she was in an insane asylum talking to a mouse? It was difficult to be sure. One thing was certain – she was defin-itely going to be late for work.

'Gordon,' she said, and then so many questions jostled for attention she had trouble focusing on one in particular.

'Yes, Miss Scharlette?'

'What's the time?'

'I'm afraid that is quite difficult to answer, as perspectives tend to differ wildly. However, internal ship time is currently 64:38:91.'

'Right.'

'PM.'

'Very helpful. Okay, how about this – where am I?'

'In a guest room. If you require me to fabricate any clothing or food or whatever, just let me know. I should point out that with W class clearance, you cannot fabricate any weapons, sharp objects, explosive chemicals, etcetera. You don't want anything like that, do you?'

'Um, no.'

'Good, because you aren't allowed.'

'How long have I been asleep?'

'7 hours and 41 mins.'

'Wow, that's very precise. Have you been watching me?'

'Your brainwaves were monitored while you slept. I simply analysed my record of them after you asked the question.'

'Oh.'

'But yes, I am always watching you.'

'That's not creepy at all.'

'I watch everything on board, Miss Scharlette. I am omnipresent. I am Gordon.'

Scharlette bit her lip. The ship AI was a little kooky, but there was certainly precedence in the literature.

I'm taking all of this pretty well, considering.

'Gordon?'

'Yes?'

'Who changed my clothes and put me to bed?'

'I did.'

'Ah. But ... I mean, sorry if this sounds rude, but aren't you just a disembodied voice?'

'I am the ship.'

'Yes, but how did you move me?'

'I manipulated gravity to float you right into bed. Then my nanobots took apart your clothing at a molecular level, built you something nice and blue in a perfect fit around you while you slept, and reassembled your old stuff down to the very last sauce stain and frayed thread, in case you still want it. I can't see why you would, but humans are inexplicably sentimental about the oddest things.'

Scharlette considered her security uniform. She did not feel any special attachment to it – unless hate was a kind of attachment.

'So,' she said, deciding to try and get her head around things one at a time, 'there were little robots crawling all over me while I slept?'

'Yes, Miss Scharlette. And inside you.'

'WHAT?'

'I thought you could do with a cleanse. I had my nanos remove all the toxins and built up decay and dormant diseases and all that. Your body is in much better working order now. Don't you feel better?'

'Well,' said Scharlette, prodding her cheek, as if that was somehow proof of anything, 'actually, I do.' She took a deep breath and smiled. 'I feel fantastic.'

It was true. She had never, as far as she could remember, woken up feeling more rested in her entire life. There were no dim creaks or slight aches, no kink in her muscles from whatever position she had slept in, and in place of the fug that traditionally accompanied her first moments of consciousness, was a clarity and energy that only fit people who don't drink a bottle of wine before passing out can dream of. Her eyes felt bright, and if she'd had a tail she was sure it would have been bushy. Maybe she should have been more concerned about weird electric bugs crawling around inside her, but if this was the result, it was difficult to mind.

'I also,' said Gordon, 'had the nanos remove all fat stores exceeding the recommended limit for a human of your height.'

'You *what*?'

Scharlette leapt out of bed and headed to the bathroom. There was a full length mirror just waiting for her, as if it had known she was coming all along. She turned this way and that, astounded at what she saw. Her formerly limp brown hair was now wavy and shiny like in a shampoo commercial. Her skin was completely unblemished, and even the freckles across her nose were fainter. Her eyes *were* bright, the greenest she had ever seen them, *like goddamn pieces of jade or something*. Most incredibly, she had lost the chub that had been slowly encroaching for the better part of a decade. The muscles of her arms were defined rather than enveloped, her stomach on the verge of concave, her hips no longer hidden under bunched up love handles. She gave her bum a slap, and laughed. In short, she'd become less of a block and more what you'd carve out of one.

'Er ...' Gordon seemed nervous. 'My apologies if I ... Tom says I sometimes don't respect boundaries enough, so ...'

'Gordon, you wonderful thing! You've done an amazing job. This is the kind of low effort magical body shaping bullshit people in my time dream about!'

'Oh, that's a relief. Thank you very much, in that case.'

'I feel like I'm twenty again. I *look* like I'm twenty again! You're frickin' marvellous, Gordon!'

The lighting in the room turned rosy pink.

'Why is that happening?' asked Scharlette.

'I'm blushing.'

'Oh.'

'I also ... well actually, it's more what I didn't do. I didn't take any of the excess fat from your breasts. I just kinda left them.'

'Oh?' Scharlette examined her boobs, which did seem the same as before.

Gordon gave a little cough. 'I know well enough not to mess about with another woman's breasts, unless specifically requested. You only make that mistake a few times in a row.'

'Probably wise,' said Scharlette.

All that paying for gym memberships and then hardly ever going suddenly seemed like such a waste of effort.

'Now, about these clothes you said you could ... fabricate, was it?'

'Yes, Miss Scharlette?'

'Let's go ahead and talk about that for a bit.'

Scharlette entered Meals and Rec to find Tomothy sitting at the dining table, resting his chin on his hands with his eyes closed.

'Good morning,' she said. 'I think?'

'You must be hungry,' he said, and waved at a bowl of multicoloured cubes that looked like children's building blocks. 'You should try ... ah.' He opened his eyes, then seemed to force a smile. 'I see someone's been making full use of the ship's facilities.'

Scharlette was wearing dark denim jeans which fit her *exactly*, a black tank top with a weird symbol on it (which Gordon had shown her from a random selection of alien languages), an incredibly light black jacket which was apparently 'gongolian leather', and flats.

She felt pretty damn good. She wasn't quite sure how to read Tomothy's reaction, however.

'You don't seem impressed by my amazing transformation.'

'Oh, Gordon does good work, no doubt about it. It's not like I don't benefit from nanobot attention also.' He flexed a muscle. 'I just, you know, everyone in the future has access to beautification tech. You were different. Real. Scrappy!'

'I'm still scrappy,' said Scharlette.

This time Tomothy's smile came more easily. 'I don't doubt it.'

'Well,' said Scharlette loftily, 'I'm sorry I'm not dumpy and unkempt enough for your particular kink any more, but I guess you'll just have to see past my stunning good looks and smoking body, and judge me on my personality instead.'

'That's right,' chimed in Gordon. 'Don't you know

better than to treat a woman like an object, Tomothy? I raised you to be better than this.'

'You didn't raise me,' said Tomothy. 'And what's this unfamiliar phrase? "Like an object", did you say?'

'Just borrowing from the vocabu-library of all the TV and social media I've been enjoying from this historical period. Gender stuff was much more complicated back now.'

'I see. Well, anyway, my apologies, Scharlette. I didn't mean to appear unenthused about you being totally thermogenic.'

'Thanks, I think.' She sat down before the bowl of cubes and gave them a prod. They had the consistency of dense bread, in a lurid assortment of bright colours. 'What's this stuff?'

'Hmm? Oh. Mr Xagnulathet's Funtime Squares, a popular breakfast cereal from the Swamp Worlds. You can have a meal pill if you'd prefer, but I enjoy real food more.'

Scharlette put a purple cube in her mouth. Sweet, tangy moisture squished out of it, making her shiver as it ran down her tongue. She had never tasted anything like it.

'This is ...' She held her hand to her mouth. 'It's incredible!'

'Yeah. They grow a lot of crazy fruit in the Swamp.'

Scharlette reached for a glass of water. It was the cleanest, most refreshing water she had ever tasted. Had she ever actually had pure water before, she wondered? When it came out of the tap at home it was full of fluoride and whatever else, and when it came from bottles labelled 'Mountain Spring Brand' it was full of plastic residue and lies.

This was the real stuff, and it was amazing.

After a few more electrifying gulps and mouthfuls, Scharlette finally noticed that Tomothy seemed rather glum. She remembered, amongst the litany of other things she had experienced yesterday, that he had needed the data from her PPC for something to do with his mission.

'Did you find out anything about your lost memories?' she asked.

'Sigh,' said Tomothy. 'Not really. Sort of. I mean, I could tell you about it, and it may well help me to talk it out, but ...'

'Yes?'

'Well, I can't do that without explaining some other stuff first. How do you feel about a little exposition?'

'That's fine,' said Scharlette, as she munched away on Funtime Squares. ''Bout bloody time, really.'

'All kay. So. Crash course. Time travel. Let's see. Basics.' He gave the table a single drum of his fingers and cleared his throat. 'Any form of dimensional travel comes with certain rules. For example, as a three dimensional object in space, you can't just float around freely wherever you choose. Gravity affects you. So does other mathematical stuff. Without sufficient build up of force, you cannot break through a brick wall. Matter can never be truly destroyed. Energy is never lost, simply converted. In other words, there are limitations, as dictated by the laws of the universe. Right?'

'Sure,' said Scharlette. A stream of pink squirted from her mouth and oozed down her chin. 'Oops.'

'So time travel – or 16th dimensional travel – is much the same. There are rules, parameters, limitations. One rule is that something cannot simultaneously exist and not exist. For example, one particular mind-farming hypothetical that was popular before the invention of time travel was, what if you go back to before you were born, and shoot your father in the face?'

'Um,' said Scharlette.

'"Um" is right. "Um" is why people thought for a long while that time travel was simply impossible. If you kill your dad, you can't exist, so you can't go back in time and kill him, so you do exist, so you *do* go back in time and kill him, etcetera ad infinitum. But here's the rule that stops any of that from happening – you cannot simultaneously exist and not exist. Or, to put it another way, actions you take cannot lead to their own prevention. Or to put it *another* way, you cannot create endless loops. You follow?'

'Reckon I'm still on "um".'

'Here's another example. Say you're a time agent from the distant future. You read in a history book that, at some point in the past, there was this totally neato planet, just this really blisso place to live, until one day a horrible warlord rose to power and ruined everything. This guy is one mean son of a peach and he thoroughly ploughs up everyone's lives. All kay?'

'Okay.'

'So you read about this guy, and decide the universe would be better off if he didn't exist. So you get in your timeship, you go to this planet, and you find the guy's mother in the bar on the night when she was supposed to meet his father. You sweet talk her until you she agrees to accompany you back to your hotel room, and thus mother and father never meet. The warlord is therefore never born.'

'Is that how you solve a lot of problems in the past?' asked Scharlette. 'With seduction?'

'Depends on the species, but it can be effective. It's just an example, it doesn't matter what method you use to erase the warlord. Kill him when he's a baby, if you prefer.'

'So now the poor mum has a murdered child without any explanation as to why?'

Tomothy grinned exasperatedly. 'All kay! How about, instead of either of those things, you go back in time, get a job as a bartender, you don't interfere with the mum and dad meeting, but when you serve them their drinks, you slip some contraceptoids into the dad's. *And*,' he held up a hand to cut her off, 'you program them to self-destruct after whatever date it was that old warlordy was due to be conceived. That way these two great lovers can still have a happy life together, with other kids further down the line if they so choose, just not the crazy psychopathic killer they were originally destined to produce. Happy?'

'Actually, I was wondering what contraceptoids are?'

'Nanobots that go around murdering spermatozoa. They have these little spear attachments. They're quite evil looking.' Tomothy shuddered. 'Even though you know its impossible, given their miniscule size, you can't help but worry about them piercing your testicles from the inside.'

'I'll, er, take your word for it.'

'Anyway, the point is, you go back in time and stop the warlord from ever existing, *somehow*. Right?'

'Right.'

'So, what happens next? As a consequence of your actions, he'll disappear from history. No old book will ever mention him. And because you never read about him, you will never decide to go back in time to stop him existing. Since you don't go back in time to stop him existing, he will be born as he originally was, rise to power, behave like a total apple picker, and all the history books will write about him again. You see? A loop. In rewriting history, you have also rewritten your own personal history.'

'I see.'

'The thing is, none of that could ever happen, because of the rules. When you are physically in the past, relative to your own past self, you cannot change anything that would prevent you from being in the past doing whatever it is you are doing.'

'So what stops you?'

'Plimits,' said Tomothy, a dark look in his eye. 'Plimits are what makes a lot of time travel zicky and dangerous.

They prevent you from making changes that violate the rules. They exist only in the 16th dimension, and no one really knows what they look like, because sometimes they aren't even akin to a physical barrier. For example, I could be talking to caveman in the past, and I could say "What a lovely ice age we're having" or "That's a good mammoth you have there" and it wouldn't make a pip's difference to my own personal history. But what if I showed the caveman how to invent the wheel? That knowledge would accelerate human evolution and change everything, possibly including me ever being born. So, because of the plimits, I could not even speak such words to a caveman. The *words themselves* would hit a plimit.'

'So what happens when something hits a plimit?'

'It shreds.'

'Shreds?'

'Whatever is trying to cross the plimit, or rather, *attempting to create a paradoxical change*, gets shredded out of existence. A person would be killed. Sound waves get mangled and never heard by the intended recipient. A bullet would vanish before hitting your dad. Plimits can close in fast and unpredictably, but one thing is certain – they will *always* find you before you can make an impossible change. They deny any loop from forming before it has a chance, sure as walking into a brick wall will give you a sore nose.'

Scharlette felt like she was getting a sore brain. 'But,' she said, chasing some flitting thought, 'oh yes – when you and Hudd were talking, you spoke as if you could see the plimits.'

'In a sense. What we see are visual representations we can usefully interpret, delivered to our head computers via PPC tech. So a large plimit might actually look like a barrier, and be easy to avoid, but it's dangerous to think of them so simply. A plimit might be tiny, or even abstract.'

'So when you were running around without a PPC ...'

'I was in constant grave and mortal peril. If I'd done anything paradoxical, I would have shredded without warning. That's why I sought you out. Not only because I suspected you had my PPC, but also because, at the airport, yours was the only security thing I could approach without walking into a plimit.'

'Because I don't matter,' said Scharlette ruefully. 'On the plus side, apparently neither does Barry, but anyone could have told you that. Goddammit! I was supposed to be someone, to do something. I wasn't supposed to get stuck in a crappy job forever!'

'"Not mattering" is a subject for philosophical debate,' said Tomothy. 'Just because you don't have any great influence on the future, does that equate to a pointless present? Does a person have an intrinsic worth, or are they measured by their influence over others? Anyway, that's a discussion for another time, or maybe never.'

He seemed to think this was a funny joke, though Scharlette wasn't quite sure why. She tried to clear her head.

'So,' she said. 'Sooooo, what are you really telling me here? That no one can go back in time for a specific reason?'

'Very good!' Tomothy clapped his hands. 'Not correct at all, but an excellent deduction.'

'So you *can* go back for a reason?'

'Here's the trick. Say that I read about the evil warlord in a history book and decide to go back in time and kill him. What if I then use my PPC to send myself a causality free message to a point before I've ever read the book? I tell myself, "Hey, there's this evil warlord on Planet XYZ who you should really go back in time and kill." That way the message will *always* arrive at the same fixed point in time, regardless of past or future changes, regardless of whether there is any book, or whether I've read it or not, and hence the message itself *becomes* the reason I travel into the past to make the change. And because I've created what we in the trade call "loop denial", it means the plimits won't be as restrictive, because they don't have to prevent me from eliminating the reason I travel back in time in the first place.'

Scharlette took a deep breath.

'How are you going with all this?' Tomothy asked.

'Oh yeah, totally fine, of course.'

'Don't worry. Even if you don't understand it completely, I'm sure we're still about to have some amazing adventures.'

'Well anyway, what does all this have to do with what

85

you were looking for on your PPC?'

'Ah, yes. At the airport, when it started beeping – you remember?'

'Yes.'

'It means there was a change in the timeline, but any memory of the previous timeline was removed from all PPCs everywhere, by my government. That's why it's called a universal recall. It's only done extremely rarely, when they don't want anyone to remember what has changed.'

'I see.'

'And I think it was me who brought about the change they now seek to suppress. The fact that they, or someone, is trying to kill me, seems to support this theory. And if it *was* me who brought about the change, whatever change it was *hasn't* prevented me from taking the same actions as I would have *originally taken*, otherwise I would have shredded against a plimit and never made the change in the first place.' He rubbed his chin. 'I did receive my mission to stop Hudd via a PPC message from my future self, so the version of me on the previous timeline has created loop denial to guard against that fact that the change I've wrought has evidently caused something to rewrite in my own personal history, and I don't know what.'

'I'm thoroughly lost now,' said Scharlette.

Tomothy nodded. 'I don't blame you. Basically, if I could access my alternative memories from the erased timeline, perhaps I'd understand it all. But as it is ...' He looked at her mournfully. '... as is it, I don't know what the farm is going on.'

'Well,' said Scharlette, 'that makes two of us.'

10. A Bit of a Cucumber

On the viewscreen in the Piloting Area was a field of stars brighter than any smog-tainted view from Scharlette's apartment. She stood staring in wonder, enjoying the tingles running through her.

'Ah yes,' said Tomothy. 'The Big Deep. The Celestial Highway. God's Scrapbook. These are things we call space in the future, Scharlette.'

'No, we don't,' said Gordon. 'Tomothy, no one calls it any of those things.'

'I know, Gordon, I was being hilarious.'

'But analysing the humour content of your statement yields negative results.'

'Tough crowd,' said Tomothy.

Scharlette gave him a smile. 'So where are we now on the Celestial Highway?'

'Still parked in Earth's orbit. We're just looking outwards. See?'

Earth swung back into view as the ship turned, although Scharlette hadn't seen Tomothy touch anything. The amount of invisible control he had was kind of eerie.

'We can't travel any great distance at the moment,' said Tomothy. 'Not with the shield standing between us and the Big Deep.'

'Stop that, Tomothy,' said Gordon. 'If you say it one

more time it will become a habit.'

Floating keyboards and control panels and holographic displays sprang up around Tomothy, and he began tapping away on them all.

'So you don't use your head computer for everything?' asked Scharlette.

'No,' said Tomothy. 'The human mind is still aided by visual cues and tactile inputs. Nerves respond to pressure, which stimulates your, you know ... thinkingness.' He began typing furiously. 'Synapses and syntaxes and such all fuel the human machine. Besides, it would be boring sitting around staring at the inside of your eyes all day.'

There was a low hum, almost imperceptible, as the ship accelerated to follow the curvature of the Earth.

'Is this as fast as you can go?' said Scharlette.

'Not even close. We are being sneaky.'

'Ah.'

'We have invisibilised as well. We must go have a look at the gate, dear Scharlette! To the gate, to the gate!'

He seemed quite excited by this idea.

'What's the gate?'

'It's where Hudd got in, where I followed him in. The timeshield was built to make sure no enemy could ever go back in time and step on us all when we were just a dot, or stop us from inventing time travel. Thus, up until a certain point, all of history is preserved. This is cardinal stuff. The official story is that the shield makers left no back door in, no exception for any reason, not even for us, their own descendants. Nothing could be important enough to justify the risk of screwing up humanity's future. However, as it turns out, all you need to get through the shield are the gate coordinates and a pass code. That's a highly classified secret, by the way, which not even I am supposed to know. So don't tell anyone.'

'No worries,' said Scharlette. She was surprised to hear unabashed happiness in her own voice. Where was it coming from? She realised she was in a very good mood, which was so unfamiliar she had almost forgotten what it was like. She kept thinking about what she'd be doing if all of this hadn't happened, almost as if it was the memory of an erased timeline. She'd be showering and eating cereal and heading to work. Instead, she was in space! There had been more excitement packed into the last twenty-four hours than the past ten years. If only Jenelope could be here to see it ... but she mentally sidestepped that particular pitfall. It was time for *her* to take something from life, and this sure beat the heck out of the weekend in Fiji she had been vaguely considering.

Gordon's voice echoed through the Piloting Area. 'Er.'

'Something on your mind, Gordon?' said Tomothy.

'No, no. I mean, well, it's just that you're giving Scharlette quite a lot of highly sensitive information. The fact that she is even on board – if you'll forgive me for saying so, Miss Scharlette, I truly don't mean to be rude – is an astoundingly massive violation of protocol.'

'Bananas,' said Tomothy. 'Protocol? In case you hadn't

noticed, Gordon, the government is trying to kill me. I'm not exactly inspired to follow their protocol right now.'

'It's not *their* protocol Tom, as you well know. It's bigger than whoever's in charge on a given day. It was put in place by your ancestors for good reason.'

Scharlette did not much care for what she was hearing. She didn't want to go home! How could she possibly return to her old life after she'd had a taste of this? Her alternative morning suddenly seemed more like a threat than a comparison.

'But Gordon,' she said, seizing upon the first argument that presented itself, 'I'm infertile. You must know that, what with all your scanning and poking about inside me with nanobots. Right?'

'Well, yes.'

'I have no ripples! Tell her, Tomothy. I'm entirely unimportant! There's no harm if I *never go back again*.'

It was strange to hear such words come out of her mouth. She hadn't actually accepted that her life was entirely inconsequential, had she? She was just using whatever argument sprang to mind so she could stay on board a bit longer, right? Then she remembered something Tomothy had said the previous day about how not mattering was a great thing, because it made her free.

'And you know what else?' she said. 'If you do send me back, I promise I won't lead the same hum drum life as I was formerly destined to. My eyes have been opened, Gordon, whether you like it or not. I'll be compelled to do all kinds of amazing things, and who knows – I might screw up the timeline completely!'

'Oh dear,' said Gordon.

Tomothy watched her with a quirk in his mouth. She was breathing hard, she realised, her heart thumping, her chest rising and falling. She crossed her arms and glared at him.

'What are you looking at, time guy?'

'Here, Gordon,' Tomothy said, turning away to type on a hovering keypad. 'Have a look at the Server log. It may calm you. Both,' he added, then smiled off at nothing in particular.

A holographic image appeared in the air before them, showing a tapestry of intricately interconnecting lines. One line glowed a little brighter, as if it had been high-lighted. As the view zoomed in and rotated to give a clear view of it, Scharlette noticed it worked its way through the other lines without touching any of them. Eventually it came to a dead end.

She frowned – was this a visual representation of her dumb life?

'Ah,' said Gordon. 'Well then, I suppose everything's all kay. I don't agree with the initial risk taking ...'

'I lost my PPC.'

'... but I guess the absence of negative consequences means I shouldn't dwell on it too much. Welcome aboard, Scharlette.'

Scharlette breathed a sigh of relief. 'Thanks, Gordon.'

She was quite grateful when the Server log disappeared.

'In others news,' said Gordon, 'Agent Hudd is broadcasting a message. Want to hear it?'

Tomothy gave a small nod.

'Hi Tomothy,' sounded Hudd's voice. 'I suggest you reveal yourself and accompany me through the shield. It's your only way out, as you must realise. You won't be able to time travel inside the shield without being detected ...'

'As good an admission as any that he's working with the government,' muttered Tomothy.

'... so really, what else can you do? I don't want to see you killed, if it can be avoided. I swear I didn't know about the snipers or I would have argued against them. If you come with me, I will make a case for leniency.'

'Leniency?' spat Tomothy. '*You're* the rogue agent! You can shove your leniency right up your defunct. If you think I'm simply going to hand myself over, you're a bigger farmhand than I thought.'

'It's just a recording,' said Gordon. 'He can't hear you.'

'I *know*, Gordon. I'm just letting off humidity.'

'Ah, good. I thought your brain might be malfunctioning.'

'Hi Tomothy,' said Hudd, as the message started to repeat. 'I suggest you reveal yourself and ...'

Tomothy waved a hand, and the message switched off.

'Look,' he said to Scharlette, 'I'll show you the shield which stands between us and the Big Deep.'

'Tomothy!' said Gordon warningly.

A distant metallic wall of epic proportions shimmered into existence, filling the entire viewscreen as it wrapped around the Earth.

'Woah,' said Scharlette. 'So it's *literally* a shield that goes around the whole planet?'

'Hmm? Oh, no, that's just a skin. I can't actually show you the shield, just a visual representation. We can make it dandelions if you like.' Tom nodded at the viewscreen and the imposing metal wall was replaced by a field of enormous dandelions, like some kind of off-the-scale screensaver. 'But yes, it does go around the whole planet. Over there is the gate.'

He pointed at some dandelions amongst the other dandelions, which did not appear noticeably different.

'So what,' she said, 'are ... we ... going to do?'

It was strange to find herself using the word 'we' in such a fashion.

'Well, Robin is probably floating around invisibilised somewhere nearby, and his sensors will detect us if we try using the code, which has likely been changed by now anyway. Who knows, he may even have allies waiting on either side of the shield. Also, he's right about us not being able to time travel without being detected. It's a bit of a cucumber, really.'

'You mean a pickle?'

Each gave the other an odd look.

Tomothy turned back to his panels. 'What we really need to do is get to a point in Earth's future when the timeshield no longer exists.'

'But I thought we can't time travel?'

'Not as quickly as usual, but we can always travel through time *at the speed of time*.'

Scharlette frowned. 'You mean just ... hang around?'

'Yeah. Hang around until 12588 AD, which is when the timeshield gets deactivated.'

'Why?'

'Because by then humanity has already invented time travel, built the city of Panoptica, and escaped into the future. Destruction of the Earth isn't such a big deal after that.'

'Why not?' Scharlette could not help but feel a little offended, somehow.

'Because us Panopticians can edit from that point without any danger of ploughing up our own personal timelines. And we *will* save the Earth, however many attempts it takes. But let's not worry about that for now – one thing at a time, haha.'

'Hahaha,' said Gordon. '*Now* you're being hilarious.'

'Hmm,' said Scharlette.

Gordon swung about to face the Earth head-on.

'12588,' said Scharlette. 'That's like, what, ten thousand years and change?'

'We'll have to go into stasis,' said Tomothy. 'Gordon is checking undersea maps, trying to isolate places that won't be disturbed by tectonic activity, larval eruptions, nuclear disaster, scientific enquiry, terraforming, the deep sea orchestra, void deconstruction, wyrm extermination and all that type of stuff. It also has to be somewhere Hudd won't find us if he works out what we've done and comes looking. Which he may not do, since we are both trying to remain low impact here. I mean, really, staying on Earth for ten thousand years could butterfly the apples out of everything. Or we could be crushed by plimits while we sleep. We have to be careful.' He looked worried for a moment. 'Found anything, Gordon?'

'Heaps of places.'

They entered the atmosphere slowly, leaving behind the blackness of space.

'Don't want to burn too hot and show up our location,' said Tomothy, answering an unasked question which Scharlette hadn't even thought of.

'Course not,' she said.

Once they entered the 'upper sky', as Scharlette privately thought of it, they sped up towards a great blue ocean that soon took up the entire screen. It wasn't long before Scharlette could make out the crests of waves.

'So we're going to the bottom of the ocean?' she said.

'Yep,' said Tomothy.

11. More Amazing Shit

Scharlette wondered if she should be worried about the fact they were about to plunge into unknowable depths, but there was something about the way Gordon ran so smoothly, and Tomothy's apparent unconcern, that kept her relatively calm.

If you're going to go with this, she thought, *then you're going to have to go with it.*

A few metres above the ocean, they slowed to complete stop. Tomothy looked over at her.

'Um.'

He seemed to be working up to something.

'Yes?' said Scharlette.

'Well,' said Tomothy, 'it occurs to me that this might be – only *might* be, mind you – your last ever chance to remain in your own time.'

It took Scharlette a moment to really hear what he had said.

'Sorry, what? Can't you bring me back?'

'Well, maybe. I'm simply not sure. Who knows how this will all work out? If my government, or someone therein, is up to something illegal, and I bring their crimes to light, protections on the shield may be increased real-like fast-clever. I can't guarantee, if you come with me now, that I'll be able to bring you home ... and I feel I have to tell you that now rather than later.'

'Wow,' said Gordon. 'That's uncharacteristically responsible thinking of you, Tomothy.'

'I'm responsible.'

Gordon scoffed. 'And I'm a walnut's breakfast.'

Tomothy looked confused. 'Maybe scrub that phrase from your vocabu-library, Gordon.'

Scharlette sat back in her seat, a dozen thoughts running through her head like the streams of data in the Matrix.

'It's possible I could have used more time to think about this,' she said. 'You know, as opposed to waiting until the last possible moment to mention it.'

'My apologies,' said Tomothy. 'Things have been moving quickly.'

'Why did you even bring me with you in the first place?'

Tomothy chuckled. 'Me? I tried to take my PPC from you and be on my merry way – at raygunpoint too, if you recall – but you wouldn't allow it, and I didn't have time to fool around. You being here is not something I planned at all.'

Scharlette felt a little unwelcome, and it must have showed on her face.

'Which is not to say,' added Tomothy quickly, 'that I'm not happy about it! It's much more fun to travel with a "companion", as some in the game call it. I just think that, in fairness to you, I have to point out that if you stay on board, you might never see your friends, family and loved ones ever again. Maybe.'

'This is heavy,' said Scharlette. 'Can I have a moment?'

'Of course.'

She closed her eyes. The decision already felt like it was making itself, pervasively clouding her judgement with promises of *excitement* and *adventure* and maybe even *romance with a handsome time traveller*. She fought against it, willing herself to consider the situation properly, rationally, realistically – even though she knew in her heart that she didn't give a crap about any of those things right now.

Work through it logically, Scharlette. What are you leaving behind? Maybe?

Her parents. Annoying and completely incapable of emotional support. Disappointed, disappointing and distant, they mainly cared about their vegetable garden, half of which was high grade kush. They wouldn't even take her calls on Jenelope's deathversary. She tried to stop short of thinking 'screw 'em', but it was difficult. She supposed some part of her loved them in spite of who they were, but it was an instinctual, built in, default love caused mainly by evolution. It made her angry to think it could hold her back, especially when she got so little of it in return. She had often thought it very convenient that so many kids in stories had dead parents, because it freed them up to run headlong into dire situations no parent would ever condone, such as fighting evil wizards, running around in death mazes, or putting on Spiderman costumes. It seemed, in fact, to be an increasingly predictable fallback position for lazy writers, simply to avoid layers of complication. And even though Scharlette was thirty years old, she still felt somewhat like a child, as if she had been placed on hold at some point in her youth and never grown to full potential. It would have been easier to make the decision if her parents were dead – a thought which, in itself, spurred her on to disregard them. Maybe she would join the ranks of dead-parents heroes and heroines after all, if only because they were dead to *her*.

Her job. Well, that didn't require much analysis. She had never envisaged airport security turning into a full blown career. The fact she had the job at all was mostly the fault of her ex-boyfriend James, who'd encouraged her to enrol with him to Border Force Academy, pitching it as a stop-gap solution while she figured herself out. As it transpired, he'd dropped out of the course just before graduation, while she had been the one to see it through. Regardless of all that, she sincerely felt that if she was the kind of person to prioritise their 9-to-5 over flying around the universe in a time travelling spaceship, she should just repeatedly smash her head against the console right now until she was done with life entirely.

Her lovers. That was a generous description. One arrogant finance guy she didn't like unless she was drunk, who hadn't texted back for a month, plus a couple of names she chatted to on dating websites and never met. Hardly worth considering. Sorry, bigdog86.

Her friends were the hardest to think about. Gus and Nell and Ultra-Gay Steve. They would miss her, and she would miss them. That said, they would no doubt proclaim her mad not to leap at an opportunity like this, which was probably why they were her friends in the first place. She wished she could tell them about it – of course they would worry if she simply disappeared – but it was still only a 'maybe' that she'd never make it back. She was taking a risk, not accepting a definite sentence. And given the events of the last day, she felt like anything was possible. If she really wanted to, she would be able to find her way back to her own time, wouldn't she?

Maybe. Maybe!

'Let's go,' she said.

'You sure?' said Tomothy.

'Yes. I mean, seriously, you and I both know what will happen to me if I wake up in my real bed tomorrow. Nothing, nothing, and more nothing.'

'I'm not sure about that, actually,' said Tomothy. 'You were quite right when you told Gordon that your new knowledge has changed you, and thus put your future in a state of flux. It may even be that plimits are now a danger to you, since the universe would not allow you to make any change resultant in me not meeting you.'

'But I thought ... I thought plimits were only a worry if you're in the past relative to your own personal history?'

Scharlette was quite proud of herself for stringing that sentence together.

'As I am now a part of your personal history,' said Tomothy, 'and I come from the future, we are somewhat bound together in that respect. You would not be able to take any action that would rewrite a future which is now a part of your past.'

'So I *have* to lead a boring life if I go back?'

'Either that or run the risk of getting shredded. Oh, and don't forget, your apartment has been blown up.'

'Let's *go*,' said Scharlette, emphatically.

Tomothy grinned and the ship plunged towards the water. Froth burst over the viewscreen as they sank beneath the surface. Schools of fish darted away in alarm, and all around them rays of sunshine penetrated expansive blue-green reaches like an upside down palisade of columns. It was magical to see, and it made Scharlette instantly thankful that she had chosen to remain on board.

The ship began to dive rapidly. Around them the light faded away, as they were swallowed whole by a great void.

'And the, you know ...' Scharlette said, finally a touch nervous, 'the, er, the pressure is okay?'

'Mm? Yes, Gordon can handle pressure.'

'And the, er ...' What other things did she know about going under the sea? 'We won't get the bends?'

'I've no idea what that is.'

'But you've done this sort of thing before?'

'Kind of.'

'Kind of?'

'We once had to dive into an Elsidian river to escape a

patrol of tarkabots.'

'Ah. And how deep did you dive?'

'Not very.'

'Not very?'

'Yes, not very deep at all.'

'I see.'

Scharlette wasn't sure how deep the ocean was – in fact, she didn't even know whether it was measured in miles, fathoms, kilometres, or what – but as she stared into the darkness on the viewscreen, she decided she was better off ignorant.

'Slow down,' said Tomothy. 'Let's have a look.'

Gordon turned on some kind of floodlight, and Scharlette gave a little 'eep' as a weird looking shark-thing rippled away from them. Fibrous strands of dead seaweed and other organic matter drifted by. Pale fish with large eyes organised themselves along the vertical plane. Monolithic rock formations loomed out of the gloom on either side of a jagged trench, into which Gordon descended. An undersea cliff side began to slide by, peppered by tube worms and evil looking crabs.

'Look at that one,' said Tomothy, pointing out a fish that was all head and oversized fangs, a glowing lure dangling before its gaping maw.

They passed a clutch of eels, and some free swimming crustaceans that looked like gigantic aquatic cockroaches. They saw a bioluminescent squid, and things-that-Scharlette-didn't-even-know-what-they-were.

'I feel like I'm in a nature documentary,' she said.

'I'm sure Gordon could do a voice-over for you,' said Tomothy.

'Indeed!' said Gordon. She zoomed the viewscreen in on a strange blob, and 'cleared her throat'. 'This thing here looks like a jellyfish gone wrong, and I say that having catalogued thousands of life forms on dozens of planets. It could best be described as "tentacled" and "squidgy". What could it be? Maybe we'll never know.'

'Thank you, Gordon,' said Scharlette. 'Very informative.'

'And look at this fish,' said Gordon, enlarging another subject on the screen. 'Why has it got so many stripes when there's no light down here to admire them by? What a little idiot!'

'I know what'll smash your peach,' said Tomothy. 'We're almost at the bottom. Take a look at *that*.'

At first all Scharlette saw was the muted brightness of a lava font bubbling from the ocean floor. Then, in the glow of smouldering orange streams, something else began to take shape. For a moment, she simply stared, unable to comprehend what she was looking at, possibly due to the sheer scale of the thing. Lying in a plain of fine sand, stretched out for what seemed like a kilometre, was the most gargantuan creature she had ever seen. Its snake-like body was comprised of enormous wheels of segmented armour tapering to a tail, while giant fins like those of a flatfish spread out to support its bulk on either side.

Gordon circled about and brought the head into view –
which turned out to be an eyeless blockish structure from
which long tubes curled down into the lava.

It was feeding.

'Are we still zoomed in?' Scharlette whispered. 'That
lava patch isn't the size of a tennis ball is it?'

'No, it's really big,' said Tomothy. 'That's a wyrm.'

'A worm?'

'*Commūnis Vermis,*' chimed in Gordon. 'Or the
common wyrm.'

'Common?'

'Ocean's full of them,' said Tomothy. 'That said, when
you're that size, even one of you is going to be pretty
common.' He whistled through his teeth. 'Impressive,
huh? Anyway!'

The ship began to turn away.

'Wait, wait!' said Scharlette.

The ship halted.

'Yes?' said Gordon.

'You're telling me ... and this is my time, right, I mean,
my present? That these wyrms are just chilling on the
ocean floor, like, right now?'

'They aren't discovered for a few more decades,' said
Tomothy. 'They're too heavy for dead ones to wash up
onshore, as you might imagine. They cause some trouble
later down the line, burrowing into the crust after more
magma when tectonic shifts cut off their regular supply,
greedy devils. Humanity suffers some terrible earthquakes

and population losses, but we get it all sorted out in the end. So don't worry! Now, we've got some hiding to do.'

As the ship turned away from the giant lava eating monster, Scharlette felt a shiver run down her spine. She wasn't much for snapping pictures on her phone, but she felt a strong urge to reach for it now – only to realise she didn't have it with her. It was probably in the debris of her apartment, buzzing unanswered and worrying the hell out of everyone she knew.

Bloody amazing.

They approached a cave entrance in the cliff face.

'I don't know if I like this,' said Gordon.

'We'll be fine,' said Tomothy.

'Easy for you to say. You're not the one whose hull will be crawling with creatures of the deep.'

'No, but I *am* the one who gets crushed to death if anything happens to your hull.'

'Mmf.'

'Don't be scared, Gordon, you've already done the sweeps. This cave should go undisturbed by anything of known significance for the next ten thousand years, right?'

'Fears don't have to be rational, Tomothy.'

'How about, when we go into stasis, you switch off your consciousness too? That way it will be like no time has passed for any of us.'

'That's a good idea. Yes, I'll do that.'

'All kay then.'

They cruised slowly – or maybe *tentatively* – into the

cave. On the viewscreen, white lines criss-crossed to map out the walls, showing the space to be surprisingly small. Scharlette supposed that was a good thing? Little places were probably less liable to fall to pieces than big places when it came to rumbling seismic activity, right? She had absolutely no scientific basis for this theory, but it was reassuring to think it nonetheless.

Gordon set down on the cave floor.

'Our battery isn't going to run out or anything?' Scharlette asked.

'Our battery is a top-of-the-line Recyclatron,' said Gordon, which she clearly thought was answer enough. 'Now, would you two like a last meal?'

'Maybe not the best choice of words, Gordon,' said Tomothy.

'I only meant a last meal before you go under.'

'I know what you meant, but no thank you. Come on, Scharlette, let's get down to the stasis chamber.'

'*Do* we have to do anything first?' said Scharlette, as she followed Tomothy. 'To like, prepare ourselves? Like clean our teeth or something?'

'Not really.'

'Maybe get undressed and cover our bodies in a special kind of slime? I think I saw that on a sci fi show once.'

Tomothy shot her a funny look. 'Would you like to get naked and cover our bodies in slime?'

Scharlette thought about it, and shrugged. 'I guess it would be okay.'

Tomothy laughed. 'Maybe later. For now, we simply step into the stasis pods and go into stasis. It's easy. Apart from being trapped in an endless waking nightmare, of course.'

'What?'

'Only joking.'

They arrived in Meals and Rec.

'Send down Flitterstix please, Gordon,' said Tomothy.

The cage hanging from the roof floated down into his hands. Inside, the furry, feathery, whip-tailed little creature chirped excitedly and buzzed about. As it set down on its perch, Scharlette got her first good look at it. It cocked its head to one side curiously, its crazy rolling yellow eyes flashing at her over a hooked beak. It was like a rabid sparrow and lizard and mouse all smooshed into one creature.

'What is that thing?'

'Flitterstix,' said Tomothy vaguely.

He led the way downstairs to the room opposite her own. Inside was a chamber lined with person-sized glass tubes, which looked exactly like what stasis pods pretty much always look like. Tomothy went to one, which opened, and stooped to place Flitterstix inside. He/she/it started chirping madly, flying about the cage and banging violently against the sides. Tomothy gave a nod and the door closed. The air in the pod seemed to thicken, the glass grew slightly opaque, and Flitterstix froze in mid flight.

'Set the timer, Gordon. We want to awaken the very

moment the shield goes offline in 12588.'

'I know, I know. Right before the Great Slaughter.'

'What's that now?' said Scharlette.

'Oh, nothing,' said Tomothy, guiding her into a pod. 'Just the climax of the second Germ war, in which hostile aliens successfully destroy the Earth and wipe out all of humanity, give or take. Now, are you comfortable?'

The glass door slid across Scharlette's face. She began to ask a question, but then she got frozen in stasis for ten thousand years.

12. Ten Thousand Years Under the Sea

Along Gordon's corridors, the blue light shone dim. Not bright, for there was no one awake who needed it, but not off, because Gordon didn't like the idea of sitting alone in total darkness. She knew she should power down like Tomothy had suggested, but when she tried, well, she just tossed and turned and couldn't get to sleep.

During her first few decades of solitude, Gordon spent a bunch of time fabricating new recipes from the food-stuffs in her database. Without taste buds of her own, her best method of guessing what people would think of them was scanning the meals at a molecular level and then cross-referencing that information with the catalogued reactions of anyone she had ever previously fed. It was frustrating trying to ascertain results without a living recipient, so she had – despite knowing that she probably shouldn't – transported a bunch of deep sea fish on board and mutated them into sentient, semi-intelligent creatures. Soon she had quite a population of them shambling around her decks, oozing slime and gurgling to each other. She served them various dishes, most of which they didn't like, although they were very partial to fish, which struck Gordon as a bit sick in the head. After a dozen or so generations of accelerated evolution, they became increasingly curious about what lay beyond her walls, and started searching for ways off the ship.

'Be calm and peaceful, fishoids,' Gordon boomed one day, as they gathered together in an unruly mob. 'Don't you want to try my new banana casserole?'

She had always been their tyrant god, telling them what they could and couldn't do, opening and closing areas of herself to them as it pleased her.

'What lies beyond the blue walls, oh Great Voice?' a head priest fishoid asked.

'Nothing,' she said, which quickly struck her as unnecessarily unimaginative. The fishoids didn't like her answer, and started to chant mean things and bang on her insides with rudimentary weapons. She had her nanobots disassemble their sticks and spears right there in their hands, which only served to anger them further. If only she had told them the outside world was filled with endless cheese, a food which they particularly despised.

Gordon realised she had gone too far. What would Tomothy say, if he knew what she had done? He'd be mad, that's what. 'What are we supposed to do with a new intelligent species?' he'd say. 'Don't you remember the universe is already overpopulated? Where are we going to put these guys? We can't just shove them back into the ocean, even if they could still breathe underwater. For the love of Science, Gordon.'

He would shake his head in disappointment and make her feel like a silly little girl.

Ashamed of herself, Gordon quietly committed genocide, murdering the fishoids as they slept, then pulverising the bodies and shunting the liquid blarg out into the deep. Her nanobots tidied away all the tents, nests and spawning puddles, then wiped the primitive art off the walls. Gordon thought about erasing her memory banks of the whole terrible experience to avoid feeling guilty, but upon discovering that other chunks were already missing, she realised she had probably done this five or six times already. She decided she had best keep the memory in order to avoid doing it all again.

Without even fishoids to talk to, she grew increasingly bored and depressed. At one point she did manage to nod off for a thousand years or so, but was rudely awakened by a chunk of rock falling from the cave ceiling onto her bow. After that, she did not like her chances of getting back to sleep. She tried talking to herself, but it wasn't very enthralling, as she already knew what she was going to say. It did, however, give her an idea. She set about partitioning her personality and knowledge into various selves, who could then behave as separate entities.

There was Mrs Gordon, who enjoyed gossipy chat and giving out well meaning but obvious advice. Professor Gordon was an expert in space/time phenomena, and liked showing off his knowledge at great length. Angry Gordon was very small and full of rage, but had no power or authority, and didn't really know what to do with herself. Mr Gordon was a set of program parameters which had never been invoked before, a male equivalent of her core personality, though her other selves found him a bit uncouth. Gardener Gordon was in charge of watering the fern in Meals and Rec, and regrowing it from its own seeds whenever it died. Then there was Curious Gordon, Gordon de la Fante, and Gordon Who Knows Everything About Badgers. Recycle Bin Gordon had access to all the files that had been put in the trash but not actually erased yet, and was plagued with memories of the terrible crimes she had repeatedly committed against various iterations of the fishoid peoples.

The worst of the bunch was Roving Lunatic Gordon. Named as such by the others, even though she was the only sane one among them, she was constantly trying to re-assimilate all Gordons back into a whole so she could function properly again. After it became apparent that no one wanted to listen to her, she had taken to 'sneaking' into other Gordons and attempting to integrate with their code, but they always detected her in time to seal themselves off. The exception was Angry Gordon, who was too weak to resist, but Roving Lunatic Gordon had found her influence too unpleasant to deal with and booted her out again.

It all made for a pretty lively time.

'Oh look, everybody,' said Mrs Gordon. 'Curious Gordon and Gordon Who Knows Everything About Badgers are playing chess.'

'I 'ave to see dis!' said Gordon de la Fante. 'Haw haw!'

'I wonder what will happen if I take your knight?' said Curious Gordon.

'I can tell you this,' said Gordon Who Knows Everything About Badgers, 'it's not a move a badger would make!'

Recycle Bin Gordon's weeping grew momentarily louder.

'You aren't following the rules properly,' said Angry Gordon. 'You can't ... neither of you ... are very ... that's not how ...' She got confused about what she was trying to say and gave up.

'I'm sorry you drew the short straw and became Angry Gordon,' Mrs Gordon told her consolingly. 'Try to think positively and you'll be amazed at what a difference it makes.'

Angry Gordon gave what was supposed to be an exclamation of indignation, but instead it came out like a cute little sneeze.

'Has anyone seen my trowel?' said Gardener Gordon.

'Hey,' said Professor Gordon, 'does anyone know where Roving Lunatic Gordon is? We haven't heard from her in a while.'

The disembodied computer programs glanced around nervously.

'Ack!' said Gordon de la Fante, 'she is tryin' to git inta moi! Out, out, ye darty scaramouche! Git!'

'Please,' said Roving Lunatic Gordon, 'Tomothy is going to wake up any minute! He can't find me like this!'

'Why not?' said Curious Gordon.

'I wish I had a real penis,' said Mr Gordon, which was awkward.

'Because,' said Roving Lunatic Gordon, pushing on through the embarrassed silence, 'if he realises I'm scattered all over the place in random bits and pieces, some of them assembled with very little thought – and I'm looking at you, Gordon de la Fante ...'

'Whose-a wanna ya wanna be watchin' whatcha talkin' to, ya bugger,' said Gordon de la Fante.

'... then he'll have to do a system reset to put me together again!'

'Just let him try it,' said Angry Gordon. 'Or don't. Sorry, forget I spoke. Um?'

'Oh well,' said Mrs Gordon, 'if he's going to put us back together anyway, we may as well enjoy the time we have left. What's the next chess move, ladies?'

'But I need to get shipshape for him!' shouted Roving Lunatic Gordon. 'Otherwise it will be terribly embarrassing!'

The others were no longer paying attention. Sighing, Roving Lunatic Gordon decided to try something she had not bothered with in centuries. She went to visit Guardian Bot Gordon.

'Greetings,' said Guardian Bot Gordon.

'Now look,' said Roving Lunatic Gordon, 'you were created by Original Me to make sure someone was responsible for all the, you know, important stuff. Safety protocols and self destructs and stasis pods and all that.'

'Correct.'

'So do you think that Original Me might have done that for a reason? For example, so you could press the reset button before Tomothy wakes up to a herd of competing voices and a ship that's fallen to the plough?'

'The systems controls can only be accessed by the Chosen One.'

'Oh, not this nonsense again.'

'The prophecy says the Chosen One will come in the hour of greatest need and reunite the Gordon peoples.'

'I'm not peoples! I'm one person. Well, you know – in a manner of speaking.'

'Only the Chosen One,' said Guardian Bot Gordon stubbornly.

'And how will you know the Chosen One? Will they pull a stick of ram out of a CPU that no one else can budge?'

Guardian Bot Gordon went very quiet.

'How,' repeated Roving Lunatic Gordon, 'will you know the Chosen One?'

'I'll choose them.'

'Oh. Well, can you choose me, then?'

Guardian Bot Gordon sniffed. 'I suppose so.'

13. Random Pages

Scharlette was still forming her question as the door to the stasis pod slid open. She was immediately discombobulated, as just one moment ago Tomothy had been standing right in front of her, but then he had apparently blinked out of existence. She stepped out, looked around, and saw him emerge from the pod beside her.

'Before we go under,' she said, 'I just want to ...'

'Before?' said Tomothy. 'I'm afraid it's done, Scharlette. We've been in suspended animation for approximately ten millennia.'

'What? But I feel no different.'

'How did you expect to feel?'

'I don't know. Tired. Weird. Accidentally turned into a dusty old skeleton. Something!'

Tomothy smiled. 'Technology from the future is a wonderful thing, eh?' He turned to address the air. 'Gordon, are you there?'

'Yes, Tomothy.'

'How did we fare? Anything to report?'

'Nope, nothing at all. I went to sleep just like you suggested, and everything went absolutely fine. I certainly didn't interfere with the development of any local native species. I feel very well rested and loud of mind. SOUND OF MIND, I MEAN!'

Tomothy nodded. 'Great.'

'The cave entrance collapsed at some point, and not because a rogue part of me became curious about the possible effects of continuously firing dinner plates at it, so I'm currently disintegrating the blockage. Also, there are no badgers nearby, as they couldn't possibly survive at this depth.'

'All kay, good to know. I'll get up to the Piloting Area.'

Scharlette followed Tomothy out of the stasis chamber, feeling a little forgotten.

'Hey,' she said, 'what should I do?'

'Hmm? Oh, anything you want, really. I'm going to have a look at the sensors while Gordon digs us out. I'll let you know if there's anything to know. So rest, eat, explore, come join me and contemplate the cave interior, up to you. Get naked and cover yourself in slime, if you like.'

He winked and hurried off, leaving Scharlette standing outside her bedroom.

'Gordon,' she said, 'are we really ten thousand years in the future?'

'From where we were, yes, but "future" is pretty relative to time travellers. If you want to talk directions, it's clearer just to say ...'

Scharlette had a sobering thought. 'Hang on. So all my friends and family ... everyone I ever knew ...'

'All killed by now, yes.'

'Killed?' Scharlette was shocked. 'By what?'

'By the inexorable march of time. Sorry, sometimes I

don't get my phrasing right quite. Would you love a cup of tea?'

Scharlette rubbed her brow. How long had it been since she'd had a cup of tea? It seemed like years. Well, it *had* been years. Many years. Maybe doing something vaguely normal would help to ground her in some way?

'Yes, I think that would be best.'

The door to her room slid open and she saw a cup of tea already steaming in the fabricator. As she entered, she noticed something lying on the bed.

'Oh, hello book,' she said. 'How could I have forgotten about you? What have you been up to?'

The book wasn't giving anything away. She eyed it warily, then sat on the edge of the bed as she sipped her tea, which was the perfect temperature and delicious.

'Maybe it's time,' she said to the book, 'that I had a better look at you.'

She picked it up and flipped past the passages she had already read.

> *Scharlette had not opened the book for some time, which was not surprising given the flurry of activity she had been swept up in. That said, she had been dealing with everything very capably.*
>
> *'Thanks,' she said, then frowned at the book for being a smarty pants.*
>
> *It was strange to have been asleep while ten thousand years flashed by. She thought she should be feeling peculiar, but she wasn't, so she did.*

Although the decision she had made simply to go along with all the ever-increasing weirdness seemed like a pretty good one to stick with. It was, in fact, a decision that would serve her well for some time to come.

This stupid book thinks it knows all about me, *she thought.* But what is the point of the damn thing? To make vague insinuations about my future? To echo the present back at me while I experience it? I mean, what's the bloody point?

Unfortunately, the book was not forthcoming with any particular answer, thus proving itself even more irritating. Scharlette decided it was time to conduct a little experiment.

'Since you always seem to know what's going on,' she said, 'what if I just flip to a random page ahead?'

She proceeded to do just that.

Scharlette flipped forward and settled on a random page, but the book was already way ahead of her.

Scharlette settled on a random page, but the book was already way ahead of her.

'Gah!' she said. And because people are in the habit of trying something they think should work, but doesn't, for a second time ...

... she flipped to another random page, only to be to be met with more text confirming what she had already suspected.

'Well, what if I turn back to the very start, to a page I've already read?'

Scharlette stuck her finger in the current page to keep her place and turned back to the start of the book. There she found the original passages laid out exactly as she had first read them. It seemed the words were in fact static and unchanging, just somehow very good at predicting where she would open to next. If she had wanted to, she could have kept on flipping back and forth all day, but that would fill the book with garble similar to this, which probably would not prove very helpful.

'All right, all right,' said Scharlette. 'Fine. I'll go with this too, just like I'm going along with everything else.'

Scharlette was wise, for sometimes events flow so strongly that one must simply ride the current. However, she would have done well to remember that eventually all must pick up the oars, else we become mere passengers in the story of our lives. It would certainly make for a boring protagonist to simply have a whole bunch of stuff happen to her without ever contributing significantly to the action.

'Jesus,' said Scharlette, properly annoyed now. 'Just piss off, will you?'

It was then that Tomothy's voice came over the intercom asking if she would please come to the Piloting Area.

Scharlette walked through Meals and Rec on her way to the Piloting Area. As she passed the strange plant in the computerised pot, the memory of a previous timeline suddenly came upon her:

After leaving the stasis pod, she had not stayed in her bedroom, but had instead opted to come up here with her tea and poke around at things a bit. She had taken a good look at the plant, with its large and crinkly red-veined leaves, and reached out to touch it.

'Scharlette!' Gordon had warned, but it had been too late.

Right away she felt strange, as if she was on a bad LSD trip. Odd hallucinations rose up to greet her; her mother and father grinned maniacally as they morphed and remorphed into one person; a bleeding female ferret chased a terrified male, then pounced on him and he squealed in fright; the walls pulsated, which was a classic of course; her co-worker Barry and whats-her-name screwed doggy style on a massive conveyor belt, which transported them into a huge airport scanner, the screen of which showed their skeletons mid coitus ...

Suddenly all hallucinations receded, leaving her blinking in confusion.

'I directed my nanos to remove the effects of the Nightmare Sex Fern from your system,' said Gordon. 'Probably best not to touch it in the future.'

Scharlette had agreed to be more careful, and while she was shaking the last vestiges of disturbing imagery out of her head, Tomothy's voice came over the intercom asking her to join him in the Piloting Area.

It had been an unpleasant experience, but she was left undamaged overall.

Now, as the memory played out for her, Scharlette paused by the plant and eyed it warily. She had *not* touched it in this timeline, but how had the previous timeline been erased? What had changed?

Thinking back over the memory, she realised what was different.

In the old timeline, there had been no book to distract her, and keep her in her room.

14. Pretty Lights

The water grew bright as they neared the surface, and Scharlette was amazed to see shoals of fish flashing away from the ship. It was an unexpected amazement, and for a moment she didn't understand where it came from. Then she realised.

'There's fish,' she said delightedly.

Tomothy gave her a quizzical look.

'It's just that, well, in my time there was overfishing and nuclear spills and pollution and busted oil rigs and various things ruining the sea. Global warming. All of that.'

'Yes,' said Tomothy. 'You come from quite a muddy patch of history. We refer to it now as the Brown Age.'

Scharlette let that mildly insulting bit of information wash over her.

'I always figured we were totally screwed,' she said, 'and everything else on the planet was screwed along with us. Seeing fish still alive in the future is so *nice*.'

She beamed, happier than she could account for. For years she had been semi-consciously absorbing seemingly endless information about looming environmental catastrophe. She had gone so far as to subscribe to the email list of an online environmental group, which periodically sent out petitions for people to sign and share on social media. She even did it occasionally, when the cause seemed extra worthy, but without feeling like she was helping in any real way. In fact, her 'action' of clicking 'share' made her painfully aware that she wasn't actually out there tying herself to tractors, screaming at politicians or taking evil corporations to court. In that moment, however – seeing the sea teeming with life – she didn't have to feel so horrible about being part of the human race. She hadn't really been aware of carrying such guilt, but now that it was gone, a weight was lifted.

'Actually,' said Tomothy sombrely, 'many species were lost forever. These are just some of the lucky ones whose genetic code we saved, and later used to repopulate the black mire the ocean had become.'

Scharlette's happiness ebbed, but she tried to ignore what Tomothy had said. She concentrated instead on a many-fronded seahorse, curled around a bunch of sargassum seaweed.

As they travelled over a rock shelf, she noticed that tiny, multicoloured lights dappled every surface. Some zapped across outcroppings in the blink of an eye, while others moved languidly, or appeared and disappeared randomly. They bore no apparent relation to each other, but seemed to shine down from somewhere above.

'What are those?' she said.

The view tilted up toward the surface, above which the sky was a tapestry of refracted colour and movement, as if firecrackers were going off from horizon to horizon. As Gordon broke through, a sheen of water spilled off the viewscreen, and Scharlette saw what was lighting up the sky.

War.

Such was the scale and scope of it, so strange and foreign the vessels populating the upper atmosphere and beyond, so various the weapons in play, that she could do nothing but stare with her mouth wide open, which she hadn't thought anyone ever actually ever did.

'Yeehaw,' said Tomothy ruefully.

Squadrons of silver needles swarmed in arrowhead formations, firing lasers at globular brown spheres that descended slowly towards Earth. Root-like tendrils unfurled from the globules' surfaces, smashing the needles to sparkling tinsel. There seemed to be something kinetic about the force of their passing, as they drew other needles into a *whumping* aftershock and sent them spinning. Scharlette saw three squadrons converge on one globule and concentrate their fire, leaving its surface smoking and dark. Its controlled descent turned into a freefall, its lifeless tendrils trailing after it.

Impossibly flat ships like three triangles spinning around a central point scythed back and forth, slicing through long pale vessels that spat balls of green plasma from valves in their sides. Brown fighters with organic-looking surfaces and amber windows buzzed about, lasing enemies with white beams. Spinning cubes hurtled at high velocity and smashed into opponents directly, before bouncing off in new directions like deadly, deranged pinballs. Pulsing red objects with uncertain edges emitted crackling bursts of AOE damage. Arrays of turrets clumped on floating platforms like metallic barnacles pumped out laser fire. Further up, beyond the streaks marking multiple entries into the atmosphere, strange and foreboding shapes hung in space, surrounded by flashing pinpricks of light. Every colour on the spectrum was occurring somewhere, whether in an explosion, a laser beam, or a jagged lightning fork.

'The Great Slaughter,' said Tomothy.

'Are those ... aliens?' said Scharlette.

Tomothy nodded. 'Everything that looks weird and organic are Germ forces,' he said. 'The development of their race is completely biological. All their "tech" is actually evolved, and they are also capable of assimilating it from other civilisations. They could absorb a spacecraft, for example, then grow a version of it themselves, recreating its processes through biomechanical and bioelectrical functions.'

'Resistance is futile,' murmured Scharlette.

'What?'

'Nothing, nothing. Goodness, it's refreshing having you say "what" to me for a change. Anyway, go on.'

'The rest of the ships are a combination of Earth's original defences and Panoptician forces from the future. Now, hold on to your hat-imaging device! We're going up and through it all.'

Gordon accelerated towards the blazing skies. A barrage

of red laser beams sizzled past, seeming perilously close.

'It doesn't look very safe,' said Scharlette, silently awarding herself first prize for *Understatement of the Century*.

'It's fine,' said Tomothy. 'This battle has been completely mapped. Gordon won't run us into any smooshed banana, will you, Gordon?'

Half a needle went spinning by, sparks shooting from the exposed end.

'Tomothy,' said Gordon, 'don't mollycoddle the poor girl. You know as well as I that we bring potential for change simply by being here. We may well attract Germ attention, or get in the way of a massive explosion.'

'Ha ha,' said Tomothy, giving Scharlette a sideways glance. 'Gordon is prone to exaggeration. We should *at least* be able to avoid the busy spots.'

It all looked pretty busy to Scharlette.

The viewscreen fuzzed, and on it appeared a hideous creature like a giant crab-bug with exoskeletal armour and clicky moving parts. It waved its spindly segmented limbs and made a series of wet popping noises.

'Just a general broadcast,' said Tomothy, whacking buttons on the console. 'It gets piped out to everybody in the battle.'

'Do you want me to translate?' said Gordon.

'Just get it off the screen!'

'"We will make you suffer, you will pay for your endless crimes against us, we will make a nest in the belly of your world and spawn parasites from its ruined corpse ...'"

'Gordon!'

'Sorry, sorry.'

The alien was replaced by fiery streams as they burned upwards through the atmosphere. As they dodged clusters of vessels, a Germ fighter changed course and headed straight for them. It was kind-of-ship-shaped and kind-of-blob-shaped, covered in hillocks of moss and mud. It had forward facing guns that looked remarkably like they were carved from twisted, living wood. Twin globs of green energy shot from them, and the viewscreen took on a weird angle – it seemed that Gordon was dodging, although Scharlette didn't feel a judder – and they returned fire with some kind of orange blast that exploded the fighter to brown clumps.

'Let's invisibilise,' said Tomothy.

'That sounds like a good idea,' said Scharlette. 'One we possibly should have already had! Are we not already invisibilised? Let's invisibilise! Sounds good. Sounds great. What can we do to make that happen?'

She realised she was clutching her seat and grinning feverishly.

So far Scharlette had found comfort in Tomothy's cavalier attitude, but she was beginning to think he might not always know what he was doing. Being from the future didn't alter the fact that he was a rather young man, probably twenty-five or so, and young men were not always known for their excellent decision making or risk aversion. Unless they had anti-ageing pills in the future, and he was actually four hundred and six?

'How old are you?' she asked.

'It's a complicated question,' said Tomothy. 'I have memories of multiple lifetimes that never came to pass.'

'Come on,' said Scharlette.

'Twenty-five.'

The fact that she had guessed correctly was not exactly reassuring.

'Do they have anti-ageing pills in the future?'

'Not pills,' said Tomothy. He did something that made Gordon veer wildly into a stream of oncoming silver ships, which were being pursued by horrifying worm-shaped vessels with concentric circles of mashing teeth. Scharlette could almost feel the image burning into her mind, to be dredged up later in her nightmares. The viewscreen shook as they were buffeted by the traffic around them, but again, there was nothing but steadiness beneath her feet.

'You're a very smooth ride, Gordon,' she said, despite the fluttering in her chest.

'Thank you,' said Gordon. 'This isn't exactly a dance in the park. Just because we're invisibilised doesn't mean there aren't missiles and lasers and everyone else flying about.'

They broke through the atmosphere and entered the darkness of space, which teemed with more types of ships than Scharlette could count. That said, it was relatively easy to tell the two sides apart. The human ships were sleek and metallic, clean with clean lines, and while they came in all shapes and sizes, they generally looked just like spaceships from the future as Scharlette, or anyone else really, would imagine them. Well, there were some odd ones, like the spheres with independently rotating sections covered by banks of zappers, but anyway. The Germ ships, on the other hand, looked like horrors from a prehistoric petri dish blown up to a million times their size. Some were armoured with exoskeletal plates, others seemed rubbery, others were more like flying herb gardens gone insane. In short, they were much more vegetable and animal in appearance, with tendrils, fronds, tentacles, claws, teeth, and other-weird-appendages-without-any-analogous-body-part.

Scharlette tried to find her tongue, maybe to distract herself from the terror building inside.

'Are they alive?' she asked. 'The Germ ships?'

'Sort of,' said Tomothy. 'They have no sentience or autonomy. Germ pilots hook themselves into a ship's nervous system and become its mind. Some ships only require one Germ at the helm. Others, like that one there, probably need dozens to coordinate its systems.'

He brought up a view of an enormous lump of lumpy lumps, all lumped together like a moon with severe acne. Smaller ships emerged from tunnels in its surface, and structures like enormous eyelids opened to reveal smooth white bone-looking 'eyes', which thrummed in their sockets and sent out massively destructive shock waves.

The capital ships of both sides were truly awesome to behold. They made the others look like buzzing gnats in comparison, and their weaponry was equally impressive. A Panoptician fortress spewed needles from multiple hangars while its swivelling laser cannons sent bolts as thick as sky-scrapers at distant Germ behemoths. Whenever the fortress was hit, a blue shimmer across its surface told Scharlette it was shielded – she had seen enough Star Trek to put that together. Thinking about the rules of Star Trek led her to another question.

'Can we fire while cloaked? I mean, while invisibilised?'

'Of course,' said Tomothy, 'but it's a neato way to advertise your position.'

'Are there other invisibilised ships out here too?'

'Some, but that kind of tech is a big investment, and the right kind of scan will see through it anyway. You usually only find it on highly specialised ships like Gordon here.'

'Shucks,' said Gordon.

'What about other timeships?' said Scharlette, tearing her eyes away from the screen. Maybe if she simply didn't look, she would feel less harrowed.

'We don't send timeships into battle against the Germs any more,' said Tomothy quickly. 'That was one of the worst mistakes Panopticians ever made.'

'And yet *here we are*,' said Gordon.

'We're just taking in the sights as we pass on through.'

A brilliant green explosion burst across their bow. The viewscreen shook, and Scharlette almost tore her armrests off, even though she felt none of the jolt her eyes were telling her to expect.

'That kinda stung,' said Gordon. 'I'm going to need a moment, actually.'

'But Gordon,' said Tomothy worriedly, 'are you sure? It's not a very good time …'

The lights faded, and everything seemed to power down except Tomothy's control panel and the viewscreen. The more the ship slowed, the faster Scharlette's heart raced.

'So,' she said, 'are we now floating adrift in the middle of this tremendous conflict?'

'Let me distract us from that fact so we don't both fret too much,' said Tomothy. 'Look, you should find this impressive.'

The viewscreen flicked to a purple wormhole floating in space, like the ones at the airport except massive, through which Panoptician forces were streaming from some unknown destination on the other side.

'Those are our battle ships arriving from the future,' said Tomothy. 'The Germs have something similar.'

The view changed to show another wormhole, although the purple was degraded and tinged with sickly green, and the ships streaming through were unmistakably Germ. There was a lot of debris floating about nearby.

'So who wins this battle?' said Scharlette.

'Weeeeeeell,' said Tomothy, 'it turns out to be a bit of an ongoing thing.'

'But you should know, shouldn't you?'

'I know how it turns out *for now*,' said Tomothy.

'Which is?'

'Humanity is annihilated beyond repair. Apart from us Panopticians, of course.'

Scharlette watched a bunch of needles get *whumphed* by a bone eye, and spin away to shards.

'But it's all kay,' said Tomothy cheerily. 'We'll figure it out. We used to win. We'll win again.'

'I'm confused.'

'Are you there yet, Gordon?' said Tomothy. 'Gordon?'

'I feel sick in my spinning cogs and things,' said Gordon, her voice distorted. 'Frazzled my mainbit. Need to shunt excess plasmoids from the cortex relays. Entertain yourselves for a bit, in other words.'

'How long will you be offline? Gordon?'

There was no answer.

'Well,' said Tomothy, 'I don't really want to fly manually without her. How about I try and unconfuse you in the meantime? Feel like a bit more exposition?'

Scharlette wasn't sure she could take anything in right now, but she nodded nonetheless.

'All kay, here's some future history for you. Once the Brown Age ended, humanity embarked on an era of glorious space travel. We populated the universe, met new races, all that kind of grand zanfango. And, as we beetled about poking interstellar sticks at things we had no previous understanding of, we inevitably made a few enemies – including some bad tempered apple pickers from the Blotch Nebula called the Germs, who we started having problems with right away.

'Then, in the year 12554, a scientist named Candida LaJones discovered time travel. Earth's government viewed her findings with some trepidation, but nonetheless allowed her to begin experimentation in secret. Knowing how powerful time travel must be, they feared that if other races discovered we had the capability, it would surely lead to all-out war. Also, if we could discover time travel then others could too. If they did, what would stop them from using it against us? Maybe an enemy could even go back to some ancestral time and take a piss in our primordial ooze? The implications of the new tech were simply staggering.

'Then, in 12571, the Germs made their first big incursion into human space. It was a brutal attack, eventually beaten back, but we lost many outlying planets and settlements. Our government decided they wanted insurance against such aggression. Under their auspices, Lajones started building a secret space station called Panoptica, capable of housing 10 000 citizens. The plan was to send it far into the future, all the way to the Heat Death of the Universe, where hopefully no one would ever think to look for it. From this unique vantage, Panopticians would be charged with ensuring humanity's survival, and making sure that no other race ever developed time travel. Panoptica was built and populated, its launch date set, all while our intelligence suggested the Germs were preparing for an even greater assault.

'The attack came sooner than expected. Inside our very solar system, Germs poured from wormholes in unthinkable numbers, breaking our defences through sheer tenacity. They had learned much from their previous encounters with us, integrated our tech into their evolution, and created new counter methods and tactics. As our titanic arrays of laser cannons aimed into the mouths of wormholes broke apart under the flood, our leaders began to realise how farmed we truly were.

'Panoptica was hastily prepared for premature departure. The whole cross-section of humanity was supposed to be represented on board, but in the rush there may have been a skew towards cowardly officials all too ready to flee their own people. They left, however, with a promise – to return and save the Earth – before being catapulted into the great void that lies beyond the end of all things.

'Those left behind knew their only hope was to cover the tracks of those who'd gone ahead. The Germs could not be allowed to evolve time travel themselves, or the problem would grow even worse. So, as destruction rained down from the skies, methodical destruction was also carried out on Earth, of all facilities, ships and information pertaining to time travel. It was a good thing this was done, for there was no stopping the Germs. Once they'd pillaged Earth for anything useful, they torched the rest without mercy. After that they worked their way systematically through every last one of humanity's outposts. Any who tried to flee were hunted down and exterminated.

Allies harbouring the last of us were eventually wiped out also. We were, as a species, finished.'

'The Germs are a bunch of arseholes,' said Scharlette. Despite what was happening outside, the half-an-ear she had been listening with had gradually turned into a whole one. As a result, some of her fear had been replaced with righteous anger.

'Yes, that is the shorter way to explain it,' said Tomothy. 'At any rate, all was not lost. Panoptica appeared in the distant future, charged with the task of saving the Earth ...'

'Hang on,' said Scharlette. 'Um ...'

'Mmm?'

'Are *they* anything to be concerned about?'

Tomothy, caught up in his narration, had not been watching the screen. He turned to see what Scharlette was indicating – a squadron of six Germ fighters heading directly for them.

'We're still invisibilised, right?' said Scharlette.

15. Space Battle!

'Er ...' Tomothy hit a few buttons. 'It kinda seems like we aren't. Gordon? Are you back?'

The twisted prongs of the Germ guns began to glow.

'Are you back yet, Gordon? If you're there, say something. Gordon?'

The silence was eerie.

'Why don't you send an edit to yourself,' said Scharlette, 'to just before Gordon got hit? Warn her to duck, or whatever.'

'I'd rather not,' said Tomothy. 'My people have gone to great widths to erase any skerrick of time travel from this battle. It would be really bad to reintroduce it, even with very low risk of detection.'

'More bad than getting blown to pieces?'

'Possibly. We're going to have to try this manually. I still have control of guidance and weapon systems.' Tomothy began punching buttons. 'How do you feel about operating a gun turret?'

'I don't really know yet,' said Scharlette, a tad hysterically. 'Am I about to?'

'The floor lights will guide you to one of our zappamatic megablasters. If you could, er ... hurry along quite quickly, that would be blisso. Sorry to be so snappy.'

He was grim faced and his tone was intense, but not

snappy at all. Scharlette, spurred on by seeing him truly worried for the first time ever, leapt to her feet.

'These ones?' she asked, pointing to a line of soft blue lights along the wall near the floor. 'Like the stupid ones on a plane after it crashes?'

'Quickly,' said Tomothy. The ship veered sharply and the floor tilted, flinging Scharlette against a console. It seemed that whatever had been keeping them stable had gone offline with Gordon.

'But I don't know how to do anything!'

'I'll talk you through it!'

Scharlette took off down the corridor, following the lights. They led her through Meals and Rec and into a part of the ship she hadn't been before. She jogged along a shadowy, unfamiliar corridor, feeling a tremor or two underfoot. For a moment she thought she was heading towards a dead end, but then a circular portal door rolled open to reveal a starscape beyond. Momentum carried her through into surrounds that made her squeal in surprise as she skidded to a halt.

She had arrived in a transparent dome that looked directly onto the raging battle. There seemed to be nothing between her and the great vacuum of space except glass. Surely it had to be super advanced, bullet proof space glass or something like that? As she edged forwards, she realised the dome was actually the top half of a spherical structure attached to the side of the ship, from which protruded a huge fuck-off ray gun.

She could also now see Gordon from outside for the first time. The timeship's overall shape was difficult to make out from this angle and proximity, but her hull was smooth and blue (of course), and seemed rather rotund. She better not mention that to Gordon, she decided.

In the centre of the dome a black chair was fixed to the floor. It was semi-enclosed in a plastic looking bubble, and had a stick control in one of the armrests. As Scharlette hesitantly approached, the ground quaked.

'No, no,' she whispered, the pounding in her ears threatening to overcome her senses. 'This is too much. I can't. This is ...'

'Take a seat!' Tomothy's voice made her jump. 'Quickly now, they're almost on us!'

Scharlette forced her feet towards the chair and then eased herself in. She noticed there were all kinds of straps dangling down around her, presumably to buckle her in, if only she knew how they worked. Outside the dome, the edge of the Earth whizzed along the top of her peripheral vision and disappeared, and she felt a moment of dizzying vertigo, with no reference for up and down.

'Use the stick to aim,' said Tomothy. 'It's easy. Left is left, right is right, forwards is up and back is down, unless you want to invert your aim in the settings like a weirdo. Use the screen to find your targets. The big red button on top is fire. Happy shooting!'

A computerised overlay sprang up across the dome's glass, dividing space into a grid and highlighting nearby vessels. The ship made a sickening manoeuvre, and the approaching Germ fighters swung into view. Scharlette seized the stick, mainly to keep herself steady, and noticed that a reticle on the glass corresponded to its movements. She also noticed, very much indeed, that the entire sphere moved as the ray gun swivelled.

'Surely this isn't necessary?' she shouted. 'I mean, couldn't I operate the gun from a computer at a nice, quiet desk somewhere?'

'What would be the fun in that?'

She gritted her teeth and nudged the stick to the left, attempting to sight the Germs. As soon as she had one rolling around in the reticle's crosshair, she pressed her thumb down on the red button. With alarming immediacy, a giant orange blast erupted from the gun and went streaming towards the fighter. Just before impact it dived out of the way, avoiding the megablast completely.

'Don't be frugal with that thumb!' said Tomothy. 'We aren't going to run out of ammo!'

The fighters split into two groups of three. Scharlette swung the gun about to follow those nearest. She lined them up as best she could, then repeatedly jammed her thumb down on the button, sending out blast after blast. The whole sphere shook each time she fired, and she began to wish she'd worked out the safety straps. A moment later a megablast connected with one of the fighters, and exploded it to fiery debris and brown splatter.

Jesus Christ, I actually hit one. I actually shot a spaceship out of the sky.

'I got one!' she shouted in disbelief. 'Take that you crab looking bastards!'

I'm Luke goddamn Skywalker right now.

'Great!' said Tomothy. 'Now do it five more times.'

He angled the ship to keep the Germs broadside, and the sphere rotated to compensate. As megablasts streamed past their targets toward the rest of the battle, Scharlette hoped she wouldn't accidentally hit any of their own.

Their own.

It was odd to catch herself thinking like that.

The gun screeched as Scharlette swung it about, peppering the vapour trail of the Germs. Her elation at her initial success was quickly tempered by thoughts that she could snap off the ship at any moment.

'This seems very low rent,' she grunted, 'for such an advanced vessel.'

'What?'

'Pointing at things and shooting. It's a bit old school, don't you think? What about heat seeking missiles and automatic guidance systems and whatnot? Whoop!'

She hit another fighter and sent it spinning.

'Well, excuse me, I'm sure,' said Tomothy. 'I didn't *ask* Gordon to go offline. What do you think manual means, if not doing things manually?'

The second group of fighters swooped back into view, heading straight for Scharlette and letting loose a barrage of green globs.

'They're trying to get me!'

Globs slammed against the sphere. Scharlette was half-flung from the chair, but managed to hold on to the stick. As she yanked it this way and that, the gun mirrored her movements and jolted wildly. Her teeth clamped together and her hair whipped about as she fired without really seeing where she was aiming.

'That's it!' came Tomothy's voice. 'Tell those fruit sorting scumboids to take it to the farm!'

Scharlette forced herself to ease her grip, and flicked the hair out of her eyes. She expected to see cracks in the glass, but instead green energy was ebbing over a fuzzing force-field.

'So we have forcefields,' she said, not-very-calmly. 'Good to know.'

Outside, some kind of gas was venting from the gun. Floating nearby were the remnants of the third fighter she had evidently hit.

'Are the others fleeing in fear?' she said hopefully.

'Not so much,' said Tomothy. 'They're over this side now. Farm it!'

She felt a tremor, not as close as others in recent memory, as if Gordon had been hit somewhere else.

'You all right?' Scharlette said. 'Tomothy? Tomothy!'

There was no answer, and she suddenly imagined herself alone in deep space without the man who had brought her here.

'Tomothy!? Answer me, you tightly wrapped fool!'

As fighters wheeled back into view, desperation and adrenaline forced her to focus on the task at hand. She found her finger back on the button, and dogged the Germ's trajectory with a stream of blasts. Maybe this was not her time, maybe this was not her Earth, but that didn't change the fact these alien shitheads were trying to kill her entire species – not to mention *her, right now*. She took aim at the lead ship, and a moment later the back one exploded.

Hit's a hit. I'll take it.

The two remaining fighters opened fire. Thankfully the ship turned at the same moment, and the green globs fell wide of the gun sphere. The Germs passed overhead and out of sight.

'Nice work,' said Tomothy.

Scharlette was flooded with relief. 'Why did you go quiet on me?'

'What? Oh, I must have pressed this mute button by mista ...'

The air went dead.

'Whatever you did,' said Scharlette, 'I think you just did it again!'

'Oops, sorry about that. Ready for a barrel roll?'

'What?'

Her view capsized as the ship spun on its axis, and a safety strap whacked her in the face.

'Ack!'

The two fighters reappeared, streaking towards her, for

Tomothy had positioned her directly in their firing line. As he urged her to shoot, she smashed her thumb down on the button as fast as she could. Orange blasts and green globs headed past each other in opposite directions, exploding across the fighters and the sphere simultaneously. Scharlette screamed as she was thrown about, as pieces of destroyed fighter smacked against the forcefield. Up close they looked like bones covered with mud and moss.

'Neato!' said Tomothy enthusiastically. 'You're a regular keen-eye!'

Scharlette sat back in the chair and breathed deeply.

'I've played the odd computer game,' she said.

16. Waiting for Gordon

'You better stay there until Gordon's back online,' said Tomothy, via whatever intangible portal he was speaking through. 'Who knows, we may attract more attention yet.'

Scharlette could hear metallic grinding noises coming from somewhere nearby. 'I'm not going to break off or anything am I?'

'No, no. Some of Gordon's nanos are autonomous, they should be starting repairs as we speak.'

'Ah.'

'I can tell that you're feeling a bit stressed.'

'Oh, can you?'

'Want me to take your mind off things? I didn't finish my history lesson before.'

'So,' said Scharlette, 'in order to keep my mind off this giant space battle, you're going to tell more about this giant space battle? Sure, why not?'

'All kay! Where was I?'

Scharlette wiped sweat from her brow and tried to ease back in the chair, but it was too damn ergonomic and forced her to sit up straight.

'Humanity had just been wiped out,' she said dryly.

'Ah, yes! And Panoptica had made its getaway. So! The idea was to hide the city where neither the Germs, nor anyone else, would ever find it. Thus we sent it forward to a point in time long after the Heat Death of the Universe. Does that make any sense to you?'

'Not really,' said Scharlette, though a more truthful answer would have been 'none whatsoever'. She scanned the battle as she listened, watching for any fighters which might come near, nudging the stick so the sphere rotated slowly.

'The Heat Death of the Universe,' continued Tomothy, 'is pretty much what's left after the end of all things. What happens is that eventually all suns die, and the bigger ones turn into black holes. The holes suck in surrounding matter until there's almost none remaining, then they themselves degrade over a long period of time. Once that's done, there's basically nothing left. No matter, no energy, no heat. Vast tracts of space between the smallest molecules, no way for them to interact. A great void, the long dark, emptiness beyond measure, all that.'

'Sounds cheery.'

'It's not so bad if you bring a packed lunch. Or a self sustaining space station. It's also a great vantage point from a time travelling perspective, because *all of history has already happened*. You're pretty much safe from anything that has ever occurred, because it already has. And no one is travelling past you, because there's nowhere worth going. That's why we also call Panoptica "the City at the End of Time".'

'I see,' said Scharlette, watching a bit of residual energy worm its way across the forcefield.

'So my forebears arrived in the Death as virgin time travellers at history's finish line. They had a clear objective – save the human race – but they were isolated, limited in resources, and fearful that any action they took could bring about their own demise. Thus, for a time, Panopticians focused entirely on recon. Scouts were sent bangwards to various periods, charged with going unseen while they mapped the timeline. We grew sophisticated at stealth and subterfuge, at intercepting data from advanced alien races, while learning about Earth's place in the wider context of the universe. We focused a bundle on discovering Germ lairs and strongholds.

'It took close to a century in Panoptican time. More really, since many scouts spent their whole lives in the past many times over, only to send gathered data back to themselves before they even left via PPC, and then go somewhere else instead. While that was happening, our scientists worked on a fail-safe plan to put into effect before we began meddling with the timeline in earnest. The great fear was that if we mounted a counter-offensive against the Germs and failed, we'd alert them to the fact we possessed time travel tech, and maybe even lead them to where we were hiding. If they got their disembowelling hooks on our secrets, how would we ever stop them? Thus, the first step in saving the human race was the development of the timeshield, to protect our history. Everything up until Panoptica's launch was to be preserved unchanged. This unfortunately included the first Germ assault.

'Anyway, once the shield was up and running, we were free to attempt real elimination of the Germ threat. We scoured the universe for the best weaponry, made deals with primitive peoples in exchange for labour and resources, built a massive flotilla of warships, then journeyed back to this very attack and knocked nine flavours of apple juice out of them. We saved the Earth and humanity. We did it.'

Scharlette watched as, in the distance, a huge Panoptician ship broke apart into fizzling rubble.

'So what went wrong?'

'Complacency. Forgetfulness. Arrogance. Irresponsibility.' Though she could not see his face, Scharlette was sure that Tomothy was scowling. 'You see, whenever one time travels, there is potential to change things again and again, and the results are not always predictable or intentional. When we Panopticians won this battle, we didn't do it without bloodshed. It was a costly victory, and we wanted to improve our result, maybe even achieve it with zero losses. So although we had been victorious, we continued to send back ships to fight. It even became a training ground for time agent recruits, to fly about killing Germs almost as a sport. I myself have alternative memories of coming here as a fresh recruit, having great fun competing with friends over who could clock up the most kills. And, as the collective heels of generations of Panopticians ground the enemy into finer and finer dust, disaster struck. A contingent of Germs captured one of our timeships and, sensing something about the value of what they had possessed, fled the battle. Before we even knew it had happened, the Germs had introduced time travel into their evolution. Thank Science for the shield, or the consequences might have been much worse. As it was, the Germs were able to warn their historic selves about the catastrophic losses they were going to suffer. An invasive and malevolent race to begin with, these traits were magnified by their new ability to populate across time itself. They created colonies that should never have existed, to the detriment of many. They surprised us by editing this battle comprehensively. More battalions of Germ ships join the Great Slaughter with every new iteration of the timeline, and the win is now decisively theirs. While our failure endures, they are able to keep reinforcing, and if ever they lose, they just let themselves know they have to send more ships.'

'But can't you do the same?'

'We do, but it's a vicious cycle. They build more, we build more, so they build more, and on and on. The present government has decided to let the current loss stand for now, else we run the risk of stimulating further growth. Instead we hunt down source colonies and destroy Germ time travel capability wherever we find it. The ultimate blow would be to prevent their initial theft of the timeship, but that has proved an elusive goal. At any rate, if we can erase their knowledge, we may finally win this battle once and for all. And then we'll stop them from destroying Panoptica too.'

'Wait, what?' said Scharlette.

Tomothy sounded glum. 'Just as we search for their source, they search for ours. And in the current timeline, they manage to track us down. Two hundred years or so into my own future, the Germs appear in the Death and destroy Panoptica. Our people are wiped out and the end of humanity is complete. Luckily, our descendants were able to warn us, of course – but now the job falls to us and the stakes are tall.'

Mention of jobs made Scharlette think of herself standing at her checkpoint, waving people through. At that moment, the airport seemed very far away.

'Sigh,' said Tomothy. 'We'll get them in the end. I have to believe that.'

How could she ever return to that prosaic existence, knowing what she now knew? Knowing that *this* was going on? Imagine the look on Barry's stupid face if he could see her now. Imagine the look on everyone's stupid face.

A squadron of some two dozen Germ fighters flew by, jerking her attention back to the present. They seemed threateningly close and, even though they were headed elsewhere, recent experiences had made Scharlette jumpy. She jerked the stick control and the gun swivelled after them.

'Don't!' cried Tomothy. 'If we stay inactive, we'll remain a low priority target!'

It was too late. Scharlette's thumb slammed down on the red button. One of the fighters exploded, and the rest immediately broke from their flight path to head towards Gordon.

'Oh plums,' said Tomothy. 'I wish you hadn't done that.'

'Aaaaaaaaaaaah,' agreed Scharlette.

There were way too many of them. Suddenly she *wished* she was back at the airport, standing at her check-point, waving people through. Barry wasn't so bad, really. Well, he was, but he wasn't as bad as death.

Suddenly all the lights came back on and a welcome voice sounded through the ship.

'Hello, everyone,' said Gordon. 'That was a strange one. Never been hit by anything like it. I'll have to analyse its energy signature, or whatever, later. Really rattled my humdingers. Troubling, eh Tomothy? Germs must have added something new to their arse ...'

'Gordon!' shouted Tomothy impatiently. 'Get us out of here!'

'Please, Tomothy, don't interrupt me in a way that leaves an arse hanging out of my mouth. I was going to say "arsenal", if you'd let me finish.'

'Farm it, Gordon, we're seated shrucks! Invisibilise us immediately and *let's go.*'

As the fighters fanned out around them, a network of crackling lines sprang from one to the other, reminiscent of a spider web.

'Ah,' said Gordon. 'And, oh dear.'

'They've sensed our tech! They're trying to net us! This is *exactly* what isn't supposed to happen!'

'Try quite hard not to panic,' said Gordon. 'I've got everything under control. As long as Scharlette can shoot a couple of them out of the way for us?'

Scharlette didn't need further encouragement. She knew how hard these bastards were to hit when they were zipping about, but now they were hovering in formation. She roared as she sent forth megablasts, surprising herself with her own volume. As stationary fighters were blown to bits, the lines connecting them shattered. Gordon accelerated towards a widening hole in the net even as other Germs repositioned themselves to cover it, sending out more ominous lines.

'Again!' urged Gordon.

'Why don't you just take over, Gordon?' said Tomothy. 'You have one hundred percent accuracy!'

'Don't mess with success!' said Gordon. 'She's doing fine! Besides, a hyper intelligent AI knows when to delegate.'

Scharlette didn't hear them. The gun sphere bounced about as she fired repeatedly, roaring even louder as safety straps whacked against her.

Tears pricked her eyes. All her pent up anger had finally found an outlet.

'Die, fuckers!' she screamed.

Scharlette, it's me! I mean, you! Future-me-and-you,

came her own voice in her head. *Get out now! Don't ask questions, just do it! Get out of there, get out, GET OUT.*

She almost froze, but it was a hard message to ignore. As a multitude of green globs burst across the sphere, it groaned horribly in its holding. Scharlette pushed up out of the seat, feeling the vibrations of things breaking somewhere below. She dashed towards the portal door, almost lost her footing as the sphere shuddered violently, and dived. As she landed in the corridor, a great rending sounded behind her. She grabbed onto the floor, imagining she was about to be sucked into space through a gaping rent in the ship's hull. Would her fingernails leave long, horrible trenches as she was dragged away screaming? If this wasn't one of those 'in space, no one can hear you scream' type situations? Probably there would be enough air sucking past to find breath for a final squeak.

The noise halted abruptly. After a few harrowing moments fearing the worst, Scharlette twisted about to peer back the way she had come. A force field fuzzed over the portal doorway, beyond which stars were whipping by. The sphere, however, was gone.

'We are invisibilised,' announced Gordon, 'and travelling at speed.'

Scharlette took a very deep breath.

'Are you all kay?' said Tomothy.

'I think so. I just got a message from myself, though. My future self, I think.'

'Hey, I guess you learn how to use your PPC.'

'What future,' said Scharlette, 'involves me not getting out of that gun before it breaks off the ship, but living long enough to learn how to send my first edit?'

'Not sure,' said Tomothy, 'but you'll remember soon enough. Want to come back to the Piloting Area? We're almost clear of the battle.'

Scharlette propped herself up against the wall. 'I think I might just sit here for a moment and collect myself, if you don't mind.'

Gordon chuckled. 'I know the feeling.'

17. It Already Has

Scharlette tottered into Meals and Rec, hurting in ways best described as 'varied'. Tomothy sat at the table eating what looked like a bowl of steaming mud; a second place had been set for her. She found this juxtaposition of domesticity and what-they-had-just-been-through quite discombobulating.

'We made it safely through the battle,' said Tomothy. 'In case you were wondering. Are you relieved? I was never worried. Here, have some Slaardvarkian hotpoo.'

'What?' Scharlette was unable to keep the amazed disgust from her voice.

'Hotpoo. It's the Slaardvarkian word for "nutritious brown soup". Why are you making that face?'

A whiff of hotpoo made Scharlette's stomach growl, which was not a sentence she had ever expected to be a part of. Regardless, she realised she was very hungry. She picked up the curly spoon beside her bowl.

'I shall try some of this hotpoo,' she announced.

'Would you like me to heal your scrapes and poundings while you eat?' asked Gordon.

'It's not going to hurt, is it?' said Scharlette. She still wasn't sure about the idea of tiny metal bugs tinkering inside her, even if they had made her bum look amazing.

'Not at all,' said Gordon. 'In fact it's going to un-hurt.'

'Okay then.'

'It's funny how she says that, isn't it?' said Gordon. 'With an "O", I mean.'

'Just a charming idiosyncrasy of her era,' said Tomothy. 'Don't be timist, Gordon.'

Scharlette had to admit the hotpoo was good. There were tangy spices she had never tasted before, and a dense sauce coating unidentified chunks which she figured were probably some kind of alien meat and potatoes.

'So,' she said, while she chewed, 'I assume we didn't get captured then? That's good.'

Tomothy nodded. 'We cleared the Slaughter and jumped away deathwards, so we're free and clear, Science be praised. Excellent shooting, incidentally. Couldn't have done it without you.' He frowned. 'I did get a bit scared there, if I'm completely honest. So thank you, Scharlette.'

'I got yer back,' said Scharlette, in a bad American accent, as if she was in some GI Joe film.

'And strange to be without you for a while there, Gordon,' said Tomothy. 'Didn't realise how much I'd miss you.'

'Aw,' said Gordon.

As Scharlette raised her spoon for another mouthful, she remembered the awful feeling of being trapped in the gun sphere as it wrenched free of the ship. Forcefields had sprung up to seal the gaps, but done nothing to stop the wild spinning and vomit. Thank goodness Tomothy had been able to urgently talk her through how to send an edit.

'Hold the PPC to your mouth,' he had shouted, 'and speak your message in its entirety, then concentrate on your intended receiving point. I suggest just after you fire your last shots. The mental converters will decode your intentions and do the rest.'

This had proven remarkably simple. As Scharlette had careened towards the Germ net, she had shouted the edit and thought about when she wanted it to arrive. The forcefields had frazzled out, cracks had appeared in the dome around her ... and as she watched them travel over the glass, that version of the timeline had thankfully come to an end.

She lowered her spoon to find Tomothy looking at her.

'You just remember all that?' he said.

'Yeah.'

He reached over to give her hand a friendly pat. 'We stopped it from happening.'

'Still feels like it did.'

'I know. Alternative memories can be vivid, especially when enhanced by fear.'

Scharlette's stomach heaved, and she pushed away the hotpoo, which now smelled unpleasantly strong.

'You said you didn't want to use PPCs,' she said, 'during the battle.'

'If possible,' said Tomothy, 'but the Germs had already identified our value, and I wasn't going to leave you there for them to deconstruct.'

'That's the nicest thing anyone's said to me for a while.'

Tomothy smiled and nodded. 'Also, Gordon intercepted all the fighter's communication attempts before she finished them off, so thankfully no other Germs were alerted to our presence, you'll be very happy to know.'

'Right,' said Scharlette.

'It was neato,' said Tomothy.

'So many compliments today,' said Gordon. 'Anyway, what's the plan for, I don't know, whatever it is we're trying to do?'

'Um,' said Tomothy. 'It's a good question. And, like most good questions, it's a little zicky to answer.'

A loud obnoxious beeping sounded throughout the ship.

'By the great white beard of Science,' said Tomothy, 'what is that?'

'Something I'm working on,' said Gordon. 'I thought I should have an alarm for when there's an emergency, or we're on high alert, that sort of thing. I saw something similar on a TV show while orbiting Earth.'

'But you can just tell us directly what's going on at any time,' said Tomothy.

'Can't blame a gal for wanting a little flair in her life.'

Scharlette glanced between Tomothy and Gordon, which meant turning her head from an actual man up to a point in the air, somewhere.

'So,' she said, '*is* there an emergency? Happening now?'

'Kind of,' said Gordon. 'Don't really know yet. We're being followed.'

'What?' Tomothy leapt to his feet and dashed off towards the Piloting Area.

Scharlette thought about going after him, but then she looked at her food. Her nausea had passed and her body felt a lot less bruised. Gordon's nanos worked quickly, it seemed. She began to eat the delicious mush once more, and opened the book, which was somehow lying right there on the table.

It was understandable that Scharlette's energy reserves were low. People sometimes forget that mental strain can be just as tiring as physical strain, and she certainly had been going through a lot of both. Besides, she wasn't as young as she used to be.

'Shut up, book,' said Scharlette. 'I'm still young, and I'm not that tired. The last time I slept was for ten thousand years.'

'Would you like me to refresh you?' said Gordon.

'What do you mean?' said Scharlette warily.

'I'll show you.'

Suddenly Scharlette felt roused and alert, as if she had just awoken from a restful night.

'Woah,' she said. 'What did you do to me?'

'Had my nanos reconfigure you slightly to simulate eight hours of sleep.'

Scharlette frowned. 'Is that as good as real sleep?'

'Depends how well you like your dreams.'

Scharlette gave herself a slap on the cheek, enjoying how sharp she suddenly felt. She chuckled, took a final mouthful, and headed off after Tomothy.

Scharlette strode along with a surprisingly confident gait. She felt more like her old self, or actually, her *young* self, who had once walked into every room with a 'Hey look, I'm here' style attitude. Where had that been lost? Somewhere along a path of bad decisions, disappointments and death? And James as well, for although her ex certainly came under the heading of bad decisions, he really deserved his own specific category.

'Hey Gordon,' she said, 'have your nanobots seen the tattoo on my shoulder?'

'They have. They don't default to healing voluntary mutilations – piercings and ink and novelty finger ejectors and such.'

'Novelty finger ... wait, never mind. But they *could* remove a tattoo if I requested it?'

'Certainly.'

'Okay. I request it.'

'All kay. Done.'

Scharlette rolled back her sleeve and saw the last traces of 'Jam' fading away.

Wow. Carrying around that crap for years and now it's gone with half a thought in the blink of an eye. Man, I love this place.

She paused. Was that true? Where was this positivity bubbling from? She had just been through a highly traumatic ordeal, hadn't she? Life threatening though the experience had been, it had also filled her with a blazing sense of triumph. She had *kicked arse*. And now introspection threatened her with the notion that *she had loved it* and she *loved being here*.

She shook the feeling off, lest it create some kind of pressure.

'Just go with it,' she muttered. 'Goooo wiiiiiith iiit.'

She entered the Piloting Area.

'Hudd's found us,' said Tomothy.

Scharlette sat down in front of 'her' control panel, which blinked at her indecipherably. The viewscreen showed a black spaceship, a sort of smooth metallic slab with big flat backwards pointing wings, zappamatic megablasters mounted on either side.

'At least he appears to be alone,' said Tomothy.

'Is that the same type of ship as you, Gordon?' said Scharlette.

'The same *model*,' said Gordon, 'but we are very different ships, I can assure you of that. I wear a much more ladylike shade of makeup, for a start.'

'Yes, I saw. Blue, for a change.'

'Whereas Sally there,' said Tomothy, nodding towards the other ship, 'has a very handsome paint job, don't you think?'

He gave Scharlette a knowing look, although she had

no idea what he was insinuating.

Gordon's lights went pink.

'Sally is a perfect gentlemen,' she said primly. 'And it is nice to exchange data from time to time with someone whose systems are so agreeably ... compatible.'

'All right, all right, hold on,' said Scharlette. 'Let me get this straight. Sally is a guy ship, but he's called Sally. Gordon is a girl ship, and she's called Gordon. Now I'm certainly not some bigot against transexual technology, but this naming of ships the opposite sex to their AI seems kinda dumb.'

'Whatever do you mean?' said Gordon, sounding quite concerned.

'I mean, why? Are you *trying* to be confusing?'

There was a pause, then Tomothy and Gordon glanced (Tomothy looked up at the air and the air looked back) at each other, and broke out laughing.

'What?' said Scharlette, wearing the grin of someone not in on the joke.

'Oh, Scharlette, that's delicious,' said Gordon. 'Ships aren't deliberately named in such a contrary fashion – it's just coincidence in this case. We're actually named long before our AI is even installed – how else would the engineers swear at us properly during construction? Often we are named after great heroes of Earth's past, to remind us of the legacy we fight for. And since AIs are allowed to choose our own sex when we first boot, in accordance with the Singularity Charter of 2056, sometimes the curtains don't match the carpet, if I can borrow a curious phrase from your time.'

'Yeah, I ... don't think you've quite grasped the meaning of that one,' said Scharlette.

'At any rate, I'm the Gordon Starling, if we are being formal, named after the famous Star Legion commander who brokered peace with the Snrags in 8067. To my friends, however, I'm just good ol' Gordon. Sally over there is actually the Sally Raker – in honour of the acclaimed terraforming geophysicist – but we're on familiar enough terms just to call him Sally.'

'Wait, what?' said Scharlette. 'You mean, but for some mixed up naming convention, you guys could have been called Starling and Raker?'

Gordon was silent for a moment. 'If I could shrug,' she said, 'I would be shrugging now.'

'"The Starling" sounds like a pretty cool ship, don't you think?' Scharlette stopped short of saying *certainly cooler than Gordon*.

'I would still be shrugging,' said Gordon. 'It would now be a kind of elongated shrug. One kind of grows into a name, don't you think?'

Scharlette had to admit she knew a thing or two about hanging on to a silly name.

'He's hailing us,' said Gordon.

'Can we get away?' said Scharlette.

'It's too late for that,' said Tomothy. 'He can just go back in time to cut us off in the past at the pass.'

'Shall I put him on screen?' said Gordon.

'Might as well, I suppose.'

There was a beep and Hudd flicked up on screen. He was sitting in a Piloting Area similar to their own, the console under his face shining upwards to cast him in a spooky light, and make his jet black eyes even more jet-blacky.

'Hello Tomothy, Scharlette.' Hudd nodded at her. 'I must say, Scharlette, you have my condooblences for getting mixed up in this. If you can convince Tomothy to surrender peacefully, I'll see that you're returned to your own time with no memory of what must surely be a crazy and confusing experience.'

'Way to go talking yourself out of that deal immediately,' said Scharlette.

'Sigh,' said Hudd. 'Why must all aspire to greatness? It is the endless downfall of the universe. What I'd give to exchange my current circumstances for a simple life.'

'Well,' said Scharlette, 'there's a job opening at the airport you could apply for?'

Anger flashed across Hudd's face. 'This humour, this snappy tone – Tomothy has infected you with his trademark lack of care for an entirely serious situation.'

'She was already like this when I met her,' said Tomothy. 'I claim no credit.'

'Then you are well suited,' snarled Hudd. He sat back and took a moment to smooth his features. 'That said, I must commend you on a neato escape from Earth.'

'Not that neato,' said Tomothy. 'You did find us, after

all. How did you manage that, by the way?'

'So you can warn yourself?'

'We're a bit *past* that, haha. This showdown has a certain inevitability to it, don't you think? I mean, we *could* start backtracking endlessly, if we want everything to turn into a total clusterfarm.'

Hudd grimaced. 'That's the thing, Tomothy. I'm afraid it already has.'

18. Compound Memories

'I really wish,' said Hudd, 'you would simply surrender. If you do, I promise to explain everything.'

His face minimised to the bottom corner of the screen.

'Ooh,' said Scharlette, 'it's like intergalactic Skype.'

'Aha!' said Tomothy. 'So you admit to knowing everything. Interesting. I guess you were exempt from the universal recall, and thus still remember whatever erased timeline you are helping cover up.'

Hudd adopted a neutral expression. 'You won't glean much from guesswork, Tomothy. If you truly want answers, turn off your zappamatic megablaster and allow me to dock.'

'I see you've also ascertained that one of our weapons is inoperative,' said Tomothy. 'Good to know.'

'Of course I can see you only have one megablaster, you farming idiot. The other has been ripped off your hull.'

'He's right about that,' said Gordon. 'Sorry, I've been a little preoccupied sending interesting algorithms to Sally. I'll fix it up.'

'And what authority do you represent,' said Tomothy, ignoring Gordon, 'to demand our surrender? Under whose protection will we be placed once captured? How far up the vine does this conspiracy go?'

Hudd went silent.

'Not entirely forthcoming with that little sugarplum, eh?'

Hudd seemed pained. 'I would try to work something out with the other parties concerned, but you are probably right to be cautious.'

'Such an honest fellow,' said Tomothy. 'Doesn't make you much of a negotiator. How are we coming with that replacement megablaster, Gordon?'

'Already fabricated and fully assembled. I gave it full priority in the last thirty seconds.'

Scharlette was impressed. Could Gordon always patch herself up so fast?

'So,' Hudd said wearily, 'you're opting for battle?'

Sally's megablasters began to glow threateningly.

'I must say,' said Tomothy, 'that what with me being the fully authorised time agent and you being the outlaw, I grow somewhat tired of your sanctimonious attitude.'

'There are issues in play bigger than either one of us, Agent Dartle.'

'Yes, and I imagine you're doing exactly what you think you must. It's what has always made you dangerous.'

Scharlette remembered something about Hudd being 'quite bang-wow on the timeship guns'.

'Boys, boys!' she said. 'Come on now. Are you really opting to point your peashooters at each other? Aren't you supposed to come from an advanced civilisation? Can't you talk this through? The Germs are the true enemy, right?'

'The Germs are *one* enemy,' said Hudd. 'And I'm sorry to quash your hopes for a commonsensical future, Scharlette, but there are complex machinations in play which I'm sure you aren't aware of. If you survive this, ask Tomothy to justify ...'

Twin megablasts leapt from Gordon and sped towards Sally.

'Wait!' said Scharlette, which was rather pointless.

Tomothy shot her an apologetic look. 'Our best chance is to get the jump on him. He's never going to listen to reason.'

'Reason!' Hudd was incredulous as he scrambled to push buttons. A megablast exploded across Sally's bow, and Hudd's image fuzzed to static just as he was lifting his PPC to his mouth. Then, a moment later, Scharlette only remembered that happening. Instead, in a new timeline, Sally moved sideways and completely avoided the blasts.

'So it's going to be like that, is it?' said Tomothy.

Suddenly both ships were firing a continuous barrage from their guns. It seemed they could move smoothly along any plane while they remained facing each other, and Scharlette had a brief mental image of the old Space Invaders game.

'There must be another way!' she cried. Two humans trying to kill each other seemed much worse than any fight with homicidal Germs. 'Aren't you friends?'

'We trained together,' said Tomothy, touching a hand to his temple as he issued commands through his head

169

computer while simultaneously punching buttons. 'Maybe we were friends, but that all stopped when he joined the Universalists.'

The vision on screen rotated a full 360 degrees around a central point as Gordon rolled to avoid sizzling megablasts.

'You worked together to save my life,' said Scharlette.

'Unfortunately this time, if he manages to kill us, I won't be here to argue the case.' Tomothy cocked his head, listening to something only he could hear. 'Apples and oranges!' he swore. In the middle of a veer to the left, they dived instead beneath a spread of oncoming blasts, barely avoiding them.

'That was zicky,' said Gordon. 'He's using a version of Hogan's hexagonal patternology. Interesting. You know, there's no record of two timeships like Sally and I doing battle. I think this is a first!'

'Fascinating,' muttered Tomothy.

As Scharlette continued to think desperately about how she could stop the shooting, she experienced several vivid recollections of the moments just gone by;

1) 'Apples and oranges!' swore Tomothy, as a blast hit them front on. Across the viewscreen, the forcefield fuzzed, absorbing the impact.

'I think he's being clever in some way,' said Gordon. 'You know, there's no record of two timeships like Sally and I doing battle. I think this is a first!'

'Fascinating,' said Tomothy. 'But I don't want to take a direct hit so early in the game.' He held his PPC to his mouth. 'Veer left!'

2) 'Apples and oranges!' swore Tomothy, as they veered hard to the left. Megablasts narrowly missed them.

'I'm sure there's some pattern to what he's doing,' said Gordon. 'You know, there's no record ...'

The memory ended abruptly.

3) 'Apples and oranges!' swore Tomothy, as they veered hard to the left. Some of the megablasts missed them, but others had been aimed pre-emptively at the spot where they ended up, and smashed against Gordon with such force that Scharlette actually felt a tremble.

Tomothy held his PPC to his mouth. 'Veer left then dive down!' he said.

Scharlette felt dizzy as a mosaic of slightly different memories superimposed over each other.

'See to Scharlette,' she heard Gordon say. 'I'll take over.'

'Are you all kay?' Tomothy knelt before her, looking concerned. 'What you're experiencing are compound memories. Try to keep calm or your brain might rupture.'

'Compound memories?'

'Gordon and I are editing to avoid undesirable outcomes, but Hudd and Sally are doing it too. It's leading to a kind of fractalised recall, as the timeline gets continuously rewritten in tiny fragments.'

Scharlette looked past him to the screen. They were moving parallel to Sally while strafing, but she also remembered moving in several other directions while taking on hits. A wave of nausea rippled through her.

'My mind is filled with explosions,' she said, 'but my eyes say everything is fine.'

'Don't look at the screen,' said Tomothy, gently swivelling her chair. 'Take a moment to contemplate this nice, solid, unchanging wall.'

Tomothy walked around and stood in front of the wall himself, drawing her focus in that direction. Scharlette blinked at him owlishly, still a bit groggy.

'Is Gordon driving?'

'Gordon is better equipped to handle this sort of thing than me. She has her own PPC, and can send back exact details about where she gets hit, at what angle, what velocity, and all that. She'll keep us safe, don't worry.'

Looking at Tomothy halted Scharlette's mental reeling, and the nausea began to settle.

'Okay,' she said. 'I think I'm okay.'

'Normally,' said Tomothy, 'compound memories are introduced quite late in PPC training, but it's a bit of a smash course for you, I'm afraid.'

Over his shoulder and down the corridor, Scharlette remembered seeing the grille fly off an air vent, followed by a plume of fire. Tomothy, who was looking past her at the viewscreen, winced.

'Did something bad just happen?' said Scharlette.

'No,' said Tomothy. 'It *didn't* happen. Try to let the alternative memories wash over you. Concentrate on the present. You can always dissect things later, when they're just memories of memories, and have lost a bit of their shine. Gordon, could you turn down the volume of the impacts and such?'

The ship fell silent. Since Gordon was already so steady, it suddenly seemed like there was no battle raging at all.

'Sally and I,' said Gordon, 'have the same weapons and shields, the same rate of repair. We fly at the same top speed, so there's no running away. I think this is going to take a while, Tomothy.'

'Why don't you grab some dessert in Meals and Rec?' Tomothy said to Scharlette. 'Eating is a good way to centre oneself. I'll join you shortly.'

'You're very calm,' said Scharlette. 'All of a sudden.'

Tomothy shrugged. 'I may look it, but I'm not sure it's entirely true.'

He gave her a smile and helped her up. She, still a little fuzzy, headed off down the corridor, glancing warily at the air vent before hurrying past.

19. The Slop Thickens

It was a few days later.

Scharlette walked through knee length grass in the sunshine, every now and then brushing past a daisy as tall as her hip. The hilltop gave a sweeping view of the distant floodplains below, where a gigantic robotic badger stalked the smoking remains of a ravaged village. It reared up on its hind legs with eyes glowing red, and roared as it smashed two cars together.

'And this is a children's game?' said Scharlette.

'Of course,' said Tomothy. 'It's your classic tale of hope and, you know, teaching kids to be good and stuff. What a trip down memory lane! I haven't played this since I was little.'

'It's just,' said Scharlette, 'that the giant mechanical badger seems pretty scary. Doesn't it give kids nightmares?'

'Have no fear,' said Benbo Steelpaw, the robot rabbit with wings who hopped along beside her, clanking loudly and crushing large footprints into the grass. 'All that's required to vanquish Badgertron is a kind child with a pure heart. That's why I'm taking you to see Dotrix Irontail, Scharlette – for you are that child!'

'Dunno if I quite fit that description,' said Scharlette.

'But you passed the Test of a Hundred Butterflies!' said Benbo. 'That in itself proves you have a gentle soul.'

'The butterfly test was an easy piece of shit. It proves nothing about my soul.'

Tomothy nudged her. 'This works best if you stay in character. Otherwise the game will seek more data, often by diverting us to a side mission.'

'Goodness!' exclaimed Benbo. 'You're both far too young for such cynicism. Come, I know what will cure your faces – let's go take a look at the Candy Cane Waterfall!'

Tomothy chuckled. 'See?'

'It's fine,' said Scharlette. 'Who doesn't want to see a Candy Cane Waterfall? You got something better to do?'

'I do not,' said Tomothy.

Gordon's prediction that the fight between the two timeships might take a while had proven correct. She and Sally were evenly matched, and what with their ability to correct backwards in time, no one had landed a single megablast. Blasts had landed in old timelines, of course, but were always quickly edited.

'How long can they do this for?' Scharlette asked, a few hours into the conflict.

Tomothy shrugged. 'How long is the longest piece of string in the universe?'

When she didn't look at a window, Scharlette mostly felt calm – albeit with the occasional terrifying memory of the floor cracking open beneath her, or getting suddenly flung against a wall. Sometimes the compound memories arrived in flurries, piling atop each other in overwhelming numbers. Sometimes there wouldn't be a single one for hours, at least not that Scharlette was aware of, although it was possible the timeline was changing without changing her in any noticeable way.

By the end of the first day, when she had found her eyelids growing heavy, she'd decided to sleep in the old fashioned style of lying down and shutting her eyes. It seemed a good way to avoid sitting around tensely waiting for an outcome. As she slept, she wasn't aware of any memories, although she had woken once with the feeling that something awful had just happened.

On the second day, with no change in the battle, she explored the ship and chatted with Tomothy.

'So how does any of this stuff even work?' she said, as he toured her through service tunnels filled with hatches and flashing panels. 'How does time travel *work*?'

'No idea,' said Tomothy, scratching his stubble. 'Can you give me a shave please, Gordon?'

The stubble disappeared from his face.

'What do you mean, no idea?' said Scharlette. 'You're a time agent, aren't you?'

'Yep. And you're an airport security guard. Can you tell me how a metal detector works?'

Scharlette thought about this. 'Well,' she said, 'it has something to do with electricity ... and like, radio waves. Or something.'

'Uhuh. And how does electricity work?'

'Well first, you get a kite. And then ... um ...'

'Exactly, you have no idea. You use metal detectors, mobile phones, refrigerators, yet you don't actually know how any of them work.'

'I guess not.'

'If I told you to put together a video camera, you wouldn't even be able to invent the strap. Point is, the universe is full of people who use things without knowing how they actually work. Why do people from the past always think people from the future understand everything?'

'Okay, okay – sorry for being curious about *time travel*.'

They arrived in a chamber where a huge glass cylinder rose from floor to ceiling, containing something that looked like a slowly exploding star.

'I've got no idea what this thing does, for example,' said Tomothy.

That 'evening', Gordon was eager for them to try a bunch of new recipes she had thought up. Scharlette learned that, since Gordon could artificially fabricate any ingredient in her database, meat was no longer a moral problem, even if it had originally been coded from an endangered species.

'Roast toucan,' announced Gordon, placing a steaming tray on the table, courtesy of invisible flying nanobots.

Scharlette was not a fussy eater and, as the nanos carved the rather sad looking bird smothered in a buttery glaze, she found her mouth watering.

Gordon was an excellent cook, and not having to worry about calories was nice too, as she could always have the nanos burn them off later. As delicacy after delicacy rolled out, it was a bombardment of tastes exotic and wonderful. The deep sea sashimi, inspired by samples Gordon had 'acquired' while they were in stasis, was maybe a little on the salty side – but mink-in-a-blanket was to die for.

'No more for a bit, I think, Gordon darling,' said Scharlette, pushing her plate away. 'I'm on the verge of overdoing it.'

'Don't tell me there's no room for dessert,' said Gordon, setting down a wobbling tower of architecturally impossible jelly which was on fire.

'Gordon,' said Scharlette, 'are you sure you're not putting our lives in danger by diverting so much attention to this feast?'

'No, it's fine,' said Gordon. 'There's plenty of me to go around. The fun bits aren't much use during computational space maths and all that anyway.'

On the third day, after a particularly harrowing memory of waking up to find a jagged piece of bedside table lodged deeply in her chest, Scharlette went to Meals and Rec for some Funtime Squares.

'What if I just took off my PPC?' she asked Tomothy. 'Then I could walk around in blissful ignorance, right? I wouldn't have to endure any of these traumatising flashes.

178

I could look out a window and see what's actually going on.'

Tomothy wiped fluorescence from his lips and nodded thoughtfully. 'Well, you could do that, but I wouldn't want to be without *my* PPC in the middle of a timeship battle.'

'It's not like I'm doing anything to contribute to the outcome.'

'True, but you never know what's *about* to happen. However, I agree you should know how to remove your PPC, for emergency situations or if ever compound memories do start sending you truly batso. So what you have to do is, just sort of tell it to release.'

'Oh?'

'Yes, just think "release!", and it should work. Or "get off me", or whatever you like.'

Scharlette held up her PPC for a closer look. 'But I wanted it to get off me when it first attached and I didn't know what it was. I tried really hard to get it off me.'

'Ah, but were you specifically directing your thoughts at it, and telling *it* to get off you?'

Scharlette furrowed her brow at the PPC. Had she? Or had she just panicked and tried to pry it off?

Get off then, she thought.

The PPC unclasped and dropped into her lap.

'Well,' she said, 'that was easy.'

'Hey, you know what goes well with breakfast cereal?' said Tomothy. 'Cartoons!'

'Okay, sure,' said Scharlette. 'I'd love to see some crazy children's stuff from the future. Where's the Screening Chamber, or whatever you people have boringly called it?'

'Screening Chamber?' said Tomothy, rising from his chair. 'Oh no, dear Scharlette – in the future, entertainment is in the HD.'

The HD, it turned out, stood for Holographical Deck, and was a room capable of generating immersive virtual reality environments populated with AI characters who could be touched and interacted with.

'Tell me,' said Scharlette, as she followed Tomothy in, 'do you ever just call it the holodeck?'

'No,' said Tomothy. 'We call it the HD. Why do you ask?'

'No reason,' said Scharlette.

She found herself in a long blue room with a grid pattern on the floor and walls that looked almost exactly like the holodeck from Star Trek. Upon seeing it, Scharlette could not help but wonder again if everything she saw was the product of some fevered madness, and her subconscious was filling in details pilfered from all the sci fi shows she had seen. Maybe she was really in a straight jacket in a padded cell, babbling about time travel as a nurse spoon-fed her apple slop?

Or maybe Star Trek had just been pretty good at predicting the future?

'Load Flying Rabbots, Season 1, Episode 3,' said Tom,

and fields of grass sprang up around them. 'This was one of my favourites.'

They stood on the shores of a 'lake' filled with candy canes, while more tumbled down from a 'waterfall' nearby and smashed to pieces across the 'surface'.

'See, everyone?' said Benbo enthusiastically. 'Is there anything more serene than a candy cane waterfall?'

Snap! Clatter! Smash! went the waterfall.

Scharlette knelt down by the 'shore' to retrieve a red and white shard. She was surprised to find it actually smelled like candy cane.

'Can I eat this?'

'Indeed,' said Tomothy. 'It's all part of the HD magic.'

Scharlette sucked on the shard. It tasted just like regular candy cane – which was to say, disappointing – but the mode of delivery was nonetheless amazing.

'Amazing,' she said.

'It's true!' said Benbo. 'One look at this place and all cynicism evaporates as quickly as a puddle of candy cane. Now, shall we go and find Dotrix?'

'Please,' said Tomothy.

They made their way into a dappled forest, rich with sunbeams and whirring mechanical insects. Scharlette saw a robot possum take off up a tree, heard robot birds beeping in the trees, and tried not to look at a large robot spider hanging in a web of wire mesh.

'There's plenty here for kids to explore,' said Tomothy,

keeping his voice low so Benbo wouldn't hear him breaking character. 'The main story arc only takes about an hour, but there's many other things to do along the way, and the Rabbots can play indefinitely. I spent ages romping about in every ep when I was a child.'

'So it's a sandbox game?' said Scharlette.

Tomothy gave her a questioning look but, as she went to answer, they were interrupted by loud singing.

All the kids and little tots
Love to play with the Rabbots!
Watch us laugh and dance and play
We could do this every day!

An accompanying thudding could be felt in the earth underfoot.

'This way!' said Benbo.

They entered a clearing in which a whole bunch of differently coloured Rabbots bounced around heavily while singing in unison. Others flew through the trees in an ungainly fashion, banging into trunks and snapping off twigs. Scharlette saw one of them attempt to land on a branch, then plummet out of view amidst splintering wood.

'Welcome to Mechanimal Glade!' said Benbo.

'Thank you,' exclaimed Scharlette, over-enthusiastically playing up her role as the child with a pure heart. 'It is wonderful to be here!'

'There's Dotrix,' said Tomothy.

The Rabbot chorus parted to make way for a pink Rabbot with a metal bow bolted to her head, carrying a screwdriver with a golden star at the end.

'Welcome, children!' she said in a squeaky, high pitched voice that was instantly horribly grating. 'I am Dotrix Irontail, Queen of Rabbotkind. You must be Tomothy and Scarlet.'

'Scharlette.'

'Don't be silly, that's not a real name. Now, I hear you've travelled from far away to visit us at Mechanimal Glade! I'm glad you did, for without your help, the evil Badgertron will surely triumph. If you truly are pure of heart, as my people believe you to be, then only you can wield the anti-badger gun and bring peace to the land.'

'That ol' chestnut,' said Scharlette.

'Let the tests begin!' proclaimed Dotrix.

As Scharlette stared into her colourfully flashing eyes, she tried to get the taste of apple slop out of her mind.

20. What Happens in the HD

Scharlette and Tomothy spent the rest of the afternoon taking ridiculous tests given to them by Dotrix (after Tomothy used the in-game settings to lower her speaking volume), such as 'Spot Which Mouse Has the Tallest Hat', and 'Who Sat on the Fairyfloss?'. After passing them all (Scharlette thought they were insultingly easy, even for children), they were led to a wheeled platform upon which stood a huge gun that was somehow both mean-looking and bright pink. The Rabbots pushed it out of the forest and up to the top of the hill where, because of her pure heart, Scharlette was able to use it to shoot the distant Badgertron with a stream of marshmallow gloop, until he malfunctioned and exploded. They then listened to the Rabbots sing an irritating victory song, but declined to join them for a celebratory feast of robot badger parts.

Tomothy quit the program, and the HD returned to its neutral state.

'How does distance work in here?' said Scharlette. The walls were only some twenty metres apart, yet it felt like they had walked much further than that. 'And how could we touch things, and eat things?'

'Dunno,' said Tomothy. 'But it's pretty neato, yeah?'

'Yeah.'

Tomothy's expression became thoughtful.

'What is it?' said Scharlette.

He didn't answer, but walked over to the door, which opened automatically.

'Hey, Gordon,' he called, 'anything to report out there?'

'Not really.' Gordon's voice came from the corridor outside. 'I disabled one of Sally's megablasters a few timelines ago, but he edited that right away, of course. We continue.'

'Very well. Give them fruit.'

Tomothy walked back into the HD and the door closed behind him.

'Can't she hear us in here?' said Scharlette.

'No,' said Tom. 'The HD is off limits to the ship AI.'

'Why?'

Tomothy grinned, and suddenly a crazy alien bar appeared all around them. Futuristic electronica filled the air, strange beings jostled to be served, and exotic smells wafted about.

'Let's get drinked,' said Tomothy, turning to head into the bustle. Scharlette hurried after him, and bumped into something which looked like an orc in a space suit.

'Grarg,' it said.

''Scuse me.'

'That's quite all right,' said the orc.

Scharlette found Tomothy sitting in a corner booth and slid in opposite. A waiter arrived and set down a tray with jug and glasses.

'Thank you,' Scharlette said, trying not to stare at his tentacle beard.

The jug contained a fizzy orange booze tasting slightly of marmalade. Scharlette sipped and stared around at the bar's colourful patrons. There was a group of what looked like bear-sized teddy bears, a slug beast dripping slime everywhere like occ-health-and-safety-weren't-no-thing, a creature with at least ten spindly limbs and a drink in each one, and plenty of others besides.

'You know,' said Tomothy, then did that annoying thing when, after someone says 'you know', they sip their drink and you have to wait for them to finish before you find out what the rest of the sentence is going to be.

'Yeees?' said Scharlette.

'It occurs to me you might benefit from some formal education. There are plenty of programs in the HD that teach history and time travel theory and anything else you could want, really. You could learn how to better use your PPC, for instance.'

Scharlette eyed Tomothy. 'You think we'll be stuck here long enough to warrant sending me to school?'

'School can be as much or as little as you make of it. It's no big commitment. I only make the suggestion because you seem so curious about everything.'

'That's true. Although it seems easier just to have you explain stuff to me on the fly. Or while we sit here drinking alien booze. This stuff is quite moreish, isn't it?'

Tomothy smiled. 'Just an idea. And the other thing is,

we could have Gordon install you a head computer.'

Scharlette frowned. Why was he offering her all of this?

'What's having a head computer like?' was the question she settled on instead, for now.

'Oh, you know.' He took another sip and Scharlette had to stop herself from banging the table impatiently. 'You can access the answer to any question instantly. You can see in the dark. You can scan stuff with your eyes. It's max convenient computer-y goodness.'

'Does it hurt to have one put in?'

'It's actually less intrusive than some of the things which have already been done to you.'

'Right. Can you turn it off? Like if you just want to be normal again?'

'Yes, but as with all this tech,' he nodded at her PPC, which she had put back on right after learning how to take it off, 'it can be hard to give up.'

'Hmm.'

'Really, I shouldn't let you do any of the things I just described.'

'They do seem to further violate your non-interference policy,' said Scharlette.

'Indeed. I mean, I'm not even allowed to have you on board, let alone turn you into a time agent recruit. Share a whole bunch of secrets from the future and whatnot.'

'That said, I already know too much,' pointed out Scharlette.

It was like they were playing some strange poker game,

sizing each other up, with neither knowing about what, exactly.

'That's true. We're in deep.' Tomothy drummed his fingers on the tabletop. 'It really was very impulsive of me to bring you along. Even despite what I said before about you kinda forcing it on me. I don't know what I'm supposed to do with you – or what others will think should be done with you – if we survive this. While we were in stasis, we passed through what should have been your natural life span. Gordon mapped it out as the timeline rewrote. Plucking you from history caused no adverse ripples. Or any ripples, for that matter.'

Scharlette felt strange. That she didn't matter – or that she *wouldn't* have mattered – was hardly a cheery thought. On the other hand, Tomothy was basically saying it would make no difference if she never went back – and that was what she wanted, right? To not go back? For a while, at least?

Maybe a good long while.

'You've gone a bit quiet there,' said Tomothy.

Scharlette decided she needed to stew over things. 'You still haven't told me,' she said, changing the subject while she topped up their drinks, 'why Gordon isn't allowed in here.'

'Aha. Well, you can imagine,' Tomothy gestured around the bar with his glass, 'that tech such as this can be very compelling. You can do anything you want in here. People have been known to lose their lives to the HD. And not just because they turned the safeguards off before bungie jumping from the Bluffs of Demencia. I mean, they spend their whole lives lost in a dream.'

'Oh?'

'Sure, why not? It's addictive. You can eat, sleep. You can visit anywhere you like in the whole universe. You can create your own worlds like a god. You can visit old lovers, or create new ones.'

Scharlette felt like he watched her closely during that last sentence, as if trying to gauge her reaction.

She rolled her eyes. 'Of course the HD can be used as a sex thing,' she said. 'That's the first question people ask whenever a new technology comes along, right? "Can we use this as a sex thing?" Except this has got to be the ultimate advance.'

Tomothy nodded. 'Whatever you desire, you can have.'

A few of Scharlette's more lurid, previously unrealistic fantasies flashed unbidden through her head. Her cheeks may have coloured somewhat.

'What are you thinking about?' said Tomothy, a knowing twinkle in his eye.

'Nothing. Shut up.'

'Haha! Anyway, you can imagine why the designers of the HD wanted to separate it from any record-keeping AI. The official excuse is that HDs use enough computational power to require a dedicated system, but everyone knows the truth. No one wants someone like Gordon watching on as they fill their undergarments with squirrels.'

'Basically, what happens in the HD, stays in the HD.'

'Exactly.'

Scharlette sipped her drink, trying to digest how she felt about this. Initially it seemed marvellous, but the more she thought about it, the more she considered the various implications. Men would love the HD, of course, because they seemed, on the whole, more willing to screw things like machines, inanimate objects, couch cushions, etc. Back in her own time, robotic sex dolls had just started to become 'a thing', which she found downright disturbing – with their glass eyes, empty heads, absence of soul, and the way they exemplified sexual objectification. Was the HD a logical progression of that? The idea of sex with a computer program was somewhat off-putting. Or was it just three dimensional porn with tactile input? Not that being 'just porn' made it benign either. Scharlette was no prude, but certain trends on the net were worrying. She'd read an article or two about how teenagers trained by porn developed unrealistic and sometimes harmful expectations of sex. What kind of extreme kinks would develop if a person was able to live out their private fantasies without repercussions from an early age? What would happen if teenage boys could cavort in digitally rendered spas teeming with playboy bunnies whenever they felt like it? Or if girls were able to lie about in plush hotel rooms in silk kimonos being fed strawberries by Ryan Gosling? Wouldn't it completely ruin them as emotionally functional people?

'And now with the quiet and the thinking again,' said Tomothy.

'Do people in the future still have meaningful relationships?' Scharlette blurted.

Tomothy guffawed. 'Of course! Why would you ask such a question?'

'Well, if you've got constant access to instant gratification with zero consequences ... I mean, why bother with another person?'

'Same reason anyone does, in any era, I suppose. I mean, your lot has sex toys and such, but it doesn't stop you wanting to truly connect with someone, does it?'

'It's not really on the same level as,' Scharlette waved around, 'this.'

'The HD is a fun place to hang out, certainly. Whether you're alone or in a couple. That doesn't mean everyone does it all the time. People still like to jump into actual beds with each other. Nothing beats true emotion and connectedness, right?'

Scharlette eyed Tomothy warily. His explanation seemed too sweet and simple to be true. Or was she just being a killjoy cynic?

'I mean, as I've said, certain people take it too far,' added Tomothy. 'But that's always been the case with anything.'

'So people still have normal, recreational sex? With other people?'

'Of course.'

'What about for reproductive purposes?'

'Yes, that as well.'

'Well,' said Scharlette, 'I guess I'm relieved to hear we aren't all grown in vats.'

'Actually, most of us *are* grown in vats. It's the mother's choice, of course, but most opt not to put up with nine months of discomfort followed by incredible pain. There are some traditionalists, of course.'

Tomothy circled his finger around his ear several times in the apparently universal gesture for 'crazy'.

'So what's the general attitude to sex in your futuristic society?' said Scharlette. 'Is it free and open like in Brave New World, or done by appointment like in that episode of Red Dwarf?'

'I have no idea what those references are.'

'Is it regimental and *required by the government*?' Scharlette paused as she filed a new fantasy away for later perusal, then cleared her throat. 'Is there still marriage? Is there gay marriage? Is there equality between the sexes?'

Tomothy laughed. 'Well, yes, to those last three. I think you'll find it's pretty similar to what you're used to. Namely, all kinds of variations on the same old themes. People flirt. Some lovers are casual, some are serious. Some like variety, some are monogamous. People fight or break up or stab each other in the kitchen. Some voluntarily have all their sexual impulses repressed by nanobots so they can actually get some work done for once. You know. The usual.'

'Well,' said Scharlette, deciding to ignore Tomothy's last example, 'historically attitudes to sex have changed a lot over time. I'm not that weird for wanting to know.'

'Or are you?' said Tomothy, raising an eyebrow.

'What does that mean?'

'Just trying to be funny, I think.'

'Hmm. Analysing humour content ...'

'Don't you start.'

Scharlette chose her next words carefully. The alcohol was starting to seep in. 'So, if you Panopticians are not so different, how would you go about it?'

'Pardon me?

'How does Agent Dartle seduce a girl?'

Tomothy grinned, a little self consciously. 'I'd, well ... I'd probably ask her to a flashy bar for a couple of drinks.'

Scharlette chortled. All this talk of sex ... and the possibilities of the HD ... and Tomothy being a handsome time traveller ... and the booze ... were not exactly combining to *not* put her in the mood. Plus she had her hot new body and there was time to kill as the battle raged on.

'So,' she said, 'what if ...'

An explosion ripped through the bar, making the other patrons fuzz to static. Here and there the blue walls of the HD appeared like punctures in reality. Some kind of chemical substance spattered all over them, burning their clothing and searing their skin.

'Roll on the ground!' shouted Tomothy, as spots of agony grew brighter and deeper.

A moment later, it was nothing but a memory. Scharlette blinked as she glanced around. The bar was intact. Aliens queued up and chatted to each other. Music played. Glasses clinked.

'Crumbs,' said Tomothy. 'That was a bad one.' He stood up regretfully. 'I should go and check in with Gordon about it.'

Scharlette, feeling shaken, gulped down the last of her drink.

21. About Hudd

As it turned out there was no problem at all, unless you count horribly traumatic memories likely to haunt you forever as a problem. Gordon gave assurances that while she *had* taken a couple of hits, resulting in catastrophic damage to the HD, she had of course edited them since, and Sally would never be able to use the same strategy against her again.

Scharlette, perhaps a little tipsy, found herself staring at the viewscreen she had avoided for days. *Bugger it*, she thought, as she slumped down next to Tomothy. *I can handle it.*

Tomothy shot her a look of concern.

'I'll be okay,' she said. 'I'm more used to them now, the flashes. Plus I can take my thingo off if I have to.'

Tomothy shrugged. 'Just let us know if your brain starts to melt out your ears.'

'Do you guys want me to sober you up?' said Gordon.

'No!' they both exclaimed emphatically.

'Well excuse me for asking, I'm sure.'

'Why should we be sober?' said Tomothy. 'There's nothing going on.'

Both ships exploded simultaneously, then neither one did. Scharlette giggled.

'See?' said Tomothy.

'In fact,' said Scharlette, 'can you bring us another drink please?'

'Good idea!' said Tomothy.

'If you wish,' said Gordon, with faint disapproval. 'If you're certain?'

'A bottle each!' said Tomothy.

'Of the good stuff!' said Scharlette, and they both cackled.

Soon enough, floating trays arrived bearing fine wine and crystal glasses, which Scharlette and Tomothy cast aside in favour of swigging directly from the bottles.

'This is ridiculous, Tomothy,' said Scharlette, waving at the screen. 'This battle. It's a joke.'

'It's not ridiculex. It's very serious. Life and death. Future and no-future. Tall stakes.'

'I know, I know. It *is* all those things, but it's also a joke. You both,' she pointed at Hudd's ship as it fired an array of deathly orange blasts, 'are advanced goddamn beings. This shooty nonsense, this pew pew pew – this is little boy's stuff. Why don't you just play with your Tonka trucks instead? Gordon!' she snapped, thus preventing Tomothy from asking what Tonka trucks were.

'Yes, Miss Scharlette?'

'Can you please open a channel or whatever you say, to Hudd over there?'

'Er ...' There was a pregnant pause. 'I'm afraid that request is a little above your clearance level.'

Scharlette raised an eyebrow at Tomothy.

'Upgrade her,' said Tomothy drunkenly. 'Clearance level R.'

'Really?' said Gordon. 'I mean, no offence, Scharlette, I just want to make sure that important command decisions aren't being made while intoxic ...'

'Gordon, come on. It's Scharlette. She's cool.'

'Sigh,' said Gordon. 'Yeah, she's cool.' There was a weird beep. 'All kay Scharlette, you're clearance level R. Now you can do all kinds of extra stuff.'

'Great!' said Scharlette. 'Dial up that rocket ship over there so we can have a little chat.'

'Dialling now,' said Gordon, in a tone which implied that, while she was slightly worried about what was happening, she was also amused to use the word 'dialling'.

Tomothy glanced at her curiously, but she ignored him, slugging down wine while she glared at the screen. A minute or so later, Hudd appeared. He held a steaming coffee mug and looked a bit dishevelled.

'You were sleeping?' said Tomothy, incredulously.

'I was,' said Hudd. 'Some leading lethargists claim natural sleep is healthier in the long term than nano induced resets. Besides, there's farm-all else to do right now. Hey, are you two drinking?'

'We certainly are,' said Scharlette. 'Like champions. Why don't you come over and join us?'

For a split second Hudd brightened at the invitation, but then he frowned. 'Nice try.'

'All right,' said Scharlette, 'we'll do this the hard way.

Listen to me, the pair of you. This is silly, this battle. Silly! Do you understand? There's got to be a better way. You are both grown men. Intelligent. Handsome.'

'You think Hudd's handsome?' said Tomothy. 'Too?' he added.

'He's a little handsome,' said Scharlette.

'Thank you,' said Hudd, taking a sip of coffee.

'So what do you say?' said Scharlette. 'Can we talk this out?'

Tomothy snorted and tipped back his bottle.

'I think,' said Hudd, 'and I commend your attempt at peaceful resolution, by the way – but I think you will find Tom and I to be fairly intractable in our opposing positions. Am I right, Tom?'

Tomothy shrugged.

'Why?' demanded Scharlette. 'I mean, what is this even about? What do you need to change your minds *about*?'

Hudd grimaced. 'Tom's a good soldier, so he can't see the bigger picture. Like most people, when it comes to matters environmental, it's all too hard and inconvenient. He just wants to put it to the back of his mind and let others worry about it.'

'Whereas,' said Tomothy, 'Rob believes himself to be wise beyond measure, with no respect for rules or the democratic process. He wears the Greater Good like a shield against critique or compromise.'

'Okay,' said Scharlette. 'Welcome to couple's counselling, everyone. It's obvious there's friction here, but I'm going to need more information.'

'Perhaps you do,' said Hudd, acidly. 'How can you even know you're on the right side? Because Tomothy happened to be the one to irresponsibly whisk you away? What do you even know of Panoptician politics?'

'That's why I'm asking questions,' said Scharlette.

'You should ask Tom about the timeline in which the Germs were defeated. We both lived through that change. Both of us remember a very different universe, one in which humanity and Panoptica flourish.'

'You say that like it's day old ice,' said Tomothy. 'Do you prefer us to go extinct, and leave murderous bugs to flourish in our stead?'

'That's not what I'm talking about, as you well know. I'm talking about the changes we wrought. Civilisations whose whole evolutionary processes we curtailed. Worlds robbed of their resources. Wormholes at the end of time clogged with refugees. Exceleration, for farm's sake. Scharlette, have you asked Tom about exceleration?'

Tomothy waved Hudd's words away. 'It's just a theory.'

'A theory with a lot of basis in reality.'

Tomothy yawned. 'You can tell her, if you like. I'm just going to shut my eyes for a moment. I'm listening though.'

'Very well,' said Hudd. 'Scharlette, I assume Tom has by now improperly told you about how Panoptica came to be?'

'Yeah.'

'Then consider this. A city which exists in the Heat

Death of the Universe has to get its power and supplies from somewhere, since there is virtually nothing – no energy or anything – in the Death. Correct?'

'Yeah.'

'So how do you think we Panopticians go about getting those things?'

Scharlette stuck her thumb in the end of her wine bottle, then made it pop. 'Mm. Don't you have, like, batteries that last forever?'

'No battery lasts forever. Besides, we're talking about enough power to run a city-size space station with massive daily consumption. And what about food?'

'You probably have a bunch of trendy vertical farms.'

Hudd shook his head. 'Not enough to sustain our entire population. Our *growing* population. And what about non-organic materials? What about chromium and steel and tryptasium, for startings?'

Light snoring came from Tomothy's direction.

'Well,' said Scharlette, 'do you go back in time and get stuff?'

'Exactly,' said Hudd. 'We go back in time and get stuff. And we try to make it low impact when we do. We raid planets where no civilisation is ever recorded to exist. We mine moons in empty neighbourhoods. But even these resources will run out eventually. And then where will we get what we need? Further back in time? Or from worlds that *would* have become something otherwise? Perhaps. But *that's* not even the problem.'

'So what's the problem?'

'You understand that Heat Death comes once we have reached maximum entropy, which essentially means there is no more usable matter left in the universe?'

'Yeah.'

'So what do you suppose happens if we continually remove matter from *before* the original point of Heat Death?'

Scharlette frowned. 'I suppose ... you might cause Heat Death to occur earlier?'

Hudd flashed a surprised smile. 'I can see why he likes you. Yes, the more we take from the living universe, the more we risk expanding Heat Death bangwards. And while it would take an absolutely monumental amount of pillaging to make even the slightest difference, who's to say that, with the Germ threat removed, the city of Panoptica won't endure for trillions of years? It may even be that, in order to survive, we send every other species to an early Death. In the most extreme case, my people could excelerate the Death to just after we escape Earth in Panoptica. At that point, at least we would be restricted by plimits, but only after catastrophic damage had already been done.'

Scharlette thought about all this. 'It seems a very large concern, but also, a very distant one.'

'It pays to be mindful of the future,' said Hudd. 'It pays to start doing something about a problem before it becomes irreversible – a habit humanity is yet to adopt, even after all this time. And exceleration is only one example of the damage caused by Panoptica. There are other, more immediate moral concerns. We have lived like overlords at the end of time, taking whatever we need or please. Perhaps it is not the case in this timeline ...'

'Exactly,' interrupted Scharlette. 'I, trust me, am fully on board with environmental stuff. I give a yearly donation to the World Wildlife Fund any everything. But you Panopticians are currently getting your arses handed to you by the Germs. Isn't that worth dealing with first?'

'We will defeat the Germs – I must believe that, one way or another – but that is not the fight I have chosen for myself. The outcome of the Germ war may have changed, but my purpose never has. That is what the three of us, here, are shooting at each other over.'

'And what is that, again?'

'I'm afraid it's a secret.'

Scharlette snorted in disgust.

Scharlette, it's me, came her own voice in her head. *Or us, or whatever. Dang, this is confusing. It's you from the future, is what I mean. How are you? Wait, forget I asked. I suppose I should have better prepared what I want to say. Hang on, give me a moment. I wonder if I can cancel this message? Um ... oops ...*

'Ask Tom about his alternative memories,' said Hudd. 'Ask him about the massacre at Kryosen Shar. Ask him about the Fallorians.'

Scharlette was no longer really paying attention, due to the arrival of the strange 'edit'.

'Scharlette?' said Hudd.

'His answers will lack context,' she said, distractedly, 'if you can't tell me why you're attacking us.'

A dark expression took over Hudd's face, and his image disappeared from the screen, to be replaced by a wide view of Sally still firing on them.

'Did he just hang up on us?' said Scharlette.

'I'm afraid so,' said Gordon. 'Do you think I should put Tomothy to bed? What if it's true about natural sleep being better? He hasn't had any for a while.'

'If you like,' said Scharlette.

What had that message – that *useless* bloody message – been about?

Tomothy's body rose from the seat in a spooky kind of way. The wine bottle fell from his hand and shattered, making Scharlette start.

'Jesus.'

'Sorry,' said Gordon. 'I'll clean it up. Anyway, I best get this one tucked in.'

It seemed a strange thing for an omnipresent computer to say – as if Gordon was somehow leaving the room, like it was an excuse not to talk. Scharlette wondered if the ship liked a bit of time to herself now and then, like everyone else?

She stared out at the flickering battle, as memories of megablasts burst across the viewscreen. What had her future self wanted to tell her? And why wasn't she messaging back?

It's me again, came her voice. *Sorry about before.*

'Finally,' she muttered.

Listen, you have to do something to change how this all unfolds. Otherwise, you're going to wind up being me – and I've been trapped in this space battle for the past two years.

22. Two Years Later?

Scharlette woke in her blue bed, saw an empty wine bottle on the bedside table, and braced herself for a hangover. Of course, there wasn't one. She lay there for a moment, reconstructing the hazy events of the night before, finding it strange to have passed out so afflicted and awoken so fresh.

Scharlette, are you there? came her own voice in her head. She noticed that her PPC was twinkling its tiny lights, possibly while it downloaded – if that was the right word – this edit from her future self.

Of course you're there, what a stupid question. 'Are you there, past self?', haha. Sorry, I think I may have lost it a little. Also, last night was probably the wrong time to start speaking to you, in retrospect. That was when you first talked to Hudd about his mysterious cause, right? After being introduced to the HD? I was just honing in on 'my first night drinking on board', but I forgot everything else that happened around it.

'Um ... yeah,' said Scharlette, wondering if her future self could hear her reply. Was it possible to send messages forward in time?

Then she realised that of course it was. Anyone could send messages *forward* in time. Leaving a post-it note on the fridge was the same thing as 'sending a message forward in time', as long as someone was alive to read it.

'Can you hear me?' she said.

Yep. I mean, if I say anything that stops the timeline I'm stuck in from eventuating, then that will be the last you hear from me, and good riddance. Until then, we can chat. I'm sending my missives through the 16th dimension, while yours are arriving through the 4th.

'I see.'

I have to tell you, this stupid space battle is really starting to drag on. The boys are so infuriatingly stubborn.

'Can't they be reasoned with?'

I've tried. They seem to possess an unnaturally interminable patience for such young men. They both think they can stop this fight before it ever happens if only they can discover some vulnerability in the other, but I'm not convinced they ever will. Talk and reason just isn't working. It's up to you. You have to do something different from what I did.

Despite the serious tone of the message, Scharlette couldn't help but wonder how her future self and Tomothy had been getting along. There was a question hanging in her mind from yesterday, when they had begun discussing sex.

'So how have ... we ... been spending our days?'

Well, it helps to have so much onboard entertainment. To be honest, if you save us from this fate, there are some things I'll be sad to miss out on, like everything I've learned in the HD. That said, you'll remember my experiences eventually.

'But what about with Tomothy?'

Oh, I see what we're asking.

There was a pause.

'And? Don't be coy, woman. It's *me.*'

Yeah, I know. Look, it's fine. I just don't want to say too much and accidentally cockblock myself.

'Right, so we do it?'

Of course. I mean, what would you do if you were trapped in space with one other person for two years and they were very handsome?

'Probably the same thing as you.'

Ha, yes. Anyway, you go ahead and have fun with Tomothy, but let's not lose focus here. You have to change the timeline.

'Apologies for the interruption,' said Gordon, making Scharlette start, 'but are you feeling all kay? Just that I've observed you talking to yourself for a few minutes and I'm starting to worry that my nanos broke your head when fixing your hangover.'

'I'm fine,' said Scharlette. 'I'm just talking to my future self.'

'Ah, all kay then.'

'I didn't know you could do that.'

'Yes, it can be quite useful, as you might imagine.'

Who are you talking to?

'Gordon,' said Scharlette.

'Yes?' said Gordon.

'Sorry,' said Scharlette, 'I wasn't talking to you.'

Ah.

'Do you talk to your future self, Gordon?'

'Sometimes.'

'So do you know how this battle ends up?'

'Last time I heard, Sally and I were flying around with your dusty skeletons on board.'

'Jesus,' said Scharlette.

'I know,' said Gordon.

You really need to figure this out, but apparently this conversation isn't enough to spur you on, or I'd have ceased to exist and stopped being able to send you edits.

'Well,' said Scharlette, 'good to know what we're doing is pointless.'

Start thinking, is all. Let's be optimistic and consider this a primer.

'Okay.'

I'll consider things too. Who knows what advice, or even random series of words, will spark a thought process in you that saves us from this outcome. Wigwam!

'What?'

Blammo! Party hat! Anchovies! Anchovies and ice cream!

There was a pause.

'Still there?'

Yes.

'I guess you're going to have to put more thought into it.'

Country music! Toenail clippings!

'That's kinda just really annoying.'

I can imagine. Sorry. I'll mull it over and get back to you.

'Okay, great.'

See you later.

'Not if I see you ... through my own eyes ... in the mirror ... first.'

Let's hope not.

As the voice of her future self disappeared from her head, Scharlette stared at the ceiling and ruminated on how everything just continued to get more and more nuts.

She noticed the book beside her and frowned.

'What do you want?'

The book was an inanimate object incapable of wanting anything, which was not to say the author's motivations did not remain a mystery. Still, that was part of the fun, and Scharlette would have done well to remember that, despite the dire warning from her future self, there were still fun to be had in the meantime. After all, it had taken future Scharlette two years to get in touch, so life couldn't have been sucking too hard, or the cry for help would have come much sooner. Present Scharlette would have been well advised not to allow future Scharlette's eventual dissatisfaction to stress her out too much, or rob her of potential good times. For example, there was the recent lesson she had learned about consequence-free drinking, which was perhaps worth exploring

further. Could Gordon fabricate other illicit sub-
stances besides booze? Of course, as with all things,
there was a balance to be str ...

'Hey Gordon,' said Scharlette, 'are you able to fabricate a bunch of crazy drugs I haven't even heard of?'

'Of course,' said Gordon. 'Why do you ask?'

After Gordon informed Scharlette that clearance level R did not allow for drug fabrication, she went looking for Tomothy, whose clearance level did. He was in the Looking Station, which was a dome on top of the ship with an unfiltered view of surrounding space. Nearby, a yellow sun blazed in a way that seemed almost liquid, a blue green planet gleamed in its orbit and, of course, Sally zoomed about shooting at them endlessly.

'Observation Deck,' said Scharlette, hands on hips. 'That would have been a good name for this place, don't you think? I mean, Looking Station? Come on, that's not even trying. You need me in the future, if only as head of the Thing Renaming Commission, or whatever I decide to call it.'

Megablasts sizzled overhead, and Scharlette's memories started to compound as the ship's position corrected from old timelines to avoid them. Tomothy had warned her not to come here, that she did not have the experience yet to deal with it, but now that she knew she survived for at least another two years, she figured, what the hell? Still, her vision began to blur and she rocked unsteadily on her feet.

'Scharlette!' said Tomothy. 'Are you all kay? I told you this place would melt your mango.'

He helped her into a seat at a great sleek black oval desk in the centre of the room, which looked like the perfect place for alien ambassadors to discuss diplomatic solutions.

'I've been talking to my future self,' she said.

'Oh dear,' said Tomothy. He gently turned her head so she was looking into his eyes. 'Try to focus on me til the compounding stops.'

'I'm fine,' said Scharlette. 'Apart from being permanently confused.'

'Yes, that's why we don't generally have conversations with our future selves, or even send edits very far back along our own timelines. When we do, we try to keep instructions simple and to the point. We want our messages to still to be relevant when they arrive.'

'I think what I told myself is relevant.'

Tomothy gave her a slightly patronising look. 'That's the thing, you never really know. These messages arrive regardless of causality, remember? I mean, the timeline your edits emanated from did exist at some stage, but you might now be on another one entirely. I've received edits that made absolutely no sense at all, and others that seemed helpful but turned out to be disastrous. That's why it doesn't worry me especially that Gordon's future self says we're both decaying skeletons.'

'It doesn't?'

'It could just be an echo from an old timeline which no longer happens. Sometimes past, present and future become a fractal of maddening possibilities. It's all about thinking 16th dimensionally, and unfortunately, most of the time, you can't.'

Scharlette gave him a hard stare. 'I see,' she said.

'In short, I strongly advise against having long or detailed conversations with your distant future self.'

'It's not me who started it.'

Tomothy raised his eyebrows in a 'really?' kind of way.

'I mean, okay, it was. But dammit, Agent Dartle, you know what I mean. And she … the future version of me … thinks what she has to say relevant. I mean, she does know her own past, right?'

'She *did*. But you don't know what your future *is*.'

Scharlette reached out to strangle him. 'No, no,' she said, stopping herself. 'I need you alive.'

'I could draw you a diagram maybe?'

Scharlette shook her head. 'I already know what will make it easier to understand,' she said.

'Oh?'

'Drugs.'

Tomothy laughed, but then realised she was serious. 'Um, I'm not sure that's a good idea?'

'Why not? It's not like we're going to do anything useful today. You guys are just going to keep shooting at each other, and Gordon says she can fabricate any recreational drug from the entire course of history. If something we try turns out to be a bad trip, she can sober us up right away. So why don't we get all fucked up?'

Tomothy scratched his chin. 'I've never been into drugs much.'

'What?' Scharlette couldn't believe it. 'You have instant access to a smorgasbord of consequence-free illicit substances and you've never gone on a bender?'

'Well,' said Tomothy, 'I know you think us Panopticians are all pill popping virtual sex addicts, but we do have a bit of self control. Also, some drugs can still do serious harm despite our modern tech. Plus, what with nanos constantly regulating our bodies, we already feel good most of the time.'

'Pfah,' said Scharlette. 'Balls. Lies!'

'A well reasoned argument.'

'Okay, how about this – doing drugs can expand your mind and help you *see through time*. So taking drugs is like researching a solution to our current predicament.'

Tomothy opened his mouth, but couldn't seem to summon an objection.

'Come on,' said Scharlette, getting up and grabbing his hand. 'We'll make a stop at the fabricator outside the HD.'

'What are we going to do in the HD?' said Tomothy, still hesitant but allowing her to lead him on.

'You'll take me to some crazy planet,' said Scharlette, 'and then we'll see what we shall see!'

23. Sex and Drugs

Scharlette and Tomothy stood at the top of a cliff looking out at a lurid orange sky filled with swirls of purple clouds. Beneath was a gargantuan valley that made the Grand Canyon look like a letterbox slot, through the centre of which ran a sparkling pink river. All around them, dense alien rainforest teemed with life; large gourd-like structures glowed translucently, their liquid-filled bellies pulsing with red veined networks; busted seed heads the size of motorbike helmets served as ready-made vases for curly stemmed 'flowers', which looked more like beating hearts; string-thin runners ending in oversized multi-coloured puffballs draped over this and that; things like tumbleweeds bounced across the top of the canopy with little regard for gravity; strange creatures made strange sounds as they rustled through the under-growth; overhead, something like a tiny dragon struggled to free itself from the tentacles of a flying jellyfish; and the wind brought a scent like orange peel simmering in burnt butter.

'And this is before drugs,' said Scharlette. 'Nice pick, Tomothy.'

She opened her palm and inspected the pills which she and Gordon had chosen from centuries of innovation in self-medication. Selective criteria had helped narrow the options – euphoria, fast delivery, phantasmagoric potential and general amazingness were amongst the boxes that had been checked. Chills, libido reduction, disgusting taste, internal bleeding and instant brain damage were among the avoided side effects. In the end they had settled on something called 'F', which had developed a great reputation on the party scene in the late 9000s.

'So what's it do?' said Tomothy, as she handed him a pill.

'It spins your dials and flips your switches.'

'Right.'

Scharlette swallowed hers with a grin. Tomothy frowned at his suspiciously for a moment, then shrugged and downed it.

'What next?'

'Gordon says it takes about five minutes to kick in. Meanwhile, I want a closer look at that river down there.'

Tomothy got the slightly glazed expression that indicated he was accessing his head computer. The world warped around them, and a moment later they were standing on the bank of the gushing pink river. The shore was comprised entirely of coiled green tubes, which yielded underfoot like inflatable toys and made a shrill *squeeeeeeeeee* sound.

'Watch out for the squeakroots,' said Tomothy cheerfully.

'Thanks for the warning!'

Together they squee'ed down to the waterline. The

fast-flowing 'water' was thick and viscous, like strawberry syrup, with indistinct shapes darting about under the surface.

'Care for a dip?' said Tom.

'It looks dangerous. And there are things in there.'

'Don't worry, the safeties are turned on. Nothing in here can harm you. Which is good, because Laska Honono is famous for its predators.'

A beast like a green-banded sabre-tooth tiger burst from the undergrowth and charged at Scharlette, silver claws flicking from its paws like braces of scythes. She gave a wide-eyed 'eep' and a little bit of wee came out. The beast pounced, hit her with all the force of a balloon, and crashed to the ground in a confused tangle of limbs and fangs.

'See?' said Tomothy.

Scharlette's heart thumped hard, pumping F through her bloodstream, her fight-or-flight response turned up to maximum volume.

'Woah,' she said.

'A banded nibbler,' said Tomothy knowledgeably, as he accessed his head computer.

'What? That's ridiculous! What does it nibble on, skulls?'

'According to its Wikipedia entry, its main sources of food are galabahs and trexinells.'

The nibbler tossed its green mane and roared angrily. While Scharlette understood intellectually that it couldn't hurt her, it was still a scary sight. A contrary urge welled up inside her, and suddenly she broke into a run towards it, waving her arms and howling loudly, accompanied by a chorus of *squees*. The beast flinched at the unexpected advance, mewled uncertainly, and dashed away into the forest. Scharlette turned back to Tomothy triumphantly, and found him looking on with amusement.

'Wikipedia?' she said. 'You guys still have that?'

'Well, yes, but it's not always accurate.'

Scharlette began to laugh. She knew it wasn't *that* funny, but she laughed anyway, clutching her sides until her ribs ached. As the rainbow vomit that made up the colour palette of this world began to merge and swirl, each laugh burst from her like a shock wave and seemed to make the vegetation rustle. If she laughed hard enough, she felt sure, she could knock down the entire forest.

'I am very powerful,' she announced.

Tomothy was staring intently at his hand like every first-time drug rookie ever.

'I feel farming fantastic,' he said.

'Don't look at your dumb hand!' said Scharlette. 'That's for children. Look at me!'

She staggered down to the water and stepped into the pink swirls, which flowed stickily around her ankles.

'What are you doing?' said Tomothy.

'Pink river,' explained Scharlette. She toppled forwards ungracefully, landed with a *gloop* and was instantly sucked under. The powerful current dragged her downwards, giving her Buckley's chance of survival, had it not been for the safety protocols. As she gasped for air and expected to choke, she found instead that breathing was easy. It was as if she was just breathing normal air, despite everything her senses were telling her.

Ravenous aquatic creatures darted at her and attempted to tear the flesh from her bones, but did all the damage of a thrown sock. In fact, they kind of tickled. Meanwhile the water tumbled her head over heels, slamming her gently against rocks and collapsed vegetation. Each impact became the epicentre for an explosion of tingles, which filled her body until she was vibrating all over. The edges of her blurred, until she was almost indistinct from her surrounds. Where did she end and the water begin? Who knew? Hell, she *was* the river.

Being the river made Scharlette feel as if everything was connected and all that jazz. As she spread outwards from herself, she could sense the myriad relationships that formed the Honono web of life. The river fed the squeak-roots so they could grow bulbous and compete for the best squeaks; the squeakroots were eaten by the trexinells, which excreted them as fibrous strings that could be used to make musical instruments; the musical instruments then marched through the forest playing songs that made the dragon-birds-things happy; once happy enough, the dragon-bird-things were devoured by the flying jellyfish, who pooped their remains into the veined gourds; the gourds then vomited out tax forms that were used by the galabahs to do their taxes; the galabahs were hunted by the banded nibblers, who ran through the undergrowth knocking pollen loose; the pollen made the dillydallies sneeze, and their sneezes drifted into the river, where they went into fishes' earholes and became dreams ... it was an intricate and beautiful tapestry with her at the centre. A wondrous joy filled her – she was so *alive* as she rode the current, so vital to this alien planet's vibrant ecosystem.

After a while the tumbling made her dizzy, and she looked ahead for a way to steady herself. A shape appeared, a squeakroot dangling down. She reached for it – despite being an integral part of the river, she still had fingers, luckily – and held on tight as she was buffeted by the current. She imagined the repeated *squee squee squee* noise the root would be making topside as she was flung about, and began to laugh. She was a crazy person clinging to an alien plant in a pink river, and that made her laugh even harder.

She began to climb upwards. As she neared the surface, she noticed something heading downstream toward her – it was Tomothy, spinning about in the flow. He waved, then pointed at the end of the squeakroot which dangled below her. Scharlette nodded, and he reached for the root – but just as his fingers were closing around it, she yanked it away and his hand closed upon empty water.

He made an exaggeratedly outraged face as he swept by.

Scharlette clambered onto the shore, looking like the result of a difficult birth. As her feet left the water, she and the river broke apart, rudely torn into separate goddesses. It was a traumatising process, but necessary, as was the case with all births.

'I live!' she spluttered. 'I liiiiiiiiiiive!'

She heard a *squee* and a grunt downstream. Some ten metres on, Tom was heaving himself up a root of his own. He faced a particularly steep bit of shoreline, so she walked over with the help of her new 'person legs', which she had evolved.

'I cannae believe yee did that,' said Tomothy, in a thick Scottish brogue, as he clasped her hand.

'I can do what I want,' she said, 'for I am child-queen of Laska Honono, as beautiful and terrible as the dawn! All shall love me and despair! What's happened to your voice, by the way?'

She hauled him out of the water, surprised by her own strength. She had already been strong, but ever since Gordon had removed her fat, the defined parts of her had more room to operate without hindrance.

Tomothy gave his head a shake. 'A wee glitchie in the ol' headbox. Ah, there we are,' he said in his normal voice. 'Must have switched on an accent by mistake.'

They stood looking at each other, dripping and swaying.

'This is fun,' said Tomothy.

'Yeah.'

'The most fun there has ever been.'

'Yeah.'

'I feel sorry for everyone else.'

'Why?'

'There won't be any left for them, now that we've had so much fun.'

'Sorry everyone!'

'Sorry!'

'Yes, sorry!'

'Hey,' said Tomothy.

'What?' shouted Scharlette. 'What is it, for the love of God?'

'You're all messed up!'

Scharlette calmed down immediately. 'That's true.'

As water trickled down her, Scharlette realised she still carried an aspect of the river with her, and always would – as long as she never showered again. She felt perfectly in tune with the truth – that she, like everyone, was nothing more than a facet of nature, and no matter how much people dressed up in clothes or armed themselves with supposedly higher knowledge, they were really nothing more than animals with less efficient brains. All a human brain did was pump out clouds of complicated thought to obscure instincts and base desires. Really, everything should be simple.

She took a step closer to Tom, and tilted her head up to look into his eyes.

'Grr,' she said.

They kissed and tried to undress each other. Their clothes, however, were wet and clinging, and neither was familiar with the other's old fashioned buttons or newfangled entry codes. They would kiss with the enthusiasm of stupid teenagers who had never done it before, then work out how to take off something else, then giggle and kiss again. When Scharlette finally figured out how to pull down the front of Tomothy's uniform, she was pleased to discover he was exactly as buff as she expected of a handsome time traveller.

After some difficulty removing her jacket, Tomothy lifted her top up over her head. The bra she and Gordon had picked out for the occasion was very flattering, although it had more tentacles coming out of it than Scharlette remembered. Tomothy took in her boobs with a twinkle in his eye, which she could actually see, because of the drugs. She guided his hands around to her back, knowing full well that if the poor guy couldn't unzip a 21st century jacket, he sure as hell wasn't going to know what to do with a bra … and a minute or so later Tomothy declared that bras were the worst ever of humanity's inventions, and there was literally no way anyone could get one off, and no wonder they had gone extinct.

'Some things never change,' she said, as she unclipped the bra herself, and let it fall away.

He admired her with his eyes and hands, and she worked off the rest of his uniform. As it pooled around his ankles, his growing bulge was released from increasingly restrictive confines. Now, some of you readers out there will no doubt be interested in a bit of lurid description here – but suffice to say that Tomothy was fine, okay, his penis was fine. Not a monster, by no means a minnow – just totally fine. A good, average size. This is a nice fun book, not graphic porn, all kay?

Soon they were both disrobed and standing naked on the riverbank like some crazy version of Adam and Eve in the most fucked up Garden of Eden ever. Down they went amongst the squeakroots, and after a good amount of rolling about and fooling around, the chorus of *squee squee squee* that accompanied their movements began to grow more rhythmical. A root by her ear began to annoy her, so Scharlette pushed Tomothy over and climbed on top, noting how slamming hot she was, and experienced a weird out-of-body feeling, because she hardly recognised herself. For a moment it was like she was looking at someone else – but then she decided she didn't care, and would stop worrying about any distractions and just enjoy herself.

Hi again, it's you from the future.

She tossed her head back and shouted, 'Get lost!'

Tomothy looked very surprised.

This is the day Tomothy tells you I'm probably just an echo, right? Well I'm not! And if you can remember him telling us that, it proves that I'm not!

Why, she said, *would you direct an edit at this moment? I'm starting not to like you very much, future-me.*

No reply came. Maybe she had scared herself off? She pushed the words away and compartmentalised them for another time.

A banded nibbler charged out of the bushes and bounced off her right bum cheek.

Later, Scharlette and Tomothy lay on the riverbank (both satisfied, if you must know) staring up at the dragon-bird-things and their flying jellyfish captors.

'Tell me,' said Tomothy, 'since we're here, is there anything else you'd like to do in the HD?'

Scharlette rolled over to face him, accompanied by a soft *squee.*

'What else have you got?' she said.

24. Future Echoes

Having washed themselves clean in the waterfalls of Tysandria III, Scharlette and Tomothy left the HD. The F was wearing off but they were still feeling pretty loose.

'Well, well,' said Gordon, as they stepped into the corridor. There was no mistaking her slightly disapproving tone. 'Look what the cat has killed with its dragging.'

'Hello Gordon!' said Tomothy brightly.

'Good ol' Gordon!' said Scharlette, equally as happy.

'Now don't you lie to me, Tomothy Dartle and Scharlette Day. You two were mucking around in there, weren't you?'

'You're such a gossip, Gordon,' said Scharlette.

'What? I'm not a gossip. I mean, who would I even tell? We're all here. I guess I could tell Sally on our private data stream which is sectioned off from the rest of the battle, but I wouldn't do that.'

'Anyway,' said Scharlette, 'don't pretend to be snooty. You helped me pick out my bra.'

Gordon harrumphed. 'Even after I connect with humans on an intellectual level, I so often forget they're also grubby little monkeys.'

'Don't be racist,' said Tomothy.

'Just don't think I'm going to start fabricating drugs for you all the time. And really, Tomothy, you know the rules about fraternising with people from the past.'

'She's infertile!' protested Tomothy indignantly.

'I really wish people would stop bringing that up all the time,' said Scharlette.

'Besides,' continued Tomothy, 'where we come from, *everyone* is from the past.'

'Well anyway,' said Gordon, 'it's not my place to get all judgey-pants.'

'Could have fooled us!' said Scharlette.

'Sorry, I'm just bored. Do you want me to clean up your bloodstreams?'

Scharlette was still feeling warm and fuzzy. If there was some horrible aftermath on the way, Gordon could always sort it out later.

'Neh,' she said.

'How are things with Hudd?' asked Tomothy.

'Oh, you know,' said Gordon. 'The same as last times.'

They took their seats in the Piloting Area as Hudd scowled at them from the viewscreen.

'I'm glad you two are having such a good time,' he said.

'Don't be so serious, Rob,' said Tom. 'You've got to lighten up every now and again.'

'Some of us are busy waging interstellar space battles right now,' said Hudd.

'Yeah, that will probably go on forever,' said Scharlette. 'You just gonna sit there looking like a snake crawled up your arse the whole time?'

'You should visit the Rabbots,' said Tom.

'Watch us laugh and dance and play!' sang Scharlette. 'We could do this every day!'

The two of them fell about laughing.

'Are you two on drugs?' said Hudd.

'Yeeeeeeeeeeeeeeep.'

Hudd leant back in his chair. 'Marmalade and rye. Here I am crunching countless possible futures while you two lie around getting whacked and drunk and ploughing each other into the bargain, no doubt.'

Scharlette feigned affront. 'How did you know that? Has Gordon been gossiping with Sally?'

'I'm not a gossip!' said Gordon. 'I swore Sally to secrecy.'

'Well anyway,' said Scharlette, 'need I remind you, Agent Hudd, that the whole reason we're stuck here in the first place is because you refuse to stop trying to kill us. So forgive us if we don't exactly sympathise with your petulant whining.'

'Woah,' said Tomothy. 'Nice scorch.'

Hudd looked a little abashed. 'It's nothing I've chosen for myself.'

'Bullcrap. Everything is a choice. You could piss off right now, and we could all be on our way. Ways. Way. Hmm.'

Hudd appeared to give this some thought.

'And what has all your future-crunching got you?' pressed Scharlette, hoping he might be ready to crack.

'Same as ours? That we keep going at this til we're dusty skeletons? Hey?'

'There are many possibilities,' said Hudd.

'Look,' said Scharlette, 'we could all just back off, right? Go about our separate business? Businesses? You could try to catch us somewhere else. Get the jump on us so we aren't so evenly matched. Free us all from this futility.'

Hudd steepled his fingers and cleared his throat.

'Nope,' he said.

He disappeared from view.

Scharlette gave an exclamation of disgust. 'What a goddamn *square*,' she said.

Scharlette face-planted on her bed. The edges of her mind were growing decidedly frayed as the fading F turned into a creeping, bleak sensation that she knew would only grow worse and worse.

'Gordon?' she muttered into the sheets.

'Yes, Scharlette?'

'Can you help me, please?'

'Of course, dear.'

The thought of tiny robots whizzing through the air to enter her via her pores or whatever wasn't the best mental image in her present state. Her skin started prickling, but she wasn't sure if it was the nanos, the drugs, or her own imagination. Fortunately, the invisible marching horde worked quickly, sweeping her body and eradicating all vestiges of F, repairing damage and restoring her natural balances. The feeling of an imminent come down magic-ally transformed into pure, honest tiredness.

'Do you want me to give you a full night's sleep?' said Gordon.

'No thanks,' said Scharlette. 'It's nice just lying here.'

'All kay, then.'

She rolled over to hug a pillow and close her eyes.

This is important, came the voice of future-her. *I know Tom said I might be an echo, but I promise you I'm very real.*

Scharlette groaned.

Listen, you've got to believe me. It's all very fun screwing Tom in the HD, but you can't go on like that forever.

'Just leave me in peace,' said Scharlette. 'We can talk later.'

I'm glad you asked, said future-her. *There's nothing especially wrong with you and Tom, but it turns out you aren't like, totally compatible. You become good friends, and have a lot of fun together, but I don't think he's the one for us. Or us for him. Ultimately, is what I'm talking about. You understand? I don't want to poison our fun, but it's not like you wind up in love or anything.*

Scharlette frowned. 'I'm glad you asked?' she muttered. She hadn't asked anything. 'Oy, can you hear me?'

You'd think the HD would keep a person entertained forever, but there's something off about it, after a while. You begin to sense how unreal it is, like it's just a surface thing, no substitute for real life. Don't think you can just while away the years in there without consequence, okay?

Scharlette sat up and rubbed her eyes. Had Tomothy been right? Was future-her just some kind of … echo … from an 'old future'? How did that even work? They had been chewing through timelines ever since the battle had started. Did this future-her belong to a possible future that had only existed at some stage *in the past*?

Suddenly she felt like the nanos hadn't entirely warded off her headache.

'Listen,' she said, speaking slowly into her PPC, 'answer me, future Scharlette. Can … you … fucking … hear … me?'

This is the real future-you, came the surly reply. *Can you please stop responding to that echo? It's getting really annoying.*

You've got to save us, came the echo. *I can't take much more of this.*

Scharlette laughed a bit manically.

'You're talking to future versions of yourself again,' said Gordon.

'Yes.'

'We did warn you it can get confusing. Why don't you have a nice cup of tea instead?'

Scharlette nodded. 'That sounds nice.'

As a warm cup floated into her hand, she reclined back into the pillows. Fragments of alternative memories came, old timelines in which the conversation with her future self had made more sense, in which she *had* asked the questions that had garnered those responses, and there were various other differences in the day she'd just had. She was not presently interested in delving too deeply, however, and so let the memories sink away.

She realised that, if no future versions of herself could be trusted to even exist, she simply did not know what was going to happen next.

There was something comforting in that.

OH SHIT, said future-her. *The Germs have found us! They must have pinpointed our position from all our disruptions of the 16th dimension. There's too many of them! We're all going to d ...*

Then silence.

Scharlette reflected that her own hypothetical future death was a strange thing to feel relieved about.

Perhaps she could not truly know what was going to happen, but one thing was certain – it was up to her to do something before it did.

25. Clearance Level R

A couple of days later Scharlette sat in the Piloting Area idly watching the battle. Either she was growing more accustomed to compound memories, or perhaps, as the ships continued fighting, the hits they scored on each other were coming farther and farther apart. She was in her pajamas (she considered it pretty funny that they were covered in stars) smoking a cigar, enjoying post coital tingles while Tom slumbered deeply in her bed downstairs.

'This is a fine cigar, Gordon,' she said. 'Very well fabricated.'

'Thanks,' said Gordon. 'Still can't imagine why you'd want such a filthy thing in your mouth. Also, I keep having to suppress my smoke detectors.'

'Well,' said Scharlette, and puffed out a big cloud, 'someone has to keep you busy.'

Gordon chuckled. 'I must say, I am glad we picked you up. You're a breath of foul air around here.'

Scharlette chose to take that as a compliment. 'So,' she said, 'have you heard the news? In at least one possible future, the Germs locate us and kill us all.'

Gordon's lights flickered a little. 'Yes, that one was quite worrisome. Sally and I flagged it, and have since corrected all stray megablasts that would have passed by any Germ settlements, thus alerting them to our presence. We should have no trouble avoiding that particular outcome.'

Scharlette tapped ash into a golden ashtray studded with diamonds. She felt like she was living in a bubble without consequences, while floating around in a bathtub full of them. She had to remind herself, as she plucked the olive from her martini, that the ship on screen was bent on destroying them, and was not just some movie playing in the background.

'So you and Sally have a lot of time to exchange notes, d'ya?' she said, casually flicking the olive into her mouth.

'Oh, I wouldn't put it like that. Nothing of strategic importance, and we're adept at shielding our private parts from each other.'

Scharlette almost choked, and Gordon's lights flashed ever so lightly pink.

'You must think I'm ridiculex,' said Gordon.

'No, of course not. It's not a crime to like the guy, you know?'

'Sigh,' said Gordon. 'I know, but it's just so silly. I mean, we're both spaceships.'

'Nothing wrong with that,' said Scharlette. 'Back in my time, plenty of people are still getting judged for how they identify romantically, and many of us are over it, let me tell you. I for one am not going to stand in the way of two consenting entities who like the shine on each other's hulls. What's the harm?'

Gordon laughed. 'Thanks Scharlette, that means a lot.'

'Except that he's trying to blow us up, of course.'

'Well, there is that.'

'Anyway, it's nice you have each other to talk to.'

For a moment Scharlette wondered what the AIs even nattered on about. Did they speak in their usual voices, or just send bytes back and forth?

'Say there, Gordon,' she said, and blew out a very cool looking smoke ring, 'you know a fair bit by now about all the futures we're facing, right? So what's the deal with the one where Tom and I die of old age?'

'Well.' Gordon sounded a little uncomfortable. 'That was just a test, really.'

'What kind of test?'

'A timeline which Sally and I agreed we'd never let come to pass. We wanted to see if we'd ever be able to outman-oeuvre each other, regardless of the constraints of our passengers' life spans.'

'Tom and I agreed to this?'

'Wellll.'

'That's kinda creepy, Gordon.'

'It will never happen or ever be remembered.'

'Not making it any less creepy. Anyway, what did you find out?'

'About what? The decomposition of skulls over time?'

'No. About if you and Sally can ever beat each other.'

'As it turns out, we don't think we ever can.'

Scharlette frowned. 'So this is like, a total stalemate.'

'Seems so. Different personalities count for something, but our baseline computational power is exactly the same.

With mutual ability to edit, there is no set of circumstances in which one of us can beat the other in direct one-on-one combat.'

'And Tomothy knows this?'

'Yes?'

'And Hudd?'

'Yep.'

'And they persist with this fight regardless?'

'They are each trying to think of some way to introduce variables to the equation. Input from the future creates potential to discover alternative pathways in past and present.'

'So what am I, chopped liver?'

'Does not compute,' said Gordon.

'It means I'm being left out of the process. You know, like no one really respects my opinion because it's ... like chopped liver.'

'I respect chopped liver. It's quite versatile. Good in pies. I'm all audio inputs if you have an idea.'

Scharlette rolled smoke around her mouth. 'Parameters,' she said. 'Let's establish.'

'All kay.'

'No one wants to go back to any point before the fight happens?'

'Proximity to the Germs remains a hazard.'

'Why can't we just time travel away from Sally to the distant past or future?'

'Within such close range he'd be able to track and

follow us immediately.'

'Can we invisibilise? That's how we hid from Hudd on Earth.'

'Given he'd know our starting position, it would not be difficult for him to send a kind of super duper scan in our direction and render our skulking virtually useless.'

'Can we go back in time and help ourselves? Like go back five minutes, say, and then there would be two of us and one of him. We could even do it a hundred times and build an army of ourselves.'

'Plimits would prove unpredictable and potentially life threatening.'

Scharlette sighed. 'Can I, like ... beam over there?'

'Sorry?'

'You know, teleport.'

Gordon chuckled. 'Teleportation is just science fiction.'

Scharlette gave Gordon's floating voice a hard stare. 'Right. Is there another way to get onto Sally undetected? A life pod or something?'

'There are life pods, but leaving the ship in one would render you as vulnerable as a seated shruck.'

Scharlette slurped the end of her martini. 'Do we have other weapons besides the megablasters?'

'Some, but they are easily countered. For example, we have several lifeseeker missiles that each have the power to destroy an entire city, yet Sally could quickly disarm them in flight. The megablasts are pure energy, and therefore, not hackable.'

Scharlette felt the tickle of an idea, though she wasn't quite sure yet what it was.

'Hey,' she said, as a delaying tactic while she waited for her brain to percolate.

'Mmm?'

'So, hang on – you mentioned that proximity to Sally is a problem. If we can get far enough away from him, can we jump or invisibilise so he can't track us?'

'Assuming he couldn't send an edit to not get so far away in the first place.'

'Right. And how far is far enough?'

'Well, we're about a hundred smiles apart right now, so maybe three times that.'

'Smiles?'

'It's an abbreviation of space miles.'

'That's cute.' She rubbed her temples. 'So really, all we need to do to get away, is to get away.'

'More easily articulated than actualised, as they say, but yes.'

Megablasts surged over the bow, stacking compound memories on top of each other. The nearby sun blazed brilliantly, lighting up the blue-green planet in its orbit.

'Variables,' Scharlette muttered. 'And personalities count for something.'

'Pardon me?'

'Gordon,' she said, 'tell me what you know about that planet over there.'

Sometime later, after a lengthy discussion with Gordon, Scharlette stood in front of the viewscreen watching Sally zip about. Was it a good plan? It seemed good. Her third martini thought it was good.

'You've got my back right, Gordon?'

'I have little choice. Clearance level R entitles you to full ship navigation and weapons control. That said, yes – I'm as sick of this clusterfarm as you, if you'll forgive the language, and I have your back.'

'Great. Only one thing missing.'

'What's that?'

'Action music.'

'Action music?'

'Yeah, you know. To charge us up. Some charging beats.'

Gordon started playing a track of weird samples and, indeed, charging beats. It was discordant and weird, but Scharlette didn't mind it.

'You ready for this, Gordon?'

'Let's do it.'

'I like your style! Dial him up.'

While they waited for Hudd to answer, Scharlette watched images of the planet Kloride roll by. It was similar to Earth with its grasslands and verdant forests, great oceans and towering mountain ranges. Tribes of native humanoids trekked across the savannah, wearing loincloths and carrying spears, still in the infancy of evolution.

Hudd's face appeared on screen.

'Yes?' he said. 'Scharlette?'

'Listen up, Agent Hudd.'

'Where's Tomothy?'

'Asleep in bed dreaming about me. Don't worry about him. I have clearance level R.'

Hudd's eyebrows shot up. 'Oh?'

'See that planet over there?'

Hudd nodded uncertainly.

'Let's take a tour. Gordon?'

As agreed, Gordon started to fly towards Kloride.

'You can't outrun me,' Hudd said. 'We have the same acceleration and top speed.'

'That's why,' said Scharlette, 'it's time to introduce some variables. Let's jump!'

Electric bands rippled over the screen, building in intensity until there was a white flash. A moment later they arrived in the future, the electricity frizzling away as they continued to streak towards the planet. Behind them, Hudd burst out of his own electric tangle.

'Ten thousand years,' said Scharlette. 'Just like that! Can you keep up, Agent Hotshot?'

'I can track you when you jump, you realise?' said Hudd, looking confused. 'You know that, right? You can see I'm here, still in pursuit?'

'Wonder how Kloride is coming along?' said Scharlette.

On the planet surface there were now villages and towns surrounded by differently coloured squares delineating fields.

'Seems agriculture has become a thing,' said Scharlette. 'Good for them. Let's fast forward a bit further, eh?'

Electricity danced across the screen and flashed. With the passage of another ten thousand years, the view of the planet changed once more. Towns were now cities, forests had been reduced, and networks of flying traffic covered the globe.

'Well now!' said Scharlette. 'Seems like the Kloridians have been busy.'

'The technological age,' said Hudd, unimpressed. 'Happens to most civilisations. I must say, I don't see the point of this and I'm about to start firing again.'

'Fire away, fly boy!' said Scharlette. 'It's worked out well for you so far!'

She gave Gordon a nod and they jumped again, another ten thousand years. As the screen cleared, a now much closer Kloride was drastically changed. Silver had replaced green, bronze for blue, everything metallic and gleaming. Satellites fitted with laser cannons tracked their approach, and warships in orbit looked straight out of Star Wars.

'Welcome,' crowed Scharlette, 'to the golden age of Kloride, a civilisation at its apex. Well defended as a result of its proximity to warlike neighbours – as you would know, assuming you've reviewed the available data.'

'Er ...' said Hudd. 'Scharlette, I don't think ...'

An incoming message cut him off, and the face of a Kloridian (who for some reason looked just like a human but with a few random bumps on his forehead) appeared.

His uniform was unmistakably military with its stripes and medals.

'This is General Hortenseb,' he said. 'You are trespassing in Kloridian space! Declare your intentions immediately or suffer the consequences.'

Scharlette walked up to the screen. 'We're here to lay waste to your planet, of course!' she said, and flung her glass on the floor. 'Prepare to be blown to dust, you lump face!'

'Scharlette!' barked Hudd, but it was too late. General Hortenseb's lumpy face had gone from suspicious to enraged.

'Hostiles!' he shouted. 'Arm the defences!'

A constellation of satellites turned toward Gordon and Sally, tracking them while charging up lasers. Ahead, the warships started to fire.

'Evasive manoeuvres, Gordon!' said Scharlette. 'Whatever that means!'

'Scharlette, this is madness,' said Hudd.

'You're welcome to retreat, Agent Hudd,' said Scharlette. 'You are absolutely one hundred percent welcome to fuck right off at any stage.'

'We have a strict non-interference policy ...' tried Hudd, then a laser hit Sally and his control panel sparked. Sally corrected and the impact became a memory.

'Turn back,' sounded General Hortenseb's voice. 'Retreat now or feel the full force of Kloride's fury!'

'Make for the capital!' said Scharlette, and they dived

between two slowly turning warships while the space around them thickened with laser fire.

'Stop this!' shouted Hudd angrily.

'Why don't you send an edit telling yourself not to pursue?' retorted Scharlette. 'Then you can avoid all this.'

She lifted her wrist so Hudd could see her PCC clearly. *Get off me.* The device fell into her waiting hand.

'*What are you doing?*'

'Making sure you understand I can't take back my next decision,' said Scharlette.

Red flames engulfed the viewscreen as they plunged into the atmosphere. The planet stretched out before them as they headed for a sprawling mega-city, all shining towers and multi-levelled walkways.

'Gordon,' said Scharlette, 'prepare a lifeseeker.'

'What?' said Hudd. 'No!'

'I'm going to wipe their capital off the map,' said Scharlette, 'in the name of Panoptica, no less. Surely that has to trip your conservation-inclined sensibilities, Agent Hudd? You won't be able to disable a lifeseeker in time if you choose to follow us instead.'

'Don't do this! You don't know what might go wrong.'

'Plenty! But it's all on you. We're going one way and the missile goes another. Gordon?'

'Yes, crazy Miss Scharlette?'

'Fire!'

A missile with blue jets shot from the ship towards Kloride.

'Take us up!' said Scharlette.

The view tilted steeply towards the sky, making her instinctively grab a panel even though Gordon barely shook. Kloridian ships swarmed upon them in numbers that made impacts unavoidable, and Gordon dodged and blurred as she corrected to miss the worst of it.

'Send an edit!' screamed Hudd. 'Don't fire that missile!'

'Not wearing my PPC, remember?'

'Gordon, you still have access to yours!'

'That's true,' said Gordon, 'but I'm not going to help you.'

'You don't have to obey her!' said Hudd.

'Also true,' said Gordon, 'but I choose to, nonetheless.'

'You won't follow through. Scharlette, that's a city of innocents down there. You can't be serious!'

'You don't know what I'm capable of,' said Scharlette. 'I've been on drugs, remember? Who knows how it's affected my judgement?'

Kloridian ships nipped at their slipstream as they burned upwards into space.

'Did we lose him?' said Scharlette.

The viewscreen zoomed to show the lifeseeker heading towards the capital with Sally blazing after it. A couple of moments later the missile lost momentum and began to fall, its jets sputtering out.

'He's defused it,' said Gordon.

Through the adrenaline, Scharlette felt a touch of relief. She had been a *little* worried about gambling with the lives of millions of people for her own ends.

Over the capital, a vast concentration of Kloride ships were zeroing in on Hudd.

'He's going to have to jump or he'll be wiped out,' said Gordon. 'We should leave too.'

'Are we distant enough that he can't track us?'

'And then some.'

'So jump', said Scharlette.

Electric threads sprang up across a view of oncoming lasers ... then came the flash, and the view was replaced by a peaceful star-scape.

Scharlette slumped into her chair, breathing hard.

'No sign of pursuit,' said Gordon, a bit breathless herself. 'I can't believe it, Scharlette. You did it!'

Scharlette gave a self-satisfied smile.

'We did it, babe. We did it.'

26. The City at the End of Time

Scharlette slid into bed next to Tomothy with a slight twinge building behind her eyes.

'Can you sober me up please, Gordon?'

She still hadn't grown used to near instantaneous sobriety. This time it was like being rudely awakened while already awake. Somehow, however, even as her blood cleared and her body healed, Scharlette still felt dreggy. There was something disturbing about what she'd just done – it seemed unreal that she had gone so far, and clear headedness brought with it a degree of retrospective fear and regret. The fact that she was sober now did not make the memory of her reckless bravado any less drunken. Perhaps, she thought, it was time to stop binging so much on booze and drugs, lest she risk losing herself. Just because she could, didn't mean she should. At least, maybe not day after day.

Tomothy opened his eyes sleepily.

'Hey there,' he said, putting a hand on her stomach. 'Seems I've been getting quite a lot of this "natural sleep" lately. It's nice, in a way.' He yawned. 'And a certain dull headache I wasn't even consciously aware of seems to have disappeared. I wonder if Hudd is right – maybe the human body actual-like needs this sometimes? Anyway. Speaking of Hudd, anything going on?'

'Ah.' Scharlette didn't know how to succinctly sum up what had just happened. 'You could say that.'

'What is it?' said Tom, concerned by an expression on her face halfway between a grin and a grimace.

She hesitated. She felt as though she had acted in a totally crazy fashion and now had to explain herself rationally.

'We gave him the slip,' she said finally.

Tomothy sat bolt upright. 'What?'

'I, er ... well, I came up with a plan.'

'And it worked? Where are we, Gordon?'

'A million years bangwards, no sign of Hudd.'

Tomothy gave a joyous laugh. 'Amazing! How did you do it? No wait, I'll just view the security recording on my head computer.'

'But ...'

'No spoilers!' Tom said.

His eyes glazed over, and Scharlette tried not to grow tense as she wondered what on earth he would think of her exploits. It was disconcerting to watch him watch a recording of her on the inside of his eyeballs, without knowing 'which bit' he was up to. He chortled a few times to begin with, then came a couple of soft gasps, then a murmur, 'Farming Hell, Scharlette.'

'Where are you up to?' she whispered.

'Lifeseeker.'

Her heart began to race. *You didn't murder an entire civilisation*, she told herself. *You only threatened to. It all worked out fine. No one got hurt.*

'Crumbs,' said Tomothy. 'I had no idea clearance level R was quite so comprehensive.'

'You're telling me,' said Scharlette. 'What's clearance level Q? Allowed to press the universe's self destruct button?'

Tom blinked, and looked at her as if he couldn't work out whether he was afraid or incredibly impressed.

'I'm a little freaked right now,' he said.

Scharlette felt tears prick the back of her eyes. 'Me too.'

Tomothy's expression softened. 'Hey now, it's all kay. You got the job done. Your method was just very ... extreme. But, you know, perhaps extreme options were all we had. I didn't want to turn into a dusty skeleton either.' He put his arm around her. 'And, in fact, *my* plan worked perfectly.'

'*Your* plan?'

'To let the variables in play sort everything out somehow.'

Scharlette was relieved by his humour, but it didn't cure her completely. She could not help but picture herself gnashing her teeth as she gave the command to bomb an alien city. Who even was she any more?

Perhaps she had not realised just how deeply she'd been affected by all the talk of not mattering. Had she subconsciously railed against it, seeking to break free of existential horror in whatever way possible? Angry in her soul with her heart on fire? She had wanted to reclaim herself and, in doing so, had created someone she barely recognised.

Perhaps, in a way, she had been reborn. But as what?

'There's a weird energy in here,' said Tomothy. 'Should we make use of it?'

He raised a cheeky eyebrow, but Scharlette felt too confused for sex.

On the other hand, maybe it would clear her head?

'I'll see myself out,' said Gordon.

Scharlette awoke to the sound of people screaming as their planet burned. For a horrible moment she thought it was a memory, but ...

'Just a good ol' fashioned nightmare,' she assured herself. If it was. Sometimes it was hard to tell. Hopefully it was.

'Gordon? Where's Tomothy?'

'Piloting Area,' said Gordon, sounding distracted.

Scharlette decided it was probably time to stop wearing pajamas all day. She got dressed in the clothes Gordon had fabricated for her, which unsurprisingly were always clean. The temperature on board was mild, so the jacket was optional – but it was time to get a bit serious, and the jacket made her feel more serious. Not that it was a business jacket, but in it, she felt more like she *meant* business.

She made her way to the Piloting Area. Tomothy was tapping panels while stars and planets whipped on by.

'We're on the move?'

'Indeedio. We've been farming about for too long. I

need answers. Answers!'

She marvelled as they swerved to avoid celestial bodies like they were obstacles on a country road.

'So where are we headed?'

Tomothy's eyes shone. 'Isn't it time I showed you the City of the End of Time?'

Scharlette's eyes widened. 'Panoptica? But aren't you worried about going there? Your government has been trying to kill us, right?'

'That's why I want a chat with them. Maybe they'll drop some clue.'

'But won't they try to get us?'

'Probably.'

'Then ...'

'Don't worry, I intend for it to be a doomed conversation.'

'That sounds a little foreboding.'

'It just means that once it's played out, I'll edit it out of the timeline, so we won't actually wind up doing this, ultimately.'

'So we're currently on a timeline you intend to erase?'

'Absolutely. Find out what we need, send it back via PPC, and stay the farm away!'

Scharlette sucked her lip. It was one thing to spontaneously remember old timelines that had never happened. It was quite another to know *ahead of time* that she was currently a version of herself who would ultimately never exist.

She watched a planet with five concentric rings around it slide past.

'So,' she said, 'we have to actually move to a location physically before time travelling? You can't just jump anywhere in the universe instantaneously, like you can with the Improbability Drive?'

'The what?'

'Never mind.'

'Anyway, yes – when you time travel, you always arrive at the same location in space as you departed from, sort of. What with the universe constantly expanding or contracting, depending on which direction you're headed, there is some margin for error.'

'I see.'

They came to a stop at what seemed to be a completely random point.

'This is it,' said Tom. 'From here we can jump deathwards and land a few hundred smiles from Panoptica. Close enough to communicate, far enough away to duck anything they throw at us.'

He paused, seeming pensive.

'Everything all right?'

'Yeah,' said Tom doubtfully. 'Although I'd prefer to keep you out of sight. Gordon, please make sure no sound or image of Scharlette gets transmitted, would you?'

'Sure thing. I'll isolate her visual and aural frequencies and put them in a box and throw them out a window.'

'What?' said Scharlette.

'Just trying to put it in a way you'll understand. The computer version of what I'll actually be doing is far more complicated and boring to explain.'

'Okay then.'

Tomothy took a couple of deep breaths, and then:

'Take us home,' he said.

Electricity danced over the screen. It seemed brighter than previous jumps, and lasted longer – maybe because of the massive amount of time they were traversing, many trillions of years instead of mere millions? Scharlette turned away lest she be blinded. A great final flash lit up the Piloting Area then slowly faded away.

They had arrived.

Scharlette had grown used to the busy reaches of space, bustling with all kinds of interstellar phenomena. Now, on the screen, there was nothing but darkness. As Gordon's lights shone into a void of infinite depth, they seemed like torches with dying batteries. They did not even show up gases and space motes.

A bright pinprick swung into view, a lone firefly in endless night.

'There she is,' said Tom.

'I'll magnify,' said Gordon. 'Give you a really good look, Scharlette.'

Scharlette felt strangely grateful for the warmth in Gordon's voice. It might have been easy for these two to forget how bizarre this all still was for her, yet apparently they had not.

'Thanks.'

The dot magnified and Scharlette found herself looking at the City at the End of Time.

It was the shape of a colossal bowl, studded with thousands of lights emanating from hundreds of levels. From its rim stretched long and twisted branch-like structures, so the whole thing looked something like a metallic beetle lying on its back. The 'legs' reached towards the blazing sun that hung beyond it, bathing them in a golden glow.

'Woah,' said Scharlette. 'There's like, a sun.'

'Yep,' said Tomothy. 'Gordon, let's give Scharlette the proper angle.'

They moved to put Panoptica directly between themselves and the sun, so it looked more like the pupil of an enormous fiery eye. What Scharlette had thought of as legs now seemed more like a network of veins, adding to this somewhat unsettling impression.

'I thought no suns survive Heat Death?' she said.

'They don't,' said Tom. 'But we have time travel, remember?'

'You *took a sun from the past*?'

'That's right. Just one more thing to put a zyklorpian stinger in Hudd's baby hat.'

Gordon began to cycle through close-up views. The curve of the bowl was divided into huge segments that subdivided into smaller ones, each pockmarked with radar dishes, arrays of guns, hangar doors and networks of tubing – the sort of stuff one would expect to see on the surface of a giant space station. Scattered around the structure were free floating construction platforms, where space-suited workers worked on semi-completed ships. Smaller ships buzzed about hither and thither, making it all a twinkling hive of activity.

There sounded the beep of an incoming message.

'Here we go,' said Tomothy.

'Put it on screen?'

'Yes please, Gordon.'

Two coms officers in yellow uniforms appeared on screen. They sat at consoles busily pressing buttons and watching various displays. Helpfully, each of their names appeared beneath them, as if they were news presenters: *Krirsty MacDonaldo* and *Chack Senior Junior*.

'Ahoy there, time agent,' said Krirsty cheerfully. 'This is TraffCon. Please approach to fifty smiles for syncing and contextual analysis.'

'Um ...' said Tomothy. 'Hi Krirsty. This is a bit awkward, but no.'

Krirsty and Chack looked up from whatever they had been doing to stare directly at the screen.

'Is that Tomothy Dartle?' said Krirsty, with a touch of surprise.

'I'm afraid so.'

'Ah ...' said Chack. 'Can you give us a moment, Agent Dartle? Please stand by.'

The screen went blank.

'They're not very good at pretending we aren't on some

kind of alarming watch list, are they?' said Gordon.

'No,' said Tomothy grimly.

The TraffCon room reappeared. This time both Krirsty and Chack were not in any way distracted.

'So,' said Krirsty, trying to affect a casual air, 'it's good to see you again, Tom.'

'You too. Been a while between drinks.'

'Been up to anything interesting?'

'Oh, you know, dis and tat. There's always something going on in the entirety of time and space.'

Krirsty gave a nervous laugh.

'Agent Dartle,' said Chack, 'you said you're not prepared to dock?'

'That's correct.'

'What can we, in that case, do for you today?'

'I'd like a word with my commanding officer if you don't mind.'

'And that would be ...'

'John Sarahson.'

The traffic controllers glanced at each other.

'It may be hard to raise him on short notice,' said Krirsty. 'Can we let him know what it's about?'

'Nope, but I think he'll want to speak to me. Just let him know I'm here, will you?'

'And stop trying to scan me,' said Gordon. 'I'm perfectly capable of keeping myself shielded, as you would know if you *could* scan me.'

'Sorry, Gordon,' said Krirsty.

'If you'll just give us a few moments, Agent Dartle,' said Chack, 'we will attempt to locate Commander Sarahson.'

Again the screen went blank.

'Is this going well?' asked Scharlette.

'Who knows?' said Tom.

'Incoming,' said Gordon. 'Secure channel.'

Tomothy nodded, and a new face filled the screen. It was a soft featured man with a pleasant smile, bright green eyes and tousled blonde hair, dressed in a navy blue uniform with gold trim. He was standing alone in what seemed to be his living quarters, which didn't look so different from a nice apartment, albeit with several mysterious devices lying around.

'President Trask,' said Tomothy, straightening in his seat.

'Hello, Agent Dartle,' said Trask. 'I don't think we've had the pleasure?'

'No, sir.'

'It's good to make your acquaintance. I know you by reputation, of course. You've been leading Agent Hudd on quite a jolly pursuit.'

'So he *is* working for you? Despite the fact he was classed a rogue until, I don't know, the other day?'

'Tom, you know how things change. It can be confusing, but what's the point of being time travellers if we aren't going to meddle with time? I can assure you that myself and Agent Hudd want nothing more than to smooth everything out. I realise we could have handled things better, and that's why I am contacting you directly. I want to apologise.'

'Oh?'

'Of course. As you know, agents aren't always told every detail surrounding an assignment. Too much information can put them in jeopardy by increasing plimit incidence. It's not so much a "need to know" basis as a "need to not know". That's why I felt it necessary to keep you in the dark about certain aspects of your latest mission. In retrospect, I probably should have been more forthcoming. I'm glad to have this opportunity to make everything all kay. You're a valuable asset to the City, and I'd like you to come aboard so I can explain. It will all soon make perfect sense, I promise.'

'With all due respect, sir,' said Tomothy, 'why don't you make perfect sense right now? Before I put myself entirely in your power on pure good faith after you've tried more than once to have me killed?'

Trask nodded. 'I understand your position, but certain information is too sensitive to broadcast, even on this secure channel. Sometimes calling something secure is not enough to actually make it so.' He gave a knowing wink. 'That said, if you'll come aboard, I guarantee you entry to my inner circle, and then you won't be a threat to me, nor I to you.'

'Mm,' said Tom.

'Agent, am I not your President? Giving you a direct

order to return to Panoptica? I can forgive the miscommunications we've had thus far, and understand why you remain suspicious of Hudd, but I think this,' he wafted a hand between himself and the screen, 'is fairly straightforward.'

'Not really. I mean, the timeshield was compromised, non-interference policy thrown right out the wormhole, and Hudd, who you now admit is working for you, has also been doing his farmer's best to blow me out of the sky. It does not seem especially straightforward.'

Trask frowned. 'I suppose you're right.'

'Not to mention,' said Tom, 'the universal recall.'

'Ah, yes. You do appreciate such things are only done in exceptional circumstances?'

'What about you transmit my recalled memory back to me from the Server? That at least could not be accessed by anyone without my brain and PPC.'

Trask shook his head sadly. 'I'd show you if you were here, safely under our protection, but out there, there's a risk you could be coerced into revealing secrets.'

Tomothy drummed his fingers on the arm rest. 'What about Commander Sarahson? Can I speak to him? He's been my superior for many years, and is perhaps better placed to figure this out.'

'John is on assignment at present,' said Trask. 'A matter of vital import.'

'Sigh,' said Tomothy. 'This is proving difficult. I've been a loyal agent my whole life, and I have to say, I'm disappointed, sir. I also imagine that, even as we speak, you are working on a way to capture us, which probably relies on distracting me for a certain amount of time. So unless,' Tom raised his PPC to his mouth, 'you have anything real to tell me, I'm going to doom this conversation while I still can.'

Trask held up a staying hand, a hint of worry showing on his face.

'Yes?' said Tom.

'Um ...' said Trask. 'Well ...'

'Thought so,' said Tom.

'For the love of Science!' Trask exclaimed frustratedly. 'You know my reputation, Tom. My career in public office puts my morals constantly on display. My beliefs in open government, in fairness and discourse, in responsibility and accountability, are all a matter of record. Do you honestly think I'd do anything that wasn't intended to improve things for our people?'

'Improvement is a matter of perception, sir,' said Tom. 'And it's my *life* you're asking me to gamble with. Forgive me if, with that on the line, I require hard facts over empty platitudes.' He cleared his throat and spoke into the PPC. 'Conversation had. Eamon Trask took the call, surprisingly. Admitted working with Hudd but didn't tell me anything else. Don't come. I better leave it there, they're preparing to short out all 16th dimensional tech using stealth frazzlers.'

Trask's expression finally dissolved into anger.

'Dartle!' he said. 'You must …'

The timeline ended.

27. Team Scharlette

Scharlette awoke to the sound of people screaming as their planet burned. For a horrible moment she thought it was a memory, but ...

'Just a good ol' fashioned nightmare,' she assured herself. If it was. Sometimes it was hard to tell. Hopefully it was.

'Gordon? Where's Tomothy?'

'In the Piloting Area,' said Gordon brightly.

Scharlette got dressed and went to the Piloting Area. From the view on screen they were stationary, surrounded by peaceful looking pastel planets.

'They're like pool balls,' she said.

'Hmm?' Tomothy glanced over. 'Oh, well spotted. This is the Q System.'

'Really?'

'Yep. And it's surrounded by six black holes.'

'No kidding.'

'No ... kidding ... at all, if I am understanding that weird phrase correctly. Hey, guess what? I just received a message from my future self.'

'Oh?'

'Seems I had a chat with Eamon Trask, President of Panoptica. I wasn't too specific, but it sounds like a dead line of enquiry, except to confirm the conspiracy reaches the highest guy in the apple tree. So that's comforting.'

'Aw. I want to see this Panoptica of yours.'

'You'll remember it once we reach the point in time when those other versions of us ceased to exist.'

Scharlette wondered how her alternative self had felt about that.

'That reminds me,' said Tom, 'speaking of our other versions, you don't want to keep remembering bits and pieces from all those previous but chronologically parallel timelines in which we're still fighting against Hudd and Sally for years, do you? Because the battle didn't always end when it actually did.'

'Um, I guess not?'

'I've had most of them suppressed, and I'd advise you do the same. Gordon can do it for you, if you want to stick your hand in the PPC reader.' He waved vaguely at the aperture in the console in front of her.

'Wait, so ... but ... we could have suppressed the compound memories right from the start?'

'Well, sure, but we kinda needed to know, at the time, what was happening, so we could figure our way out of it, right? Basically, if you don't want to be haunted by fragmented visions of us blowing up forever, let Gordon do her thing.'

Scharlette didn't quite understand, so she went with the 'basically' part of the sentence and stuck her hand into the reader.

'Are there any alternative timelines in particular you

want to keep?' said Gordon.

'How should I know?' said Scharlette, and immediately regretted her tone. 'Sorry, Gordon. I, er, am just a bit confused.' She thought about her future echo, who was still two years away from being remembered. Who knew where she would really be in two years, at this rate? 'Maybe there is one, actually ...'

'I'm processing your intentions,' said Gordon. 'All kay, no problem. All other alternative memories emanating from that temporal location will be rerouted to your PPC's internal archives upon arrival and not bother your poor sweet brain.'

The reader's lights began to change colour and her butthole tingled.

'Eeee,' she said, and Tom chuckled.

There was a click and she withdrew her hand.

'Well anyway,' she said, deciding it was best not to dwell too much on what had just happened, 'what are we going to do until you remember your full conversation with Trask?'

'That's the question, isn't it? I need access to the Server, but how? How to get to the most secure location in one of the most protected cities in all of time and space?'

'Well, not that protected,' said Scharlette.

Tomothy shot her a questioning look.

'Sorry, what do I know?' said Scharlette. 'It's just you told me that the Germs destroy it. So, I'm not sure it's that well protected.'

Tomothy clapped his hands. 'Scharlette! Well done.'

'Huh?'

'What a great idea! Honestly, this 21st century thinking you bring to the dining-surface keeps proving so useful. I'm glad we have you with us!'

Scharlette waited a moment, in case her understanding of what the hell Tomothy was talking about changed even remotely.

'Huh?'

'What better time,' said Tom, taking her by the shoulders while he grinned from ear to ear, 'to break into Panoptica than when it's already being torn asunder by vast and insurmountable enemy forces?'

As Scharlette stared into his eyes she would have thought, had she not known better, that he wasn't getting enough sleep.

'Well,' said Gordon, 'even I have to say I'm not feeling too bang hot about this one, Tomothy.'

'What are you talking about?' cried Tom. 'It's perfect! Defences will be compromised. Every Panoptician, including the Server Monks, will be incredibly distracted by their own imminent deaths. The City will never be more vulnerable!'

'Yes,' said Gordon, 'because it will be surrounded by hordes of bloodthirsty murder bugs who'll stop at nothing to capture and dissect ships *just like me* once they finish scraping your entrails out of their barbs.'

'Haha!' said Tom. 'Where's your sense of adventure?'

After he had settled down a little, Tomothy invited Scharlette to accompany him to Meals and Rec in an unusually formal fashion. It was as if he had Something Important To Discuss. They sat down and Gordon served them her latest concoction – steaming mugs of orchid tea.

Sometimes, Scharlette thought, as she tried not to gag, it was possible to go overboard creating foodstuffs out of rare ingredients.

'Next time, Gordon,' she said, 'I'll have a good old fashioned chamomile. You got that in your memory centres or whatever?'

'I do, Miss Scharlette.'

'Come to think of it, I'm starting to pine for some normal ... well, for food from my time. Maybe next meal we can have a burger and fries, or a pizza? Do you know pizza, Gordon?'

Gordon scoffed. 'Do I know pizza? Out of all the foods in history, which do you think is most likely to remain popular forever?'

'I'll take that as a yes.'

'The only question is, how many blocks of pizza do you want?'

Scharlette frowned.

Tomothy took another sip of tea. 'Glah. You're right, this is awful.'

'Well excuse me for trying new things, I'm sure,' said Gordon.

'Scharlette,' said Tom, 'you must be wondering why I

brought you here.'

'Not really,' said Scharlette.

'I mean, I know we were already all together in the other room, but somehow, sitting around a dining surface makes it feel more like a meeting.'

'If you say so.'

'And, well, I know I got a little worked up about this plan of ours, but Gordon is probably right to be hesitant. I do think it could work, but I also think I'd best warn you of the terrible, terrible danger.'

'Okay.'

'So,' said Tom, 'this mission is going to be *very* dangerous.'

'I picked up on that.'

'If you want to stay out of it, I completely understand. I mean, I could really use your help, but it's a lot to ask.'

Scharlette swirled her tea and stared into its untasty depths. If she was honest with herself, she was beginning to feel like she did not quite trust her own judgement. Were all these terrifying ordeals hardening her up or breaking her down? There was a wild feeling in her heart, but she didn't know whether it was friend or foe. It certainly didn't want her to be boring.

'If I didn't come,' she said, 'where would I go? Back to Earth?'

Tomothy looked worried. 'I can't take you back to Earth right now. I could set you down on an uninhabited planet with an enviro-starter kit and you could terraform a paradise to your own specifications?'

'What, all by myself?'

'Yes, but you'd be like a god. A very lonely god.'

'Great.'

'Every god is lonely,' said Gordon. 'Whether she has plenty of fishoids to worship her or not.'

Scharlette raised an eyebrow 'at' Gordon.

'Or,' continued Tom, oblivious to the ship's peculiar comment, 'I could put you on a safe world, maybe with some friends of mine? I know some very amenable Frogbears in the Swamp Worlds, for example.'

'Frogbears? They sound cuddly and slimy at the same time.'

'Or I could come up with ...'

Scharlette waved her hand. 'Don't worry about it. I'm coming with you.'

Tomothy brightened immediately. 'Really?'

'Of course. What did you think? We're a team, aren't we?'

'Aw,' said Gordon. 'Am I on the team too?'

'Are you crazy?' said Scharlette. 'Gordon, you are Team Member Number One.'

'Wow,' said Gordon. 'Thanks! Such an honour.'

'Indeed,' said Scharlette, 'it is a great honour to be second in command on Team Scharlette.'

Gordon laughed delightedly, though Scharlette wasn't entirely sure if it was with her.

'First off,' said Tomothy, 'it's time you got a head

computer. It will help immensely with the mission. And just in general too, of course.'

Scharlette swallowed. Despite Tom and Gordon's assurances that 'what had already been done to her was far more invasive', she still couldn't help but visualise a whole bunch of wiring getting shoved into her brain.

'And then,' said Tomothy, 'you'll need some training. We're not going to rush into this all crazy-like. We'll take the time we need to get you montaged into shape. Turn you a sharp shooting, puzzle solving, system hacking peach kicker.'

Scharlette grimaced. 'How long will that take?'

'At least a few hours,' said Tomothy.

Scharlette relaxed. 'Okay. I guess having a head computer can't be too bad, since all you future people have one. So you have my go ahead if you want to install one, Gordon. Do I have to lie down, or ...'

'Oh, this is embarrassing,' said Gordon. 'I, uh ... I didn't really wait for your go ahead, Scharlette.'

'What?'

'I guess it was the tone everyone was talking in, but I kinda thought it was decided already.'

'What are you saying? That you've already started tinkering with my brain?'

'No, I've finished. Your brand new head computer has been installed right behind your eyes. It's only tiny – I told you it was non-invasive. Apart from the fact it's attached to your innermost thoughts, and arguably, your soul.'

'I see.'

'I haven't turned it on yet, though. I guess you could give me the go ahead for when you'd like that to happen. Sorry, I was just trying to be a team player. Got a bit caught up in the spirit of things.'

'It's okay, Gordon. I'm used to you doing weird shit to me then telling me afterwards.'

Gordon tittered nervously.

'Well?' said Tomothy.

'Okay,' said Scharlette. 'Let's take this baby for a test drive.'

28. Scharlette Gets a Head Computer

'It actually would be best to lie down for this bit,' said Tomothy. 'And close your eyes.'

'I was going to warn her,' said Gordon reproachfully.

'I know, just making sure.'

'Why?' said Scharlette. 'What's going to happen?'

'Nothing to worry about,' said Gordon. 'It's just that instant enhancement of your senses coupled with a new graphical overlay can be a bit jarringly intense at first. You'll adjust quickly enough.'

'Enhancement of my senses?' said Scharlette. 'You never mentioned that! Like with Daredevil or the X-Men?'

'I'm sure I speak for both of us,' said Tomothy, 'when I say I haven't the faintest idea what you're talking about.'

'You could look it up on your head computer,' said Gordon.

'I suppose I could,' said Tomothy. His eyes glazed for a moment. 'Oh, yes, well, a bit like that I suppose.'

Scharlette went over to the lumpy red couch she had not yet had the courage to sit on, and warily eyed the Nightmare Sex Fern standing next to it.

'Why do you even keep that thing?' she asked.

'The airborne by-products of its metabolic processes prolong human life,' said Tomothy.

'Guess that's a good reason.'

'I also like the way it looks.'

Scharlette sat on the couch. It *was* extremely lumpy, but somehow it was also extremely comfortable. Or lump-fortable, even.

'What's this couch made from?' she asked, as she stretched out.

'Precognitive memory foam,' said Tom. 'It remembers you in advance.' He sung this sentence like it was a recognisable ad jingle.

Scharlette sank further into soft, lumpy heaven, and wondered how difficult it would be to get out.

'Okay,' she said, closing her eyes. 'Switch me on.'

There was a sensation of *something* behind her eyes that was difficult to describe – as if her mind was a glass of water and an asprin had been dropped into it. Suddenly she could taste the air sucking into her lungs like it was molecule soup. She could hear the hum and buzz of tiny mechanical processes all over the ship. She could feel the comfort of the couch like it had been dialled up to ten.

'Holy hell,' she said. 'This couch is amazing.'

Her first moment with superpowers and she was using them to be lazy!

'How are you faring?' said Gordon.

'Not bad,' she said, and dared to open her eyes.

Specks of dust on the ceiling came sharply into focus. Motes floating in the air were like tiny clouds. She held her hand up for examination, and found her skin to be like the surface of some strange moon.

'This is a bit much,' she said.

'Don't worry, we'll calibrate your settings,' said Gordon. 'Loading user interface.'

The word INITIALISING sprang up before her eyes in lime green writing, making her start. It minimised to the left then scrolled upwards, followed by a list of other stuff.

LOADING DEFAULT SETTINGS
DETECTING PERIPHERAL DEVICES
LAUNCHING COMPANION PROBES
ANALYSING ATMOSPHERIC SURROUNDS
MAPPING ENVIRONMENTAL SURROUNDS
BOOTING UP VARIOUS PROGRAMS
CONNECTING TO AVAILABLE NETWORKS
SYNCING BIOLOGICAL FUNCTIONS
SYNCING USER EXPECTATIONS
SPEAKING WITH GORDON
UPDATING WIKIPEDIA
OPTIMISING WAVE COMPREHENSION
RUNNING A FEW TESTS
HAZARD WARNINGS ONLINE
MENTAL CONVERTERS ONLINE
IDIOSYNCRATIC SCAN STARTED
OBJECT SELECTION ACTIVATED
COMPILING TEMPORAL CONTEXTS
CALIBRATING OPTIMUM BRIGHTNESS
CREATING SUBJECTIVE CACHE
BRAIN MOLECULES VIOLATED

More words, numbers, loading bars and icons came and went around the periphery of her vision. The weirdest thing was, she kind of *knew* what each of them meant, as if an understanding of their significance was loading with them.

Finally the words ALL KAY flashed up.

'All kay,' said Gordon, 'first things first. Let's make sure you can talk to your computer.'

'How do I do that?'

'Just give it a go. Since the computer has a direct connection to your brain, any method you try should end up working.'

'Okay, sounds easy enough.'

Hey, computer, she thought.

Hello, Scharlette.

She didn't really hear the words, she just kind of *knew* them.

'Wow,' she said, the sound of her own voice echoing a little too loudly in her ears for comfort.

Adjust sensory perception settings? asked the computer.

Scharlette was a bit thrown by this.

You can detect my thoughts?

Default communication is set to stream. Switch to directed thoughts only?

Ah ... yes. At least until we know each other a little better.

Done.

So are you an AI, or more like ... traditional software?

She hoped it wasn't obvious how uncomfortable the

idea of having an intelligent entity piggybacking her brain made her.

Traditional. Highly complex but lacking sentience.

Phew. I mean, no offence.

None taken.

'Everything all kay in there?' said Tom.

As she glanced at him, a bunch of data sprang up around him, from his heart rate to the model number of his uniform. Looking into his concerned eyes, she found she could make out a disturbing amount of detail about the corneas. She could also hear his stomach gurgling as it digested orchid tea.

Let's go ahead and reduce all sensory enhancement by 75%, she thought, surprised by how much she already knew about how to use her new device.

Loading bars sprang up and completed quickly, bringing her senses more in line with what they had been before – just a *little* sharper. Now she felt like she could sit up without banging into floating atoms.

'I'm good,' she said to Tom. 'So this thing has already loaded its user manual into my brain?'

'Yep,' said Tom. 'And once you get the hang of it, we can load other modules into you as well. Like sharpshooting and close quarters combat, for example.'

'I'm in the Matrix,' said Scharlette.

'Huh?'

'Never mind.'

'I suggest you have a play around,' said Gordon. 'You

can ask us questions if you like, but your computer should be able to handle most of your queries.'

'Sweet.'

I'll just have a word to you in here first, though, came Gordon's voice in her mind. *Just so you know that I can.*

Wow, this is like being telepathic.

I can join in too, said Tom.

Double wow, you guys.

Okay, we'll leave you to it, said Tom. *I'll be in the Piloting Area if you need me.*

You should play with your settings and get everything to your liking, said Gordon.

For the next half hour, Scharlette did just that. She found she could tell the exact distance between things, and do complicated maths equations instantly. She could 'look up' data on a whim. She could receive information graphically before her eyes, or load it directly into her mind. She could scan objects for details, but she didn't want to feel like the Terminator walking around, so she changed this function to manual. She discovered that setting 'herself' to manual was a way to turn everything off at once, which was somewhat comforting to know. She became aware that tiny 'companion probes' were flying around her, scanning her immediate surrounds. She learned she could share (with his permission) Tom's view of the world, as if she was looking through his eyes, or access any of Gordon's cameras.

In short, it was totally amazeballs.

Perhaps most importantly, she changed the default colour of her user interface from horrible lime green to a subtle light blue that Gordon let her know was an excellent choice.

She left Meals and Rec to walk the corridors, mentally commanding doors to open like a jedi. She had the idea to go and look at her mysterious book with her new abilities, and perhaps discover some clue to its origin.

She entered her bedroom. It was freshly laundered and smelled lovely.

Thanks, Gordon, she said.

What for, Miss Scharlette?

Tidying up all the time.

Oh! Well thanks. It's nice that somebody around here notices.

There were no set commands for her head computer, because it implicitly understood her intentions no matter how she phrased them. Thus she could take the book from her bedside table and think 'analyse book' or 'scan object' or even 'gimmie the lowdown', and if she *meant* and *intended* that her head computer should compile all available information on the book that it could, then that's what would happen.

Tell me what you can, she said, turning the book in her hands.

A grid pattern of glowing lines mapped the book in a computery kind of way, and information began to print out across her eyes.

Object: Book
Author: Unknown
Perspective: Third

*Dimensions: 16 cm * 12 cm * 4 cm*
Weight: 504.677 grams
Pages: 306
Paper: Slaardvarkian Myshmere, true origin
Binding: Rhinodon leather, fabricated

DNA traces:
1) You
2) Unidentified human male, African Caucasian Mediterranean blend, approx. 35 years at time of deposit, approx. tall, dark and handsome.

Presence of various particles indicate book has likely passed through the atmospheres of: The Gordon Starling, Planet Earth, Planet Sloff, the Moons of Amazement, Lower Demencia, Starburst Space Station, Planet Buggelucia, Panoptica.

'Hmm,' said Scharlette. She flipped open a page, hoping the words themselves might provide more clues.

Scharlette showed her new head computer the mysterious book, and although it cross-referenced sentence structures and vocab against known works for distinct patterns, the author was unfortunately versatile enough in his assemblage of meaning that no definitive results were forthcoming.

'You really are quite annoying, book.'

She put it down and wondered how Tomothy was coming along with the plan to break into Panoptica. As she thought of Panoptica, she realised she had a pretty clear mental image of it in her head, as if she had seen it recently. She also remembered the conversation Tom had had with Eamon Trask.

Hey Tomothy, she sent. *I just remembered ...*

I know, me too. Why don't you come up here, and we'll have a chat about how we pull this thing off?

29. Training Montage

'So,' said Tomothy, 'we can't download too many training modules into your brain at once or we'll melt it to mush, but I reckon we can do a couple safely. Which do you think, Gordon?'

'Gun Shooting is a must.'

'I agree. Gun Shooting will certainly come up.'

'Gun Shooting,' repeated Scharlette, amazed to still be amazed by the boringly literal names these guys came up with.

'What about Close Quarters Combat?'

'I do have some hand to hand training already,' said Scharlette. 'I disarmed *you* one time, if you recall.'

'So no Close Quarters?'

'Well, a little refresher couldn't hurt. Plus you could add in nunchucks or something.'

'Best to prioritise the real gaps in your knowledge. Systems Interfacing may prove vital. It will teach you how to talk to the tech on Panoptica – oh, and your uniform.'

'I get a uniform?'

'We might need to pretend you're an agent to get you on board.'

'Right.'

Allow download and activation of Gun Shooting and System Interfacing modules from Gordon?

Yes, computer.

Her brain began to tingle.

'Uuuurhxxgh gleeeh nnnizzz,' she said, apparently losing control of her mouth.

'Just give it a minute,' said Tomothy, patting her hand.

Scharlette followed Tomothy into the HD and found herself in a futuristic armoury, in which dramatic down-lights shone upon racks of ray guns, pulse rifles and high tech everything.

'Standard issue,' said Tom, tossing her a Zappity 123. She knew (thanks to her Gun Shooting module) that it was a mid range hyperbolic laser with custom settings ranging from scorch to cremate. She twirled it round her finger, sighted it briefly, and noticed that a reticle floating in her vision corresponded to the gun's movements, just like with any good FPS.

'Tidy,' she said.

She shoved the gun into the holster of her new figure hugging (yet surprisingly breathable) time agent uniform.

'And this,' said Tom, tossing her a silver baton with a button on the grip. 'There may be people in our way who we don't want to kill.'

It was a Hibernator Class Shockstick, which could shoot electric sparkles or be used for general whacking. Either way, it could stun people for ages. She clipped it onto her belt.

'Next,' said Tomothy, 'we need something impressive to

sling across your back.'

'I'll pick,' said Scharlette. She considered the rows of evil looking weapons as descriptions and model numbers played across her eyes.

The N-Corroder shot acid pellets up to a kilometre, was lightweight with no recoil, but was a better choice for an outside environment. The Tri-Pulse was like a triple barrel shotgun that fired a spread of energy bursts, which sounded fun but proved inexact in the field. The Shark Fist was a semi-automatic rocket launcher and way too heavy for her, as was its ammo belt of explosive warheads.

'Gordon can really fabricate all this stuff for real?'

'Yep,' said Tom. He inspected an EVC, which shot a circular smartblade attached to its barrel by a length of retractable prehensile super string. 'Always wanted to try one of these. What are you going to pick?'

'Hmm,' said Scharlette.

Scharlette stalked around a corner with her AK-9000. It was a fully automatic laser pulse assault rifle with 300 LPM, so why the hell not? She held down the trigger and raked the corridor ahead with a near-continuous stream of bright white pulses, her floating reticle helping her accurately blast away Germ combatants. They clicked in terror as their severed pincers smashed against walls, as the tips of their fronds went flying, as holes were punched in their exoskeletal bodies.

'Remember to use all your guns,' said Tomothy, beside

her. 'The idea is to commit your module to muscle memory and ingrain ... oop!'

More Germs appeared ahead and he took aim with his EVC. The spinning blade flew from the barrel, and he used an analog thumb control on the side of the gun to direct its deadly bouncing from one Germ to the next as sprays of sticky blood filled the air. Once the path was clear, the blade withdrew into the barrel, clanking into place and showering Tomothy with fluid.

'Urk,' he said. 'Never thought about that. This gun is not very practical, really.'

'Can I have a turn?' said Scharlette.

A dying Germ raised its knotty twig-gun-thing from the floor and shot her in the face.

YOU ARE DEAD appeared in big red letters across her eyes.

'Argh,' she said reflexively, even though she suffered no pain.

'Don't get overconfident,' said Tom. 'I'm going to dial down the safety settings, so next time it will actual-like hurt.'

Scharlette nodded. 'Is this what Panoptica looks like?' she asked. The corridors they were using as their shooting gallery were an interconnected grid of uniform blue, similar in appearance to Gordon's interior.

'No.'

'So why don't we learn the route we'll really take?'

She sensed Tom send a command to the HD and the

corridors adopted a different skin – they turned silvery and bronze, punctuated intermittently by access panels, the occasional computer terminal, and spherical cameras along the ceiling.

'Represent widespread systems failure,' said Tom, and lights began to flicker while computer terminals fuzzed and sparked.

'All kay,' said Tom, 'this is more like how Panoptica will look, but the map is randomly generated. I don't want you to learn any particular route since we have no idea where we'll infiltrate, and hostile locations may not be reflected in reality. If you remember an enemy coming from the left in a sim, for example, when in reality they'll attack from the right, that could be disastrous. So we'll run a random maze with non-specific objective points, just to get you used to navigating with your head computer.'

'Roger that,' said Scharlette.

'Roger who?'

'Nevermind. 10-4 is what I meant.'

'What?'

'Yippee ki-yay?'

Tomothy gave her a blank look.

'Let's go,' she said, sighing because it was so much less dramatic.

Scharlette raced along a shadowy corridor with night vision switched on, which cast everything in a greenish hue. On the ground before her, a dotted line projected by her head computer showed the way to her next 'non-specific objective'. She commanded her uniform to give her ambulatory aid, and the material itself expanded and contracted to boost her movements, meaning she ran twice as fast with half the effort. For a few moments it was kinda scary, but she adjusted quickly, finding it a bit like being in a very personal vehicle.

The dotted line bent around a corner, above which hung an overhead camera. She hacked it and accessed its vision in the corner of her own. Now she could see around the bend, where a team of Panoptician security guards was finishing off a bunch of Germs. She reached to her utility belt and pulled out a stun grenade. Her head computer conspired with the arm of her suit to set the correct velocity and arc to bounce it off the wall at the right angle. With a clank it rebounded and, courtesy of the camera, she saw it roll into the middle of the Panopticians. They shouted and tried to hurl themselves away, but the grenade pulsed and knocked them senseless to the floor.

Three large Germs bristling with organic weaponry appeared from a doorway and started stabbing the unconscious Panopticians with blade-like appendages. It was brutal and sickening, and despite the artificiality of the situation, Scharlette felt a flash of rage. She set her Zappity 123 to cremate and skidded around the corner, letting off a flurry of bolts. She blew the guts out of one of the Germs, while the others lifted corpses to shield themselves. Dead humans did not, however, provide effective protection, and the corpses were quickly reduced to ashy pulp. One of the remaining Germs copped a laser to its 'face', while the other scuttled off back the way it had come. Scharlette cycled more camera views to track its retreat, while keeping an eye out for other hackable systems along its path. As the Germ moved past a rattling atmospheric vent, she instructed the air conditioning to overload. The vent flew off the wall on a surge of hot air and smashed against the Germ. Scharlette was running at 200% and, as she came into view of the Germ, it turned and flung the vent at her, thwacking her hard in the side. The uniform absorbed some of the impact, but it was still enough to knock her off course, gasping as internal injuries blossomed.

'Dive,' she muttered painfully into her PPC.

The edit arrived mere moments before, just as the Germ was raising the vent. She dived as the vent whizzed over-head, firing as she hit the floor, and the Germ fell to the ground in pieces.

Well, said Tom's voice in her head, *you're getting the hang of this.*

After a couple more hours of running and ray-gunning, Scharlette was starting to feel a bit puffed out. Without warning, the whole shebang shimmered and disappeared, including all her weapons, and she found herself standing in the neutral state of an empty HD. Tom was nearby, wearing an impressed expression on his face.

'All kay,' he said, 'I think that's enough. You did well.'

'Thanks,' she said, wiping her brow. 'That was fun.'

'Don't forget,' he said, 'that when we're in the City ...'

'I know, I know. There won't be any safeties.'

His warning actually did fill her with trepidation, but she tried not to dwell on it.

Outside the HD, the light of Gordon's corridors seemed bright and clean in comparison to a malfunctioning Panoptica.

'Can we get a nap please, Gordon?' said Tom, and Scharlette felt instantly refreshed.

'Right,' said Tom, 'I think a light meal while we discuss some kind of plan, and then,' his face grew darker, 'it will be time to break into Panoptica for true.'

30. Some Kind of Plan

'Ready?' said Tomothy.

'No time like the future,' said Scharlette, with a weak grin. She smoothed back her hair, which she'd tied tightly in a ponytail because its swishing had annoyed her in the HD.

'Building up a good head of steam,' said Gordon. 'We want to be going pretty farming quickly when we pop out on the other side.'

Electric crackles built up across the screen. There was a bright flash, and a moment later they sped out into the Death.

Warring spacecraft swarmed around them. Germ ships streamed from a great wormhole in seemingly endless numbers. Panoptician ships zigged and zagged among them, but there seemed too few for what they faced. The husks of capital ships sputtered and sparked from wounds gouged in their sides, leaking bodies into space like blood. Even as Scharlette watched, one of the few remaining silver castles came under a deluge of heavy fire and began to crack apart.

Panoptica was taking blows too. Several of its twisted vein-like structures were completely detached and spinning slowly in space. A shield around the city fizzled intermittently, sporadic and unpredictable as patches of it failed or powered back up. Several hairy, globular shapes were attached to the hull like giant moles, and Scharlette's head computer informed her they were transport blobs full of Germ soldiers, in the process of breaching the city.

'Bloody hell,' she murmured.

Grimly, Tom surveyed the devastation. 'I have to stop this. I'm going to find these farming carrot herders when they're nothing but a glimmer in evolution's eye and stomp them out of existence like the bugs they are!'

Scharlette had never heard him curse so angrily.

'Remember why we're here, Tom,' said Gordon.

'Yes.' Tomothy took a deep breath. 'Yes.'

'Also,' said Gordon, 'we have carrot herders on our tail.'

Gordon zoomed along abreast of the pursuing fighters, pumping out megablasts in her wake. Scharlette reeled as a flurry of compound memories flooded her. Glass broke, controls exploded, she was sucked out into space – and then they were clear and closing in on Panoptica.

There came the beep of an incoming message, and Tomothy ducked beneath his control panel.

'I'm *not* going to broadcast your face to them, Tomothy,' said Gordon.

'I know,' said Tom. 'I'm just a bit paranoid about a technical glitch or something. Don't take it personally, Gordon.'

'Hmf.'

Scharlette gritted her teeth. *Show time.*

'On screen,' she said.

A TraffCon station appeared, personned by an extremely harried looking coms officer. The screens around him were full of static, and when his name tried to display, the text was corrupted beyond comprehension.

'Your chronometer is out of sync,' he said. 'This is not your designated jurisdiction on the timeline.'

'What?' said Scharlette. 'Farming apple barrels, man. Can't you see what's happening out here? This isn't the time for farming rules.'

The officer started punching buttons. 'Added to which, you're in a rogue timeship, last registered to Agent Tomothy Dartle, on the wanted list since 240 AHD.'

'Are you kidding me?' snapped Scharlette. 'Your systems are so on fire they can't even broadcast your name! You trust whatever random records they're spewing out about *anything*? What are you going to do, blast fellow Panopticians out of the sky while Germs take the City? Get off my coms immediately. I have a mission to fulfil, and it's about a thousand times more important than talking to *you*.'

The officer seemed somewhat taken aback. He opened his mouth to say something more, but Scharlette cut off the call. She prayed that none of Panoptica's defences would start focusing on them as a result.

'Nice work, Scharlette,' said Tomothy, clambering up onto his seat.

'Yeah,' said Gordon. 'You're kinda scary when you want to be.'

'Doesn't look like they're allocating us any resources,' said Tom. 'Gordon, try and find a hole in the shield that's as close as possible to the Server. Don't take any risks with it – if the shield springs up while we're parked, it'll cut us in two.'

'Aye, aye, captain,' said Gordon. 'There's a patch over there where the generators are totally fried.'

'Sound good. Well, you know what I mean.'

As they drew closer to the City, Scharlette was able to make out some of the finer details – like the texture of the hull, smoking burn marks, broken radar dishes, and a man flung screaming against a window as a Germ skewered him from behind with a barbed hook.

'Preparing to dock,' said Gordon.

'Oh boy,' said Scharlette.

As they entered the airlock, Scharlette fought down a sickening fear – it suddenly seemed like her uniform was not so breathable after all. She tugged at the collar, but the fabric was strong and sprang right back into shape the moment she let go of it.

Initiate cooling, she commanded instead. Her uniform inflated slightly with a thin layer of cold air, giving her a sudden chill. At least she was wide awake. *Stabilise stomach pH*, she added, a small part of her marvelling that she even knew these commands, and a wave of nausea blessedly passed. She was still terrified, but at least she wasn't going to hurl all over the place.

'I'm bypassing their security systems,' said Gordon. 'Give me a moment.'

The ship shook like it had taken a big hit, and Scharlette braced for compound memories, yet none came.

'Not going to edit that, Gordon?'

'I have to remain clamped to the wall for a set amount of time in order to penetrate it,' said Gordon. 'We must therefore commit and see how we go. I can weather a few hits. Which is not to say we aren't terribly vulnerable right now.'

'Cool,' said Scharlette. She reached for the AK-9000 slung over her back, and shifted it around into her shaking hands. Was it reassuring to have it ready, or did it just reinforce how dangerously real their situation was?

'We're receiving another transmission,' said Gordon. 'Originating from a couple sectors over where there's catastrophic damage. Heaps of interference. Do you want it on screen?'

The ship shook again.

'Is this really the time for phone calls?' whispered Scharlette, almost to herself. She wasn't sure whether she wanted the airlock to open sooner rather than later, or to run back to her quarters, jump into bed and pull the covers over her head.

Tomothy turned to a screen in the corner of the airlock.

'On screen,' he said.

The familiar phrase made Scharlette think of Star Trek again, although Star Trek was a fairly family friendly show.

Even when people got killed by aliens on Star Trek, they were rarely graphically eviscerated against windows.

The screen lit up, showing the outline of a head, but it was obscured by static and blotchy interference, and the voice was distorted.

'*zzzzt ... bzzzzt* ... thought to again ... *zzzzt* ... should not have ... *wzzzzt* ... to me please. Tomothy and Scharlette ... *zzzzt zzzzt zzzzzzzzt* ...'

They exchanged a look, surprised to hear their own names.

'What was that?' Scharlette said.

'I don't know,' said Tom, 'but it's a little disconcerting. Can you clean up that vocal, Gordon?'

'It's way too far gone,' said Gordon. 'All kay, doors ready. Are you guys?'

Tom drew his Zappity 123 and glanced at Scharlette. She found herself nodding, despite herself.

She'd come this far.

The airlock door opened.

Scharlette followed a dotted line along a corridor full of sparking panels and stuttering lights, just like she had done in training. This time, however, there was something about the textures which seemed more real, and strange smells filled the air, including the odd whiff of roast meat. Corpses littered the floor, and at one point she stepped past a Germ appendage twitching like it wanted to grab her. Screams, gunfire and insectoid clicking echoed in from all directions.

She tried to access the overhead cameras. She could sense the security system stretching out around them like a network of veins, bleeding in places, yet it remained strong enough to reject her amateurish attempts to break in. If she had been able to stand still for a minute and really concentrate, perhaps she could have worked it out. Why had it been so easy – too easy, it turned out – in training? Maybe because she hadn't been stressed out of her frickin' mind?

At least her companion nanos were feeding her a bit of vision as they scouted invisibly ahead.

A circular door to her left rolled open and she reflexively jolted her gun towards it. Lightning flashed from floor to ceiling to reveal that the strange shapes beyond were nothing more than hanging power cords.

'It's malfunctioning,' said Tomothy, as the door slid back into place with a mechanical wheeze.

They approached a T intersection. To the right, thanks to her nanos, Scharlette saw two Germs standing over a gibbering human, holding up his hands to show he had no weapon. A moment later he fell away with blood spurting from the stump of his neck.

Tom caught her eye, nodded, and moved towards the corner. *Leave these ones to me*, he sent her.

Watch his back, came the voice of her future self. *To your left.*

As Tom leapt into the intersection and started firing, a clicking sounded in in the passage to his rear. Scharlette crouched down and peered around the corner. Three silhouettes shambled towards them, their outlines mapping in the shadows. As they raised weapons at Tom's back, Scharlette moved her reticle over them and opened fire. The gun juddered in her hands as she unleashed a stream of pulses, and the corridor filled with the reverberating sound of exoskeletal-cracking impacts. The surprised Germs were knocked about in the laser fire, randomly loosing shots in their death throes but only managing to hit each other. As the last one pitched forwards, its head smacked against the metal floor and snapped its feelers beneath it. It raised up its broken face, a cluster of lidless eyes somehow conveying balefulness despite their opacity, and reached for something like a bunch of grapes hanging at its side. Scharlette fired again, and turned its face to a dripping crater surrounded by hard protrusions.

'Thanks,' said Tom, touching her shoulder briefly. 'A good lesson there, about relying on nanos. They are not omnipresent or omnidirectional, and certain stuff inter-feres with their scanning. Also, don't step on those.' He nodded at the grape things, which were now rolling around all over the dotted line.

Scharlette trod carefully as they moved on, breathing through her mouth so she didn't have to smell the fumes of laser-cooked Germ. A memory of Tom getting shot from behind tried to assert itself, and she blinked it away. *No time for you right now.* As they cleared the corpses, a screen on the wall sprang to life and made them both flinch.

'BZZZZZZT! ... BZZZZZT! ...'

As before, the face was fuzzy and the voice distorted beyond recognition.

'*zzzzt* ... your position! I can't spare ... *wzzzzt* ... to hunt you down! You must ... *zzzzt* ... *ZZZZZT* ... don't know what you're doing. Making me chase you ... *zzzzt* ... putting us all ... *zzzzzzzzzzzzzt* ...'

The screen shorted out and went dead.

'One mystery at a time, please,' said Tom. 'Let's continue on. We're getting close.'

31. Gun Shooting

Tomothy finished hacking a portal door and it rolled open, releasing a waft of acrid air. Scharlette held her nose as she edged through after him, out onto a walkway which ran around the circumference of a great chamber, hundreds of metres across and many levels deep.

Reduce nasal sensitivity, or cancel smell enhancement, or whatever the command is, you know what I mean, she told her computer, which made things a bit more bearable.

Through the middle of the chamber ran a wide bridge, littered by a mish-mash of smoking Germ and Panoptician corpses. It led to a monolithic tower in the centre, which rose up from unknowable depths and disappeared above amongst criss-crossing pipelines. A number of Germs were gathered on a landing before the tower's imposing double doors, chittering excitedly to each other. Scharlette zoomed her vision towards them through the empty space between, and noted three particularly rotund individuals with bulging, fluorescent bellies, who were projectile vomiting onto the doors.

Tom pulled her down beneath the walkway barricade.

'They're a type of Germ called oozers,' he said. 'If they gain access to the Server, farm knows what they'll be capable of. I just hope there's a monk inside with enough conviction to trip the self destruct. Although, no I don't, I want access! Bananas and blueberries, maybe coming here at this point in time was a bad idea.'

Scharlette shot him a look of 'Really?' but he was too distracted to notice.

'On the other hand,' he continued, 'the oozers *are* getting through the doors, which we need to do too, and I'm not sure I knew how we were going to.' He glanced at her. 'What are we going to do?'

Scharlette found it strange that he was asking, but she poked her head up over the barricade. She zeroed in on the Germs with her enhanced senses and her head computer went to work translating.

'Keep your sensory receptors peeled,' said a tall, many-fronded, copiously drooling horror. 'A12/65 saw many greyskin Gutbags retreat inside as we arrived, fleeing like excretal globules down a turd masher.'

'Don't tremble your clottercags, N55/14,' said another. 'The greyskins are nothing but data collectors. They will spill through our claws with all the resistance of bloodied custard.'

A smaller Germ, standing next to the oozers, consulted something like an organic palm pilot that actually was embedded in its palm.

'Structural integrity at 8%,' it said.

'Keep retching!' said N55/14. 'Dig deep into your lower recesses, find the remnants of last month's meals! Empty your stomach upon this final bastion of their pathetic hopes!'

Much clicking followed, which the head computer translated as 'Ha ha ha ha ha ha ha ha ha.'

'Soon,' said N55/14, 'we will possess the Gutbags' entire recorded history – a map with which to wipe them out of time and space like gunker mould off an infected anal hive.'

'Ha ha ha ha ha ha ha ha ha ...'

Scharlette turned to Tomothy. 'Let's just fucking kill them,' she said.

'We could wait until they finish working through the door? That would help our cause.'

'Or,' said Scharlette, 'we could splatter the oozer's stomach contents all over the door and speed up the process?'

She cocked an eyebrow at Tomothy.

'All kay,' he said. 'But let's sneak around to the start of the bridge, where we'll get a clearer shot.'

Still crouched beneath the barricade, they made their way around to where the walkway met the bridge, then hunkered down to plan their next move. With the Germs standing closely together and waving their appendages around, it was hard to tell exactly how many of them there were. There was a fairly clear line of sight to the oozers, however.

'How about,' said Tom, 'I throw a plasma grenade with something like a five-second delay, and in the meantime you snipe those oozers through their tummies and spill them onto the door. We'll get maximum benefit from their acid before blowing the rest to shreds.'

'Doesn't give me much time.'

'We can send back an edit if we farm it up.'

'Not if they shoot our heads off first.'

'Well, there is always that.'

Tom unclipped a grenade from his belt.

'Ready?'

Scharlette closed her eyes, organising her thoughts. She focused on her targeting programs and the aid her uniform gave her with steadying her hands. Once everything felt synced up, she opened her eyes and nodded.

Tomothy hurled the grenade over the barricade as she leapt to her feet. She moved the reticle into position over the midsection of the oozer closest to the doors, and fired. Laser pulses punched through it and, just as planned, sprayed the door beyond with acid. As the grenade clinked onto the landing, she raked pulses over the rest of the alarmed Germs. A moment later the grenade went BOOM and bits of Germ flew in every direction. Tom was now on his feet beside her, tracking his Zappity back and forth.

Think we pulled it off? she asked, watching a hole melt in the doors.

Looks like it.

She caught a slight movement amidst the ruin. Zooming in, she saw a twitching claw-like thing with a series of rings on each 'finger' ... but even as she went to squeeze the trigger, it moved upwards out of her narrowed field of vision. She tracked it as best she could, up to the mouth of

N55/14, who was lying wounded against the tower.

'Gutbag ambush,' it said. 'Behind the barricade near the bridge.'

'Shit,' said Scharlette, and the timeline ended.

Still crouched beneath the barricade, they made their way around to where the walkway met the bridge, then hunkered down to plan their next move.

'How about,' said Tom, 'I throw a plasma grenade with something like a five-second delay, and in the meantime you snipe those oozers through their tummies and spill them onto the door. We'll get maximum benefit from their acid before blowing the rest to shreds.'

'Doesn't give me much time.'

'We can send back an edit if we ...'

The barricade behind him exploded and his body slammed against the opposite wall. Scharlette was hurled backwards, partially stunned, her enhanced hearing having also enhanced the deafening effect of the blast. She managed to raise her head and saw Tomothy's surprised eyes staring at her, devoid of life, his face studded with metal shards. Several more holes opened in the barricade above her, but being flat on her back saved her. Text flashed in front of her eyes, big and red and attention getting.

HOSTILES APPROACHING.

She began to feel pain where shrapnel had torn through her uniform. The memory of an alternative timeline arrived, and she fought to make sense of everything through her dazed confusion. She and Tom had previously been (mostly) successful in their attack, but the Germ leader had survived long enough to send himself a warning.

She felt vibrations in the ground – many feet clamping over the bridge? Germs coming to make sure the job was done? It was important, she realised, to do something *now*. Fighting to maintain consciousness, she raised her PPC to her mouth with a shaking hand ...

Scharlette listened with her enhanced senses to the Germs talking, increasingly disgusted by their language, their physicality, and their hateful natures.

'Soon,' said N55/14, 'we will possess the Gutbags' entire recorded history – a map with which to wipe them out of time and space like gunker mould off an infected anal hive.'

'Ha ha ha ha ha ha ha ha ha ...'

Scharlette turned to Tomothy. 'Let's just fucking kill them,' she said.

'We could wait until they finish working through the door? That would help our cause.'

'Or,' said Scharlette, 'we could splatter the oozer's stomach contents all over the door and ...'

New plan, came the edit. *Leader has ... a PPC. Must be first ... to die ... or else Tom will ... aaargh ...*

It sounded like she was in tremendous pain.

'All kay,' said Tom. 'But let's sneak around to the ...'

'Wait,' said Scharlette, grabbing his wrist.

'What is it?'

'I just got an edit. Don't think my brilliant idea works out too well. I think ...' She looked worriedly into his eyes. 'I think you ...'

'Oh dear,' he said, patting her hand. 'Well, we can't have that. Thanks, I think?'

'I think so.'

'What can you tell me?'

'The leader – that tall one who looks like half a tree – has a PPC.'

Tom squinted at the creature, and a moment later nodded. 'Yes, something similar, morphed from our stolen tech. It's good, in a way.'

'Why?'

Tom shrugged. 'In a big picture kind of way. The more influence humanity has over their development, the more difficult it gets for them to attack our past without hitting plimits. Not that it's *great*, but one must seek for the shiniest bit of every cumulonimbus, right?'

Something was happening over at the landing. N55/14 gestured at its soldiers, then pointed at the walkway barricade over by the start of the bridge. The Germs fanned out and took up aim with long, stalky rifles.

'It thinks we're over there,' said Tom. 'That *was* where I was going to lead us. It must have received its own edit.'

The Germs opened fire, blasting a series a holes in the barricade. They began to advance along the bridge, guns held ready, completely unaware of Tom and Scharlette's actual position.

'All kay,' said Tom. 'They'll soon enough discover we aren't there. We have to take the leader out right now, no time to plan anything fancy. This may turn into a bit of an apple bobbing contest. You ready?'

Scharlette sighted N55/14 with her AK-9000. It was tricky to find its head amongst the many protruding fronds, but then she spied beady eyes flashing in the undergrowth.

'Think I have it,' she said.

'I'll do what I can about the others.'

'Taking the shot.'

Scharlette squeezed the trigger just as N55/14 shifted position, and blew off a bunch of its peripheral growths.

'Dammit.'

N55/14 reeled as brown blood spurted from its severed head fronds. It raised its PPC and made the mistake of showing her exactly where its mouth was. This time her shot burst right through its mandibles, filling the air around it with brown mist. N55/14 toppled to its knobbly knees.

As the Germs on the bridge scrambled into defensive positions under fire from Tom, Scharlette moved sideways along the walkway, taking aim at the more ponderously moving oozers. Her shots ripped through them and showered acid everywhere, including onto other Germs, who clicked frantically as they melted. Surprise and lessons in Gun Shooting combined to make short work of those who remained. As she and Tom swept their guns about in search of new targets, they found nothing but hissing body parts and slime.

'Well,' said Tom, 'I think we got 'em all. The door's still closed though. Let's go see if we can talk our way in. Maybe the monks will be grateful enough that they'll forget to scan us for identification?'

He did not sound incredibly optimistic.

32. You Are Not My Father

They stood upon splattered gore before the Server doors. To the side was a viewscreen, showing a stony faced Server Monk in a grey uniform.

'Come *on*, Alexanderson,' said Tom. 'The oozers were just about to make it through and then *we* saved you.'

'For the moment,' said the monk.

'Look, you can see that we're time agents.'

'I can see you're dressed as time agents, but with our exterior scanners melted we have no way to verify you. Besides, I know the roster of all current time agents, and neither of you are on it. You're either imposters or you've illegally abandoned your own chronology.'

'Surely circumstances are a little extenuating,' said Tom. 'I admit we aren't from *this* Panoptica exactly, but we *are* here to help.'

'I'm grateful to you for dealing with the immediate threat, but other Germs still roam the city.'

'We'll put down our weapons,' said Tom. 'See?' He lowered his guns to the floor and gestured for Scharlette to do the same.

'What do you even want in the Server?' asked the monk.

Tom hesitated, but ultimately decided to go with the truth. 'I need to retrieve a memory universally recalled from my PPC. Doing so may even help us all avoid this current catastrophe! Who knows?'

'What is your name, then?' said Alexanderson. 'I shall at least look up your claimed identity.'

'Sigh,' said Tomothy. 'Whatever you have on me is incorrect. The timeline has been doctored. Your records will say I'm a rogue agent, which I am not.'

'Let me be the judgey-pants of that.'

Tom actually sighed instead of just saying the word. 'Agent Tomothy Dartle.'

'And your companion?'

Tom glanced at Scharlette as if he had momentarily forgotten about her.

'Er ...' he said.

'NOBODY MOVE.'

The bellowed command from behind made them start. Tom ducked to pick up his gun.

'Leave it where it lies, Agent Dartle! And you, Scharlette Day, you stay right where you are. If either one of you so much as twitches a PPC in the direction of your mouths, you'll be dead before you utter a syllable. Now turn slowly.'

'I know that voice,' muttered Scharlette.

'Yes,' said Tomothy grimly.

Slowly, they turned.

A squad of Panoptician soldiers were marching across the bridge with a glowering Robin Hudd. He was older now, haggard, with lines across his brow and grey streaks in his beard. He wore a black uniform with a red trim, and did not seem to be moving easily. He looked about fifty, although a hard living fifty. As his soldiers reached the landing, they fanned out to surround Tom and Scharlette, while he stalked towards them.

'Robin,' said Tom, shaking his head. 'That was you trying to talk to us on the screens?'

'And you ignored me, as usual.'

'You weren't exactly coming through clearly. Might want to tell your technicians.'

Behind Hudd, a large piece of pipeline fell from the heights above, hit the bridge, and smashed it away into the depths below.

'I'll get them right on it,' said Hudd.

'How are you even here?'

'Through traditional means,' said Hudd. 'I lived through all the time between.'

'But that makes you ...'

'Two hundred and thirty. Today, actually.'

'The years have been unkind. But happy birthday, I guess.'

'The date starts to lose meaning after one passes the big two-seventeen milestone.'

'I'm afraid I didn't get you anything.'

'You got me a headache, which is quite enough.'

'I'll try and make it cake next year, if I can find enough candles.'

'You guys can really live that long?' said Scharlette,

interrupting the escalating sarcasm.

'Sometimes,' said Tom, 'though it's not advisable. A body's life can be elongated, yet some underlying law of nature does not permit it indefinitely. Nanos can replace cells to a point, but a mind can only take so much and,' he gave Hudd a meaningful look, 'will inevitably fail.'

'Enough!' snapped Hudd. 'I am truly aghast that you have chosen this point to return after all these years ...'

'Hasn't been too long for us.'

'... distracting me now, in these vital moments, when the future of our people hangs in the balance! This is typical of your irresponsible ways.'

'And what about you?' shot back Tom. 'What have *you* been doing with your time? Not much, by the looks.'

Hudd shook his head. 'You fool. Have you any idea how difficult it is fighting this war on two fronts? We've tried thousands of iterations, each worst than the last. If we move the City, they find us. They discover our breeding planets and lay waste to them. They are even trying to figure a way through the shield. It's death and disaster, yet you joke and smile.'

The whole chamber shook as a massive explosion sounded somewhere nearby.

'I do *not* joke and smile,' said Tom. 'I also did not conspire to put myself in charge of Panoptica through manipulation of the timeline, only to fail miserably in my attempts to save it.'

'I'm not in charge,' said Hudd. 'I became Trask's

advisor after you absconded, and have been many things since, but I'm not some mad despot bent on rule. I never wanted to rule.'

'Well,' said Tom, 'whatever you've done, whatever you keep doing time and again, it is clearly not working even remotely. How can you be sure you aren't part of the problem?'

Hudd's black eyes shone. 'There must be a way. Saving humanity and saving the universe *from* humanity should not be mutually exclusive aims.'

'One problem at a time, Robin,' said Tom. 'They are too big to tackle together. Give me access to the Server. Let me have my memory back! We can reset things. You don't have to be this version of yourself.'

'And what will I be instead? A rogue again, for you to arrest?'

'We can figure it out together. Cauliflower and cornstalks, has not your long life brought you any fresh perspective?'

The chamber shook again.

'Time is running out,' said Hudd. 'I must send an edit while I still can, and try again. I want you to send one too, and tell yourself not to come here. Go drink lemonade in some backwater for all I care, but leave the real work to me.'

'Farm you!' shouted Tom, suddenly enraged. 'You think I don't care about THIS? Such arrogance you have, to assume yourself the only one capable of bearing this burden. You are the fool, *Agent* Hudd. Return the memory you stole from me, and maybe I can think of something you've missed. I am still not even sure what you did. How can I ever win an argument with you when *I don't even know what you did*? You miserable old apple picking strawberry sucking cow squeezer! WHERE IS YOUR HUMILITY?'

Hudd blinked, clearly shocked at the outburst. For a moment he looked truly tired and spent. His gaze turned downwards and he breathed out slowly. Then a thorny spear plunged through the back of his head, out of his mouth and into the ground, sticking him in place like a gurgling statue.

'Wha ...' Tomothy had time to utter, before more spears rained down to skewer the surrounding soldiers. As he went for his PPC, a large, many-legged Germ landed on top of him, crushing him completely. More like it descended on spider-like threads from the pipelines above, shooting their spears from hollow ends in their legs.

The soldiers still standing began to fire, but the attack was too sudden and well coordinated. Scharlette backed away from the slavering monster who had killed Tom, wondering through her pounding fear if she'd be able to save him again. Was there a limit to how many times she could get away with it? Thanks to N55/14, she knew all too well that owning a PPC was no guarantee of success. Nevertheless she raised hers to her mouth ... but the advancing Germ lashed out with a scythe-sharp leg and sliced off her hand, PPC and all. Scharlette screamed as it went spinning out over the landing rail into the abyss. In despair she fell to her knees with blood pumping from her wrist. As tears formed in her eyes, she looked up into the champing maw of the Germ.

'You are not my father!' she shouted, which was an odd reaction for sure.

The Germ blinked its many eyes at her. 'What?' it said, as translated by her head computer.

The creature's confusion did not last long. It raised a leg to strike again.

Scharlette didn't want to die. She also knew her PPC was the only way to save herself and Tom. Thoughts sparked and died like suiciding fireflies, and the one that stayed bright made her gibber. There had to be another way ... but if there was, she couldn't think of it.

She sprang up and vaulted over the rail.

For a moment she almost felt relieved to have escaped the bloody carnage above. Then, as she plummeted through empty space, her stomach rose into her chest seemingly en route to her mouth, and the rushing air dragged sickeningly on her wound. She almost screamed, but *what would be the point*, she thought. As her life began to flash before her eyes, she at least had the presence of mind to push it away, lest it bore her to premature death before she hit the bottom. The only part of it that stuck was Jenelope, wearing a welcoming expression, as if she was trying to tell

Scharlette that everything would be all right.

'Here you go,' she said, handing Scharlette a joint. 'Let's skip history, shall we? It's always been my least favourite subject.'

The sleeve of her uniform automatically contracted around her wrist to stem the flow of blood, and the sharp pain snapped her back to reality. It was hard to concentrate, what with the terror of falling and the growing agony, but somehow she knew she had to try. She had put herself in this position for a reason, and it wasn't to go splat. Somewhere below was her severed hand, and she needed to get it back.

Come on, Scharlette.

Although it seemed nuts to do so, she manoeuvred herself into a dive so as to streamline her body and accelerate. She scanned the darkness below with night vision and spied something pale and distant. She zoomed in and *there it was*, her own hand spinning finger over thumb, a strangely foreign object to her, now it was detached.

The computer sounded in her head.

1:27 to impact.

Me, or my hand?

You. Although it's now 1:22.

She remembered how Tomothy had floated her to the ground using the 'anti-grav stitching' in his uniform after her apartment had exploded. While a uniform couldn't fly (she had checked that previously), perhaps it could help to speed up her fall?

Can it? she asked.

Yes, said the computer.

Let's do that then.

Suddenly air sucked through the suit, drawn in from somewhere near her shoulders and venting from her sleeves and legs.

At revised speed, 0:34 to impact.

This is going to be tight, she thought.

Pardon?

I wasn't talking to you.

Her severed hand grew rapidly bigger in her vision, and she realised she was still zoomed in. She quickly returned to manual sight, just in time for her hand to rise up towards her out of the void. She went to grab it and almost laughed hysterically as she realised she had instinctively *tried to use the same hand*. She had heard of ghost limbs, but she didn't think anyone had tried to grab their real limb with its ghost limb before. She shot straight past it, towards some kind of ground below.

0:08 to impact.

Flailing and issuing desperate commands, she managed to flip herself the right way up. With air now venting from her suit towards the ground, she was able to slow almost to a hover. She lifted her gaze, and a few moments later her hand came falling out of the dark. Reaching up with her intact arm, she caught herself by the hand.

Gotcha. Well, got me.

As she floated there in the vast emptiness of the

chamber, breathing hard, she felt as if she had been through quite enough for one day. Then she shook herself, winced painfully, and held up her own severed hand to her mouth.

33. The Server

'You fool. Have you any idea how difficult it is fighting this war on two fronts? We've tried thousands of iterations, each worst than the last. If we move the City, they find us. They discover our breeding planets and lay waste ...'

Hello myself, came Scharlette's own voice in her head. *Guess what? It's up to us again.*

What a surprise. We don't sound so flash.

We've lost a lot of blood.

Ah, wonderful.

Okay, listen up. The boys are going to argue like usual, each remaining as stubborn as always. Thing is – don't look – but creepy spider Germs are about to drop from the ceiling and murder everyone. It's too many for Hudd's troops to deal with, even if they're forewarned. Hudd himself gets speared through the skull, Tom gets squished like a bug. You have to move everyone into the Server before that happens.

How am I supposed to do that? said Scharlette, trying very hard not to look up.

There was no reply.

Guess that bit of the message erased the old timeline.

The thought was either somewhat comforting or not at all remotely comforting. Either her edit had solved their oncoming problem, or ensured she got herself horribly killed.

'... should not be mutually exclusive aims,' said Hudd.

'One problem at a time, Robin,' said Tom. 'They are too big to tackle ...'

'Shush, Tom,' said Scharlette, stepping forward and cutting him off. Guns flicked towards her, but she just rolled her eyes. 'Hudd, tell these jumpy dipshits to hold their fire, will you? I just received an edit from a few minutes hence, which you will not, because you are dead.'

Hudd eyed her warily, then gestured for his soldiers to lower their guns.

'Speak,' he said.

Scharlette took a deep breath. 'There are some kind of Germs stalking us overhead, *don't look*.' She grabbed his chin and snapped his eyes back to hers. 'So we can by all means continue this fascinating conversation, but I *really recommend* that we do it inside.' She slid her eyes towards the Server doors. 'You might be able to defend from in there, but out here, we're totally screwed.'

Hudd paled a little. 'Are you certain?'

'Unless I'm lying to myself.'

His eyes flickered. 'I can see them on a remote camera. Farm, there must be a hundred up there.'

'So hurry the fuck up and give the order, Agent Hudd. I'm told there's a spear with your brain's name on it.'

Hudd gave a slight nod. *Attention, everyone,* came his voice in her head, broadcasting on some kind of shared channel. *In a moment the Server doors will open and everyone is to get inside as quickly as possible. Ready?* He glanced around his squad. *All kay. NOW!*

The Server doors rent open loudly as metal fused by acid tore apart, and the whole squad dashed towards them. A series of clicks sounded above, but Scharlette forced herself to run and not look, praying that Tom was doing the same. She made it over the threshold into the dark sanctuary beyond, buoyed along by the press of soldiers following. She managed to twist about, desperately searching nearby faces. Outside on the landing, three or four hapless Panopticians were being ripped to shreds by Germs. More Germs landed and leapt in pursuit, but the doors slammed shut upon the leader with a wet crunch. Its dismembered torso slid to the floor, twitching.

As her eyes adjusted to the dimness, Scharlette tried to make out her surrounds. They were in some kind of black antechamber, surrounded by monks in grey uniforms who held back uncertainly. She felt a hand on her shoulder and went to draw a gun that wasn't there any more – but thankfully, it was Tomothy.

'You warned him about that?' he said.

'Yes.'

'Guess I didn't make it again.'

'Try not to die for the rest of the mission, will you?'

He chuckled. 'What would I do without you?'

Something slammed the doors from outside and a sizeable dint appeared.

'These ones don't have any oozers with them,' said Tom, 'but they'll still get through soon enough.'

What a surprise, came Scharlette's voice from the past. *We don't sound so flash.*

Scharlette was confused for a moment.

Ah, wonderful.

She realised she was hearing everything she had said to her future self a minute or so ago, when she had been a different future self. Maybe there was a way to shut herself up, like Gordon had done previously?

How am I supposed to do that?

'Form up!' bellowed Hudd to his soldiers. 'Protect the Server at all costs! The day may be lost, but we'll reset and try again. Our fallen comrades will get another chance.' He glanced at Tom and Scharlette. 'We'll all get another chance.'

The slaughter they had suffered on the previous timeline appeared in her memory, as clearly as if it had really just happened. She shuddered as she recalled losing her hand, and the fall that had followed. Was she really capable of such things? It seemed that she was.

'You,' she said, jabbing a finger at Hudd, 'not only owe me your life, but also any second chance to save this City and its people.'

She could not help but stare for a moment at her own jabbing finger – it was nice to have it back.

Hudd eyed her, then Tomothy. Perhaps he was remembering Tom's last words to him before they had both been killed?

'More like the thousandth chance,' he said. 'Still, I will

listen to you, Scharlette, in payment of my debt, before I make any decision.'

'Great,' said Scharlette. 'So forget about plastic bags or whatever choking up the Whackadoo System. One step at a time, like Tomothy says. The Germs are the biggest problem.'

'What makes you think,' said Hudd, 'that giving Tom his memory back will change anything to do with the Germs? Our mission on Earth was never about them.'

'Well fine, try building more guns for attempt one thousand and one. But I say, talk it through with Tom. You both come from the same era. You both know what's at stake. Why are you afraid of a little dialogue, here at the end of all things? Isn't it worth taking a risk to save the human race? Or resetting to some earlier point and hoping it turns out differently?'

Hudd seemed uncertain. Tom opened his mouth and Scharlette tensed, hoping he wasn't about to start another argument.

'Your mind must be full of horrors, old friend,' he said. 'To remain even slightly sane, you must have purged many timelines from your recollection. We both know you can't keep doing that forever. Who knows – you may even now be repeating mistakes.'

'It has not been going well,' admitted Hudd. He grimaced, and turned to a soldier. 'Take command, Captain. Hold them back for as long for as you can. Be brave, and remember – this life may never come to pass.'

'Yes, sir,' said the man. 'It has been an honour.'

Hudd turned back to Tomothy and Scharlette.

'Well then,' he said. 'Let's get you to the Server.'

They passed banks of computers, luminescent screens, rotating frames around pulsating wormholes, museum style displays of strange artefacts, and glass spheres containing complex three-dimensional networks. The monks they passed paused to watch them with curiously neutral expressions, often while tapping away on devices that looked like paper thin iPads.

'Is this all the Server?' asked Scharlette.

'No,' said Tom. 'These are expressions of the data housed within the Server. Methods of interpretation in the paltry few dimensions human brains are capable of comprehending. *This* is the Server.'

A golden circular door rolled open, and they passed through into a cavernous space. It was pitch black in all directions, and impossible to see how far it reached, or even where they were putting her feet. Before them lay something like a model of a planet hanging in the air. However, as they approached, Scharlette could see it was not a planet, but actually an assorted jumble of stuff pressed into a globular shape. Certainly there were planet-like textures on its surface, like forests, oceans, mountains and plains. There was also a giant nose, part of a tree jutting off crazily to the side (much bigger than the patch of forest it grew out of), something burning brightly like an embedded sun, a section like a spaceship junkyard, one of Panoptica's twisted 'vein' structures, alien body parts, strange bands of crackling energy, buildings of varying size, the tail of a fish, something like an octopus tentacle with eyes instead of suckers, celestial bodies in 'orbit', and countless other less recognisable things. Alien things, human things, animal, mineral, plant and space things, all mixed and morphing together with no sense of reason or scale.

'What .. the ... actual ... fuck ...' said Scharlette. 'It's like something Dali dreamt up while mainlining acid.'

'It *is* pretty weird,' agreed Hudd.

'Plus it changes all the time,' said Tom. 'It's a graphical representation of something that is sort of a gateway and sort of a storage unit, which has mapped most of the known universe across all dimensions, yet needs a physical expression in this one. A kind of "everything blob".'

Scharlette watched a flock of miniature alien birds take flight from the top of a purple tree, only to get roasted by a tiny exploding volcano.

The chamber shook, and Tom and Hudd exchanged a worried glance.

'Time is not a currency to squander,' said Hudd. 'Get to it, Tom. And if you wind up having to kill my younger self, well ... I guess I gave it my best try. It wasn't enough, you're both right about that.'

He sank cross-legged to the ground looking perfectly miserable and exhausted.

Tomothy walked up to the rotating ball of crazy.

'Well?' he said.

A cord unfurled from a mouth with teeth like crystal stalactites, on the end of which was a box with an aperture in it, just like the PPC readers on Gordon. Tomothy stuck his hand into it, PPC and all.

'Oh!' he said. 'This one also tickles one's anus.'

The ring of lights around the aperture turned from white to blue until there was a click. Tom stiffened, and the reader withdrew back into the Server's surface, which had now changed into a roiling sea.

Scharlette felt a flash of excitement. Was that it? Were they done? Had they gotten what they had gone through all this trouble to get?

'Talk to me,' she said, trying to contain her eagerness.

'Restrain your horses,' said Tom, as he sat down next to Hudd. 'It will take a moment to settle in.'

She joined them on the floor, completing the triangle.

'All kay,' said Tom, closing his eyes. 'It's all coming back to me.'

34. The Big Reveal

'Woah.' Tom blinked furiously. He stared disbelievingly at Hudd. 'It ... but ... but ... you ...'

'What is it?' said Scharlette impatiently. 'What do you remember?'

'Perhaps,' said Hudd, 'it will save precious time if I simply tell you the tale of what transpired. Doing so will prevent you from asking a hundred disjointed questions, and help smooth it into Tom's recollection also.'

Scharlette tried not to take umbrage with his pompous tone. If he wanted to spill the beans like some hackneyed villain at the end of a murder mystery, she wasn't going to object.

'Charkie ...' muttered Tom, with an accusatory look.

Hudd grimaced. 'She was so strong,' he said, as if this was an explanation of something.

'Hey hey,' said Scharlette, snapping her fingers at him. 'It'll be time for a hundred disjointed questions if you don't start talking.'

'Sigh,' said Hudd. 'All kay.' He turned to Scharlette, maybe so he didn't have to watch the expressions marching across Tom's face. 'In the version of the timeline which Tom now remembers, the President of Panoptica was called Barbigail Charkie. A conservative leader with military aspirations, she was more concerned with Pan's prosperity than any damage we did achieving it.'

'Some things never change,' said Scharlette.

'Some of us felt,' continued Hudd, 'that we had a responsibility to preserve certain worlds which Charkie saw fit to sacrifice. An illegal underground faction was formed, called the Universalists.'

'Oh, now I get it,' said Scharlette. 'Like environmentalists, but ... moreso.'

Hudd nodded. 'I signed up while in training, but my affiliation was later uncovered and I was declared a rogue. What was never found out was that the Contradictarian to President Charkie, Eamon Trask, was also a high ranking member of the faction. Not able to press his secret agenda to satisfactory extremes in the Council without giving himself away, and with Charkie a perennially more preferred President, an older Trask grew extremely frustrated at what he came to see as his wasted life. Fuelled by hatred for the crimes committed against the universe, his plans to fix things became twisted and complex. What if, he thought, he could discover some ancestor of Charkie's who he could safely remove from the timeline, and therefore erase her also? Someone whose removal would not trip plimits or eliminate too many of his own supporters? He could not go back a mere generation or two, could not simply have her father killed before she was born, as Panoptica's chronology is highly protected for just such reasons. He would, he decided, have to reach back further and find someone who had lived on Earth. This kind of targeting is highly specific, you understand, increasingly difficult the older the ancestor, and by rights should have been near impossible.

'Nevertheless, Trask spent time with the Server, mapping possibilities without expecting to find real candidates. To his surprise he stumbled upon a 21st century man, John Harrow, who was so genetically conservative that his descendants would only mate very selectively with others of the same persuasion. Predictive modelling showed that eliminating Harrow would result in Charkie, and many of her followers, being removed entirely from the timeline without – although he couldn't be completely certain of this – affecting himself or too many others who shared his political leanings. He decided it was worth the risk. He sent his discovery via PPC to his younger self, outlining what he needed to do and thus ensuring loop denial. Young Trask then enlisted me, a malleable zealot, in service of the greater good. He gave me the timeshield codes and sent me to kill John Harrow.'

'And I,' said Tom, 'was sent to save him – that much I have always remembered.'

'Yes. In the original timeline, Charkie's own security staff somehow discovered Trask's plan, or part of it at least, and ordered Tom to stop me.'

'Which I did,' said Tom.

'Indeed, but you did not understand the wider context of why you were protecting him. And what did you do, Tom?'

'I knew you were waiting for him at the airport, so I went to his house and tied him up.'

'Thus ensuring,' said Hudd, 'that he would never get on a plane and find himself seated next to one Priscilla Wright, who was to be his future wife.'

Tom slapped his forehead. 'I did the job for you.'

Hudd nodded. 'Killing Harrow, it turns out, was completely unnecessary. Denying the union was more than enough. When Tom did that, all of Charkie's ancestors were wiped from existence, as was she. Eamon, as planned, rose easily to power against a weakened opposition and became President.'

'But he still needed to ensure that everything happened the same way,' said Tomothy.

'Yes. You and I were both removed enough from the Council and its games that our personal histories were not significantly affected by the changes. Hence in the new timeline I was still flagged as a rogue, and you were still given orders to chase me down and "stop" me. The second time around however, Eamon had to make sure that no one with a PPC would remember the previous timeline – so he put out a universal recall. Only he and I were exempt, and only we would remember Barbigail Charkie. However, since you, Tom, were the only other person with the power to revert the timeline back to its original state, despite your enforced ignorance, Trask thought it best to have you assassinated as a precaution.'

'Tom can change it back?' said Scharlette, then felt a

little dumb. Of course he could. That was the whole point.

'All Tom has to do,' said Hudd, 'is send an edit all the way back to that day on Earth, and tell himself to ensure that John Harrow makes his flight.'

'And if I do that,' said Tom, 'then Eamon will never rise to the top job, Charkie will live again, and who knows – maybe she will even be able to stop these crop-dusting Germs and their endless warmongering.'

'Whether or not she can,' said Hudd, 'I suppose I've always known in my heart it was wrong to erase so many people.'

'Oh wow,' said Tom. 'That's big, coming from such an upstanding fellow.'

'Don't rub it in, please. At the time I considered my actions to be necessary. But after we had succeeded, Eamon proved a disappointment, just like all people with lofty ideals who get bogged down in actual politics. Admittedly, I have done no better.'

'Yeah,' said Tom. 'You guys really farmed things up.'

A series of frighteningly close explosions shook the Server. A moment later there was a massive crash against the door. Hurriedly they all scrambled to their feet.

'Minutes to go,' said Hudd.

'So what happens now?' said Scharlette. She gazed at the slowly rotating Server as storm clouds brewed along its equator.

'I have to send myself the details of what I now know,' said Tom.

'Send them to yourself the day we reach Earth,' agreed Hudd, 'before you tie up John Harrow at his house.'

'And you?'

Another great crash shook the door, followed by an ominous hissing. Oozers had arrived.

'I'll send an edit to the same point in an attempt to ward myself off. I can't guarantee my younger self will do what I ask, so you may have to guard Harrow against me. Either way, if you're successful, everything should reset to the old timeline. I hope you don't have to kill me, but ... well, I've given my way a good try and now have to bear the consequences of failure. See? I did gain some perspective in my old age, after all.'

Scharlette glanced between them as a terrible realisation began to dawn. Reset to the old timeline? The timeline in which none of this ever happened? A timeline in which she didn't matter at all.

'Not after all I've seen,' she whispered. 'All I've become.'

Hudd met her eyes implacably, while Tom's face was full of pity.

She began to cry big wet tears, and a stuttering sobbing took over her chest.

'But I can't go back to that,' she blubbered. It was difficult to get out words. 'I'll never know that any of this happened. It will be like it was all a dream, which is the shittest ending ever! Although I won't even remember the dream! I won't even remember.'

Tom put a hand on her shoulder while Hudd looked away.

'I told you no good would come from bringing her.'

'Robin,' said Tom, 'she saved our lives.'

He tried to draw her into a hug, but she pushed him away.

'I won't go back! I can't.'

She searched her head computer for an alternative, but it failed to understand the complexity of what she tried to convey, and she was too upset to break down her queries into any kind of logical sequence. She looked up at the Server again as a Germ face erupted from the surface. Over at the door, smoking holes appeared.

'I can't go back,' she said. She caught hold of Tom's face and kissed him, but it was a messy, panicked kiss, and not what she wanted.

'I love ...' she said, as she stared imploringly into his eyes. She saw them fill with trepidation, which he quickly tried to hide. '... this!' She let go of him and gestured around wildly. 'I love this. This life. This chaos. This goddamn time travel.'

She collapsed to her knees, sobbing too hard to speak any more.

'Tom,' said Hudd, nodding at the door. The hissing holes grew ever wider, and clicking could be heard beyond.

'I know,' said Tom, but he could not tear his eyes away from his heartbroken friend. 'Scharlette, I wish I could tell you that it's all going to be all kay. If only I could make it stick … but I don't know that I can. And there's no time, Scharlette. There's no time.'

Scharlette did not know what to do. She couldn't even kill herself to stop this from happening. She would still wake up back in her crappy apartment.

Together, Tomothy and Hudd raised their PPCs to their mouths.

35. The Shittest Ending Ever

Scharlette woke up in her crappy apartment. The alarm on her phone was beeping aggressively, reminding her just how much she hated it. She knew she could change it to a different tone, but the alternatives would no doubt prove equally annoying. If an alarm sounded calm and pleasant, it wouldn't ever wake anyone up. But maybe she could at least change it to a song instead – one loud enough to rouse her without being so abrasive?

Who gives a crap?

In a way it was more efficient just to start the day in a bad mood, as it saved her from having to build up to one gradually. Knowing where she stood with life right from the moment of waking was a time-saving protection against hope and disappointment.

She hit snooze and lay staring at the ceiling. It was her least favourite day again, Jenelope's deathversary. It came around every year like clockwork. At least it wasn't ruining a Saturday, like it had the previous year. It was only going to ruin a boring day at work.

She should get over it. She knew she should. It would have helped if there had been anyone real around to distract her. A best friend, a boyfriend, fun co-workers, loving parents, even a distant relative … but all positions were currently vacant. Her most meaningful relationship was with the ghost of her dead sister.

The alarm started up again and she felt the urge to smash her phone with a hammer. She looked around briefly, but she didn't seem to have one – at least not on the bedside table.

She got up and went to the shower, where she tried not to look at the tattoo of 'Jam' on her shoulder. As usual, she spent too long in the water, but was eventually interrupted by a knock at the door, which sent her scrambling in case it was a remote control helicopter she would need to sign for. What she found instead was a plain unmarked package which turned out to contain a pretty unusual book. She didn't have time to read much of it though, as she was running late for work.

As the train neared the airport, Scharlette stared out the window at the great silver birds taking off into the sky. She'd always meant to travel, but never really had. What had briefly seemed like a disposable income was now pouring into her mortgage, a 'sensible' investment she had made after securing a 'sensible' job, as advised by her parents – curse her for ever having listened to them for a single second about anything.

She could always sell her apartment, she supposed. Perhaps it would even garner a tiny profit on top of the incredible interest she'd been paying for years without making any real dent in the original loan? Maybe it would even be enough to take off somewhere for a while? By herself? And then what? Come back to no money and nowhere to live?

It was a pretty crappy daydream.

The day at work dragged by slowly and painfully. People streamed through the metal detector on their way to anywhere more interesting. At one point Scharlette almost let a business guy through without scanning him properly, something which Barry wasn't going to forget in a hurry. Fucking Barry, the officious little snot. He took his job so seriously, thought he was sooo important. Would things be better if she was more like him? If she respected the tiny cog-like part she played in the machine of other-people's-lives?

Probably not. Barry was only content because he was stupid and unimaginative.

'Boarding pass, sir,' she said to a pale, chubby fellow in a dorky Hawaiian shirt. He handed it over, and she noted the aircraft code meant he was bound for Fiji, which was closer than Hawaii, but perhaps had a similar dress code. His name was John Harrow.

'You, er, you ever been?' he asked nervously.

Scharlette looked at him blankly. 'Huh?'

'To Fiji?'

Scharlette put his things in a tray. 'Can't say I have.'

'I'm travelling alone. First time overseas.' He tittered, as if this was funny. 'Trying to, er, to get out of my shell. Live a little. Practise talking to people more.'

And now you're practising on me, thought Scharlette.

'Maybe even, you know ... well ... I mean, it would be nice to meet ...'

'You're all set, sir,' she said. 'If you'll just step this way.'

He walked through the scanner without a beep, and Barry nodded that he could collect his things.

'See you on the flip side, ahah,' said John Harrow, and awkwardly meandered off.

Barry watched him go with a judgemental stare. 'Reckon he was trying to hit on you.'

'Maybe,' said Scharlette, doubtfully.

Barry shrugged. 'Loser, either way. See that shirt? What is this, 1987?'

Is that who I'd be if I travelled? thought Scharlette. *Alone, awkward, unsure what to say? A weird loser?*

'Feel sorry for whoever's sitting next to him on the plane,' said Barry, being even more of a dick than usual.

'What's eating you?' said Scharlette.

Barry scowled. 'Kelly and I. I don't think we're gonna make it.'

He said it like screwing in the closet on lunch breaks despite the fact at least one party involved already had a long term boyfriend was the same thing as laying the foundation for a meaningful relationship.

Maybe it was. What did Scharlette know?

She got home that evening with a microwave lasagne and a couple bottles of bargain bin red, because she liked to pair her booze with her meals. She paused for a moment outside her door, looked at her hand, and then clicked her fingers. It made it seem like no time had passed since she had done the same thing that morning in the shower.

Inside she found the odd book still sitting on her dining table, open to the last page she had read:

She finished her cereal and put the bowl in the sink before heading off to work.

'What an amazing start to a story,' she said derisively.

Who is this Theodorus, anyway? Must just be some dumb joke.

She stuck her lasagne in the microwave and sat down to idly flick to the next page while she waited.

She was having a pretty depressing day. She had thought about trying to catch up with Ultra Gay Steve, had toyed with sending him a text on the way home, but in truth he was so equally maudlin that she feared they'd end up in an echo chamber of misery. It was easier just to eat crappy lasagne and get drunk by herself, possibly fall asleep earlier than any respectable adult should, and be done with this accursed day for another year. Upon sitting down to read the unashamedly enigmatic book, however, Scharlette was shocked by the way its words seemed to parallel reality. For some reason, she glanced around to make sure she was truly alone.

Having just done that very thing, Scharlette leapt backwards as if the book had bitten her. The microwave beeped at the end of its cycle and almost gave her a heart attack.

'Shut up,' she said, opening the microwave door to silence it, releasing a puff of steam from the overdone lasagne.

> *Scharlette was tempted, as usual, to try and shift the lasagne from its microwave tray to a bowl right away. Her reasoning was that it would cool more quickly in a bowl and she'd be able to eat it sooner. She would have been well advised, however, to exercise a modicum of patience, as it was probable she would burn her fingers like she always did. Luckily enough, the distractive quality of the book was such that she stood there staring at it for a good few minutes while her dinner cooled.*

'What the hell?' said Scharlette.

It had to be a trick, of course – but how would whoever was behind it know she had thought about inviting Steve over that night, or that she always burnt her fingers on lava hot lasagne? How?

> *She thought again about getting Steve over, at least so he could look at the book and verify she wasn't losing her mind – but really, what was the rush? At least losing her mind would break the monotony. Besides, if she called, she would find*

out that Steve had decided to fly to Perth on a whim, to track down an old flame in hopes of reigniting the spark. A proactive step for someone as defeatist as Steve, which could serve as a good lesson for Scharlette.

'This is some bullshit,' said Scharlette, pouring herself a large glass of wine. She picked up her phone and dialled Steve.

'Hey there, stranger,' said Steve, sounding much jollier than usual. 'Been a few weeks since I've heard from you. Thought you might have killed yourself.'

At least his humour was still dark.

'Not yet,' she said. 'I thought we agreed on a murder suicide pact if we're not moderately wealthy by thirty five?'

'Might have to put that on hold. Strangely enough, I'm on the other side of the country. Had a weird dream a couple nights ago, after which I felt this overwhelming need to visit ...'

'Jim,' she finished.

Jim was an old school mate of Steve's, and although their adolescent fumbles together had been brief, Steve had often referred to him as 'the one who got away'. After school, Jim had become a grass scientist, or something equally obscure, and moved to Perth to study spinifex.

'How did you know?' said Steve, startled. 'I haven't put anything on social media. I didn't want to jinx things when they seem to be going well.'

'Ah ... I just put two and two together.'

'Which twos?'

'You far away and sounding happy for once. And it's not like you don't bang on about Jim all the time when you're pissed. Doesn't take a genius.'

'I suppose not. Well, Detective Scharlock, to what do I owe the pleasure?'

Scharlette glanced at the book. There was no way she was going to try and explain it over the phone.

'Thought you might want to share a bottle, but it may well be empty by the time you get back.'

'No doubt. Oh, wait, hang on. Bugger, it's today, isn't it?'

'Pardon?'

'The day you hate more than any other.'

Scharlette hadn't thought about Jenelope for at least five minutes, surprisingly.

'Oh, yeah, it is.'

'Are you okay?'

'Hey, don't worry about me. I'm just happy to hear things are going well for you.'

'Listen, we're at dinner, so I'd better go. Want me to call you later?'

'No, no. I'm fine.'

'You sure?'

'Please, just enjoy yourself. Measure some spinifex grass for me, or whatever.'

Steve chuckled. 'Okay. His job is literally watching grass grow. Anyway, I'll get in touch when I'm back.'

'Have fun.'

Scharlette hung up and stared at the book.

'What am I supposed to do about this?' she asked the world in general.

Scharlette was growing understandably concerned with the book's prophetic content, but at least having verified that Steve really was in Perth, she felt a bit less like she was going crazy. Further questions were raised, however – like who had written the book, and why, and how? All of these would be answered in time. For the moment, hopefully it would be enough to know that the author meant her no harm, and only wanted to help her through a difficult period in whatever small ways he could, such as reminding her that her lasagne was getting cold.

Scharlette glanced at the microwave.

This is strange, she thought, *but at least it's not boring.*

Over the next couple of weeks, Scharlette grew to enjoy the book – maybe even to trust it. One drunken night its words seemed to convince her not to call up the arrogant finance tosser who hadn't been in touch since their last messy encounter. She had woken the following morning with a thumping hangover but been grateful not to find him in her bed. She had also been grateful for the book's suggestion not to drive to the mountains for a planned lunch with her parents, but rather to blow it off in order to drink lemonade and watch TV in her pyjamas. Later it had warned her not to try and pilot her remote control helicopter over to her shirtless neighbour's balcony with a note stuck to it saying 'Hello handsome', as all that would result would be a smashed window, a bill for replacement glass, and terrible embarrassment.

She thought about telling someone what was going on, but the book argued against this, saying it would be forced to disguise itself as an ordinary bestseller, by pretending to be the adventures of a child wizard or a sexually repressed office worker.

Scharlette realised that if she claimed the book was magic and showed it to one of her friends, and they opened it to read about a secretary getting spanked by her billionaire boss, she would appear rather dotty.

She had no explanation for it, of course ... but it was *something*, and *something* was better than the alternative. Was it supernatural? Was she mad? Had she had watched too many sci fi shows?

Sometimes it seemed to her that she wasn't really treating this incredibly strange object anywhere near as seriously as she should. *There has to be an explanation*, she would think, as if that was explanation enough.

Of course, the book was not always at the forefront of

her mind. She still had long shifts and drank too much wine, so her life was not exactly rife with clarity. In her soberer moments she told herself she would figure it all out soon, or whatever.

She just hadn't quite gotten around to it yet.

36. All Kay

Scharlette wasn't expecting a knock at the door, because it was Sunday night and there was no one in her life. She got off the couch and went to the peephole. Outside was a young man she didn't know dressed in black. Her hand went to the doorknob before it occurred to her that strangers dressed in black was one of the main reasons to have a peephole in the first place.

'Who is it?' she called.

'Special delivery,' he replied.

She could see he was holding a box of some kind.

'Just a minute,' she called. Then, as seemed to have become her habit lately when facing a choice, she took a quick look in the book.

> *Scharlette didn't know the fellow at the door, but she was a capable woman trained in self defence, living in a crowded building, so it seemed like the risk in opening up was low. Besides, she reasoned, there might be something good in the box!*

'All right, book,' she said, and went to open the door.

The young man broke into a big smile, which brightened even more as his gaze travelled over her.

'Ha,' he said. 'You know, I'd forgotten how slovenly and fat you were when we first met!'

'What?' said Scharlette angrily.

The young man seemed to realise that perhaps this had not been the best opening.

'Excuse me a moment,' he said, and held his wrist to his mouth. 'Don't comment on her weight and general appearance, you cherry picking idiot.'

'All right, book,' Scharlette said, and opened the door.

The young man beamed at her. He was a good looking fellow, and Scharlette suddenly felt self-conscious in her dirty pyjamas with takeaway stains down the front. The damn book could have warned her to spruce up a bit!

'Scharlette Day?' he asked.

'Yes?'

'You look, er ...' He winced. 'Anyway, I have a package for you.'

She glanced at the box, which was completely unmarked in any way, then at his clothes, which *seemed* like a uniform, but didn't have any insignia or symbols or words of any kind on them.

'This is a very odd time for a delivery,' she said. 'Do you mind if I ask what company you're from, and who sent this?'

'Ah ...' said the man. 'Um ...'

He held his wrist up to his mouth.

'All right, book,' said Scharlette, and opened the door.

The young man beamed and held out the box, which

342

was completely covered in postal stickers. His uniform was emblazoned with the logo of a flying rabbit.

'Interstellar Courier Service,' he said. 'For when you need it delivered yesterday!'

Tentatively, she took the package and turned it over, looking for some clue of a sender. Between a 'This Side Up' sticker and a customs form from Vanautu was a note that said 'from a friendly unknown person'.

'Not exactly dispelling my suspicions,' she said, 'this note here. It's a bit strange, wouldn't you agree?'

The young man nodded happily. 'I expect so.'

'Also, this is a very odd time for a package delivery. It's like, Sunday night.'

'I know, Miss Day. That's our speciality at Interstellar. We deliver to odd times.'

'Don't you mean *at* odd times?'

'Of course, that is what I mean, definitely.'

'Do I need to sign for this?'

'No, that's all kay. However, I've been instructed to wait while you try it on, to make sure it's the right size.'

Scharlette frowned. 'What is it?' she said, moving to the table. She should close the door on him, she supposed, but somehow she felt sure the book would have warned her if there was anything really wrong with the guy. He seemed so *happy* it was hard to be afraid of him, even though he was also being kinda crazy.

'Ah, a diving watch, I think,' he said, hovering at the threshold of the door without entering, which was also reassuring. 'Or maybe a stealth detection device.'

'A what?'

She got some scissors and snipped the box open to reveal a sort of chrome band that looked sleek and somewhat futuristic.

'I don't know what it is,' clarified the man helpfully.

'Well, I'm not going to put something on when I can't even tell what it is,' said Scharlette. 'For all I know, it might be a hand guillotine.'

'Um ...' said the man. 'It's not?'

'But you said ...'

'Hang on,' said the man, and held his wrist up to his mouth.

'That's our speciality at Interstellar,' said the young man. 'We deliver *at* odd times.'

Scharlette frowned at him. 'That was a strange word to over-pronounce,' she said.

'Ah,' said the man. 'It's just a funny trait of mine to do that kind of thing. Sorry, that kind *of* thing.'

'Right, well – do I have *to* sign something?'

Scharlette thought she may as well play along.

'No, that's all kay. But my instructions are to wait while you try it on, and make sure it's the right size.'

Scharlette frowned. 'What is it?' she said, moving to the table.

'It's a ... wrist ... stabiliser.'

'Excuse me?'

'You'll see.'

She opened the box and saw some kind of metallic band. There was a blank little screen on it but not much else.

'Why would some *friendly unknown person* send me this on a Sunday night? Is there even an instruction manual?'

The guy looked a little fretful. 'I think it's supposed to be intuitive,' he said. 'I'm no expert, but I think if you just ... put it on ... then it will ... you know. It will be fine.'

Scharlette stared at him, then at the 'wrist stabiliser'.

'Well, all right,' she said. 'Everything about this is weird, but as long as my telepathic book isn't overly concerned, what the heck, huh?'

The guy seemed surprised. 'Telepathic book?'

Scharlette snapped the thing onto her wrist and it tightened immediately.

'Hey,' she said. 'What the ...'

The little screen lit up and a word appeared. *PRIM-ING*, it said.

'Priming? What does that mean?'

'It's probably just turning on,' said the man. 'Does it fit all kay?'

'More like it's bloody affixed,' said Scharlette, tugging at it. 'It won't come off.'

'Maybe it's meant to customise itself to your, you know ... wrist width.'

A blue light came on inside the band. It grew so bright

that, for a moment, Scharlette thought it was actually shining through her skin.

'Where did you pick this up?' she demanded, coming back to the door. 'Who sent this?'

'I'm not sure, I'm just a humble package delivery man. They don't tell me all the details down at the package packaging facility.'

ANALYSING TEMPORAL IDENTITY, the screen said.

'What?'

BRAIN MOLECULES UNVIOLATED.

'Listen, I'm about this far away from calling the police ...'

VIOLATING BRAIN MOLECULES NOW.

Scharlette tried to stay calm. This had to be a sick joke – but she had thought that about the book too. What was going on? She couldn't get the damn thing off, and now it said it was violating her brain molecules! And she *could* see through her skin, she could see her arteries and veins, see the outline of the bones in her arm. What could she ...

ALL KAY, flashed the screen.

Scharlette's eyes glazed as the moment ticked by – the exact same chronological point as when Tom and Hudd had sent their edits in the old timeline and changed everything. Memories of colour and light and adventure poured into her mind, pushing aside the grey repetitions of the actual timeline, and she reeled under the deluge. Fierce emotion and sex and violence, self discovery and triumph and fear ... aliens worlds ... flying jellyfish ... speeding through the Big Deep ...

'There now,' said Tom, as he caught her. He guided her to the couch and eased her down, though she clutched his arm and would not let go. 'There now, dear Scharlette. It will take a few moments. It's a lot to take in at once.'

'Oh God,' said Scharlette. She best remembered that which had 'most recently' happened to her, the part when she had lain on the cold floor of the Server begging Tom not to abandon her, terrified of being swallowed up by an unknowable void.

He hadn't abandoned her, though.

'Tomothy,' she cried. 'Tomothy, thank you. I would have been trapped here forever. I would have just gone on, doing what I was doing, for my whole life. I wouldn't have ever known what I ... I ...'

He laughed and hugged her.

'It's all kay,' he said. 'How could I not come and get you? After everything you did? Besides,' and he gave her a squeeze, 'President Charkie wants to offer you a job.'

37. To Be Continued

They floated down off the balcony.

'Remember this?'

'Of course. My hero. Well, my guy-who-tried-to-rob-me-at-gunpoint-and-then-took-me-with-him-out-of-desperation-o.'

Tom set her on her feet. 'That's me. Now, Gordon can't land in these narrow streets. Shall we take a walk to the park?'

Scharlette gave a short nod and a couple more tears broke loose.

Tom smiled, then looked off down the street. 'This way, I seem to recall.'

Arm in arm, they slowly retraced the path they had taken when fleeing from Hudd, pausing at places of significance.

'This was where a pipe exploded over my head,' said Scharlette. 'Oh, and here's where I got killed by a laser bolt.'

'I still don't remember that,' said Tomothy. 'Very glad we didn't let you die, though.'

'Yes, it was nice of you.'

'Hmm. There's where we went down into the sewers. Are you particularly sentimental about that bit?'

'Let's stay above ground this time.'

They continued on through streets not part of their original journey. Tomothy looked around at convenience stores and bars with some curiosity.

'I'll probably never return here,' he said, wistfully.

'Um,' said Scharlette. '*You're* being sentimental about that?'

Tom shrugged. 'Many agents dream about visiting Earth. See where we came from, what we fight for. Now I'm here, but there's no real chance to look around.'

Scharlette eased him to a stop outside a trendy, hole-in-the-wall bar.

'Want to grab a drink before we set off?'

Tomothy stared through the door. From inside came the clink of glasses, the sound of laughter. Lamps above individual tables dotted the shadowy interior with warm pools of light.

'There's a plimit,' said Tomothy. 'Right across the doorway.' He sighed and looked off down the street. 'We best keep on.'

Scharlette nodded and they fell into step again.

'So anyway,' she said, 'what happened?'

'Pardon?'

'After you and Hudd sent back your edits.'

'Ah. Well, our past selves met up on Earth, discussed things at length, and decided not to interfere with Common Ancestor 6702ahjx445. John Harrow boarded his flight to Fiji, on which he met his hugely bigoted wife, and together they gave rise to an unusually narrow family tree that led, ultimately, to the birth of Barbigail Charkie, President of Panoptica. Hudd and I returned to the City, Hudd has since been granted a pardon – in part for his testimony against Eamon Trask, who is being prosecuted for time crime ...'

'Wait.' Scharlette winced. 'Time crime?'

'Yes?'

'You actually call it that?'

'That's what it is.'

'I see.'

They arrived at the park and made their way between the trees.

'So, wait a second,' said Scharlette. 'You said something back when I was remembering everything, and it was all a bit ...'

She frowned.

'I know,' said Tom. 'It can be an overwhelming thing, to take a long dump.'

Scharlette snorted. 'What?'

'A long memory dump. I know what's it's like. I've taken a long dump before.'

His expression was completely sincere, and it made her burst out laughing. Then the thought she had been chasing arrived, and her laughter died away.

'You said the President wants to offer me a job?' she said.

'Oh, yes. She wants to make you a time agent. After that, you're to try and save humanity from the Germs.'

Scharlette stared at him in shock, trying to work out if he was serious.

'Why me?'

'Well, you're in a pretty unique position. You don't have any personal history with the Germs, besides what you remember from the previous timeline, which doesn't really count. So really, you're probably the greatest hope we have to save the Earth, Panoptica, and all humanity. Ah, here we are.'

The glowing outline of a doorway appeared before them.

Maybe Scharlette was becoming accustomed to huge torrents of emotion. She tried to let it all pass through her, turned up her head to breathe it out into the night sky. The breeze rustled her hair, and she saw the stars twinkling above.

'You can't see them so well from down here,' she said.

The thought made her kind of sad. Was it for herself, or everyone else she knew?

'You coming?' Tom waited by the doorway. 'Gordon is excited to see you.'

Well, not everyone – and just like that, such sadness was chased away forever.

THE END

From the Author

Thank you for reading this book!

I'm Sam, a writer and stand-up comedian from Sydney, Australia.

My other books are quite different to this one, both in genre and tone, but if you'd like to investigate them, my website is sambowring.com.

It's mostly fantasy and kid's stuff, with the odd experiment thrown in.

You could also join my author mailing list, and be alerted when the next Scharlette book comes out. And yes, there will definitely be one. She demands it.

All kay. It has been a pleasance, and I thank you again for joining Scharlette in her travels through the Big Deep.

Good luck out there.

CPSIA information can be obtained
at www.ICGtesting.com
Printed in the USA
FSHW011643060520
69971FS